THE LONG WAY HOME

LINDA GOULD

BLACK ROSE writing

© 2016 by Linda Gould

All rights reserved. No part of this book may be reproduced, stored in a retrieval system or transmitted in any form or by any means without the prior written permission of the publishers, except by a reviewer who may quote brief passages in a review to be printed in a newspaper, magazine or journal.

The final approval for this literary material is granted by the author.

First printing

This is a work of fiction. Names, characters, businesses, places, events and incidents are either the products of the author's imagination or used in a fictitious manner. Any resemblance to actual persons, living or dead, or actual events is purely coincidental.

ISBN: 978-1-61296-675-5
PUBLISHED BY BLACK ROSE WRITING
www.blackrosewriting.com

Printed in the United States of America

Suggested retail price $16.95

The Long Way Home is printed in Adobe Caslon Pro

I'd like to dedicate this book to my family who, with unfailing regularity asked, "how's the book coming?" And to the smart women in my writing group for their sophistication, knowledge and support but most of all to my daughter Beth, for her editing and creative expertise.

To Captain Ron & Carol

THE LONG WAY HOME

with wonderful memories of Florida

Linda Gould

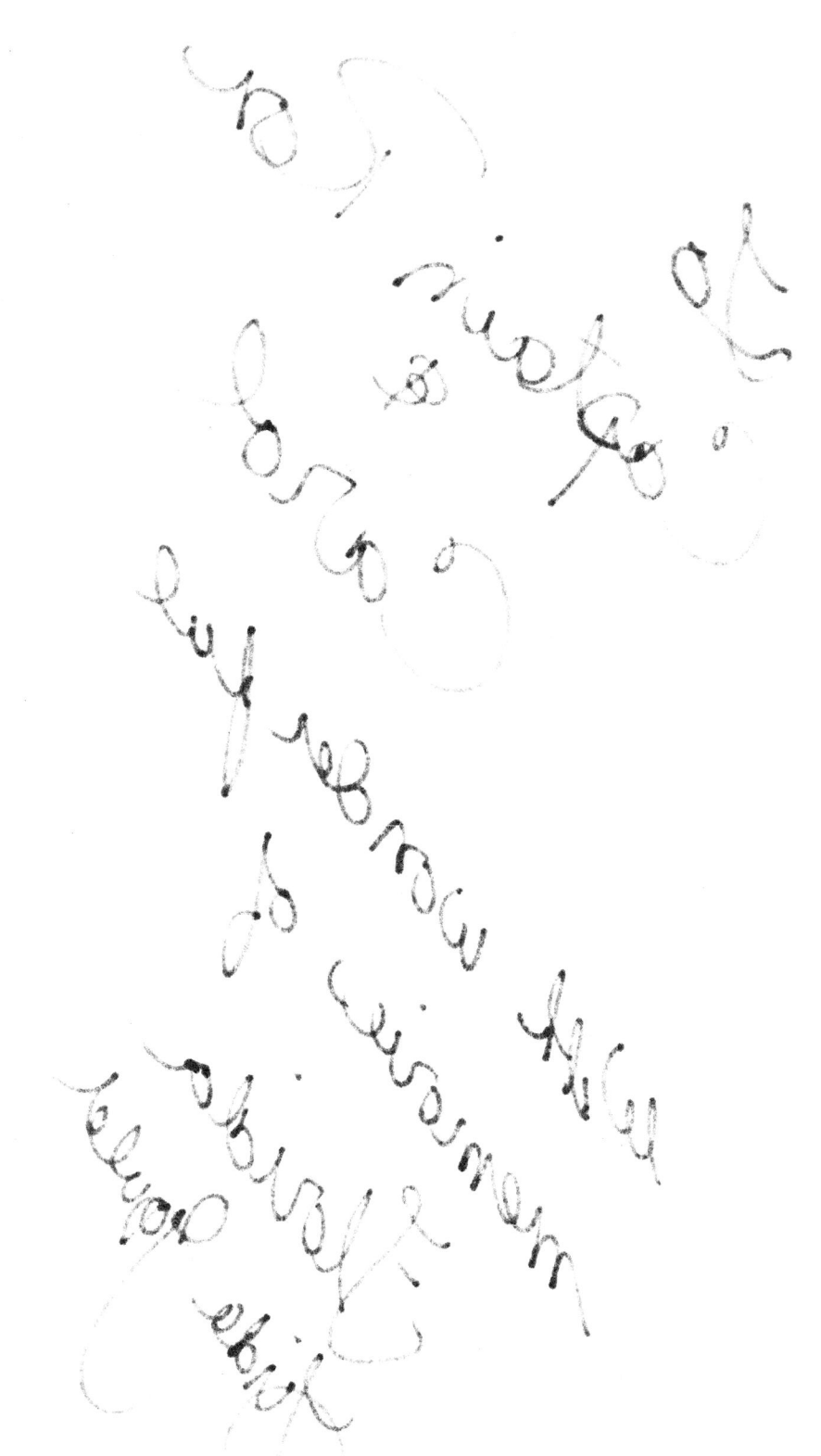

CHAPTER ONE

This was her first flambé. And even though Peaches preferred eating to cooking, she was determined to create Julia Child's elegant banana dessert in honor of her younger brother's birthday. Matthew was turning forty.

The dessert had caught her eye for two reasons. First, with so few ingredients, it couldn't possibly be fattening. She and Matthew had both inherited the fat gene and, although today wasn't the day, they had plans to diet very soon. But more importantly, there would be that spectacular flame part on top of the bananas instead of plain old candles. Peaches reasoned forty candles on one cake was a lot. They could start a fire.

Dessert had to be just right because as Peaches saw it Bananas Flambé was a perfect symbol of her sophistication and deep love for her younger brother. She was his closest relative, if you didn't count his four year old illegitimate daughter, Mimi. Aunt Blossom, who was probably the originator of the fat gene, had driven across town for the occasion and was out in the backyard at that very moment with Matthew and Mimi, watching the barbecue smoke.

The flambé was looking good. The sliced bananas were already in place and the next step was the syrupy liquid. As she poured it all over the bananas, some of it sloshed over the edge. She fixed that by running a finger around the perimeter of the plate. It cleaned up nicely. She was almost finished. There was just the flame part to work out before she would triumphantly carry the blazing delicacy outside to the picnic table. They were all looking forward to a light dinner of barbecued chicken, chili con carne, corn fritters, potato salad (made with light mayonnaise), deviled eggs and corn on the cob, which were already outside on the table. All that was left to do was the spectacular dessert. As the cook, Peaches had been working hard all day.

The directions had suggested a third of a cup of cognac. When poured on the top and lit, it would create a pleasant, but brief flame effect. But Peaches wanted something sensational that would last at least until she got out the door. She decided to add a little more. As she reached for the bottle of cognac, the front door opened and her most detested ex-friend Dawn walked in holding a cigarette.

"Don't say anything Peaches, Matthew said I should stop in." From the get-go, Dawn was on the defensive. After crushing her cigarette in an ashtray, she tossed it in the trash and headed for the back door.

Indignant, Peaches could barely contain herself. Why on earth would Dawn come now? Why would Matthew even invite her? Who cared that Matthew thought Dawn was fun and made him happy. So what if the woman was Mimi's mother? She wasn't married to Matthew. She would ruin the party.

As Peaches opened her mouth to demand that Dawn leave, Aunt Blossom stumbled through the back door offering to help with dessert. Unaware of the ongoing feud between the two younger women, Blossom welcomed Dawn joyfully. Still enraged by her ex-friend's invasion, Peaches grabbed the bottle of cognac and poured the liquor all over the bananas, emptying the bottle. Too much for the dessert, the cognac splashed onto the greasy stovetop and down the side of the oven into the trashcan. Dawn stopped to watch the action.

"Oh dear," noted Blossom, her arm around Dawn's shoulders, "You've spilt it. Do you have any more?" The older woman thought for a moment. "There might be some outside. I'll check." Moving surprisingly fast for a large woman, she left for the backyard and came back with a bottle of amber liquid. "I couldn't find any of that stuff," she indicated the empty bottle of cognac, "but let's try this."

Peaches nodded absentmindedly toward Blossom then moved to cut Dawn's progress off, preventing her from going outside to join the others. But before Peaches reached Dawn, Blossom screamed.

Peaches turned around to see her beautiful dessert engulfed in flames. Immediately it spread to the stovetop erupting into a horrific ball of fire that made Peaches leap back tripping over Dawn.

Blossom made it out the door with Dawn not far behind. The flames spread to the tablecloth, the blue and white curtains and threatened the whole house.

Peaches couldn't remember whether she should throw water on the fire or close the door. The smoke alarm shrieked as Peaches frantically ran outside with no dessert, no belongings and her life changed forever.

CHAPTER TWO

"What da ya think Matthew? It is a squeeze."

Clasping her hands, Peaches twirled with a little difficulty given the small space.

"Let's take it!" she cried with enthusiastic abandon.

Without waiting for his answer, she pushed by her brother and walked down the narrow corridor of the refurbished self-contained motor home and out the metal side door. She was impressed again at how the bottom step automatically extended out whenever the door was opened. Pushing the screen door aside and descending the steps, she daintily put her foot to the ground; her large body jigging underneath her khaki colored muumuu.

Bucky, owner of Bucky's Recreational Vehicle Sales, New and Used, greeted her outside. Through the open RV window, they could hear Matthew happily whistling the theme song from Rocky.

Her brother was examining the refrigerator door, noticing that it was kept shut by a small latch at the top.

"We'll take it," Peaches announced to the salesman. Nodding toward the motor home she added, "he'll be out in a minute."

Bucky wanted to ask how two over-sized people could possibly think they would be happy riding around in a medium-sized motor home, but decided against it.

Instead, he asked pleasantly, "Have you been in Pittsburgh long?"

"Born and bred," Peaches answered as the screen door swished open, the step extended and Matthew joined them.

Smelling an almost certain sale, Bucky launched into his well-honed pitch as he herded his two customers toward a flimsy wooden building that served as his office.

"Right this way. You've picked a beauty." With a grand gesture, he invited them into his small, crowded office.

"You beat me to it." Bucky smiled broadly. "I hate to let her go." He opened two folding chairs, and then hustled around and sat down at his desk. "I was fixing to get that one for myself."

Sensing that Peaches made the family decisions, he addressed her first.

"Which lease plan would you and your husband be interested in, two years or five? There's quite a difference in the monthly payments."

"This here's my brother and we'll be payin' cash." Peaches folded her hefty arms as her chair creaked.

"Cash? Are you sure? I can give you a special deal. Our payments are convenient and fair."

"Listen Bucky, I kept the books at Best Deals Used Cars, that's the one across town on Piedmont Avenue, so I'm wise to your game." Peaches leaned into the conversation, making sure Bucky got the message. "By the time we pay this thing off on your special deal, we could probably buy another motor home outright. Now how much is this thing gonna cost?"

Bucky moved papers around on his veneered desk, nodding toward the window where they could easily see the Fleetwood Bounder they had been looking at. "That one has a price tag of only $29,999 cash money and that includes taxes and handling." Frowning, Matthew leaned over and whispered in Peaches' ear.

She readjusted on the small chair. "Bucky, are you taking into consideration our trade in? Your sign does say you take trade-ins."

"Trade-in? What would you be trading in?"

"That car right out there."

They all turned to look at a tired blue Plymouth sitting in the parking lot.

"That thing? No, no," he protested. "You don't understand. The sign means a motor home trade-in, not a car. What year's that thing anyway?"

"1977," Matthew said.

"Good lord! What would I want with a 15-year-old car? It probably has at least 200,000 miles on it."

"221,544," Matthew corrected him.

"Let's face it, Mr. Bucky," Peaches said, "what would we want with a 15-year-old car if we're buying this almost new, reconditioned recreational vehicle with the motor and all right inside? Me and my brother expect to be traveling together."

Bucky rubbed the side of his face with the palm of his hand; business had been slow.

"Humph, I thought you were the boss."

"I am," Bucky said more defensively than he'd intended.

Peaches abruptly stood up. "Come on Matthew, let's get outda here. Let's go somewhere where there's some truth in the advertising. There must be another one of these motor home places around."

"Wait," cried Bucky. "I'll take your car, but I can only give you 300."

"500 and you've got a deal," Peaches snapped back.

"Okay, okay. It's a deal." The salesman didn't look happy.

"Draw up them papers, Mr. Bucky. Matthew, you start getting our stuff out of the Plymouth."

"Now? It's not ready. This isn't a supermarket."

"Why wait?" Peaches eyed the salesman. "You gonna change the equipment when we're not lookin'?"

"No, of course not, but there's a certain amount of preparation ... license plates, a title."

"I know all that, but motel living doesn't agree with us and we were hoping to take possession of this thing sometime in the very near future, like today. Doesn't your sign say 'quick turn around'?" Sighing loudly, she turned to Matthew, "I knew you couldn't trust someone named Bucky."

"Wait. Give me two hours."

Peaches regarded Bucky for a moment. "Okay, two hours. We'll go get some Tasty Freeze down the road. We'll be back in a while. I know all the car tricks so don't try anything funny," Peaches warned Bucky. "Your sign says a clean deal and we expect you to deliver."

. . .

A few miles down the road from Bucky's, Peaches guided the Plymouth into an empty Tasty Freeze parking lot. The attendant languidly wiping the ice cream maker didn't seem to notice them as they stood at the service window. A fan droned in the background.

"Ahem, excuse me." Peaches didn't like waiting around. "We'd like some service over here."

"I can't believe we're the only customers." Matthew mopped his brow with a McDonald's napkin he'd found in his pocket. "It sure is hot."

"It's the end of August, Matthew, it's suppose to be hot and being it's mid-week, of course there aren't any lines." Peaches surveyed the food options printed in bright colors on the glass. "That's just one of the benefits of being on vacation."

"Or between jobs, like us," Matthew said dryly.

Peaches moved on to the ice cream selections. "Let's see, I'm not very hungry, I'll just have a little something." The attendant was finally ready. "Give me a double banana split with three scoops of vanilla ice cream. Put some chocolate, caramel, and strawberry sauce on top and a good sprinkle of peanuts, but just one cherry. I don't want to go whole hog."

"Large hot fudge sundae here," Matthew took his turn. "Put extra whip cream on 'em both to celebrate."

"Oh Matthew, whipped cream?" she patted her stomach. "Just this time and only because we're celebrating. I was going to go on a diet, but it can wait 'til tomorrow." It took the attendant a while, but he finally handed their orders out the window. They headed toward an old picnic table off to the side of the parking lot, shaded by a discolored Heineken Beer umbrella. The ancient wood benches creaked and sagged as the brother and sister settled down on opposite sides.

After savoring a few mouthfuls in silence, Matthew looked thoughtfully past Peaches' shoulder. "Boy, that RV we're buying is special." He shook his head and continued. "In my forty years, I've never done anything like this. You're forty two and you've never done anything like this either, right?"

Peaches nodded, adding solemnly, "This is going to be the perfect vehicle to find ourselves in."

"Pop would have been proud we bought, not rented. I think this is making good use of his life insurance money." He took a spoonful of ice cream, dipping deep into the cup to make sure he got some of the chocolate sauce. He thought of their deceased father with affectionate relief.

"Pop was hard." Matthew tried to explain. "When he wasn't drinking, he was complaining. I always felt you and me were better together, you know, handling stuff. I was glad you came home."

After their father's stroke, Matthew had quit his bus driving job to care for their father.

"Pop always liked value." Eating a little he continued, "I like the way that table folds down into a bed. It'd be wider than that skinny couch. I think I'll sleep there. You take the bedroom."

"There's always resale value to something you own." Peaches took another spoonful thick with whipped cream.

Matthew licked the hot fudge from his upper lip. "In a way, using the insurance money from Pop is like having Pop here, only without his advice."

Peaches nodded in agreement. "Too bad the house burned down. That would have been a nice family remembrance. Pop was probably spitting fire and smoke and rolling in his grave when it burned. He loved that house."

"If it hadn't burned down, we wouldn't need to buy the RV," Matthew pointed out. He studied his sundae, growing more serious, "I'm glad we didn't have to answer to him."

Matthew looked across at his sister and asked, "Peaches, about the fire, I haven't talked to a soul like I promised, but why does it have to be such a big secret? There were other people there. People do dumb stuff all the time. I know I do. Wasn't the fire just a big accident?"

She seemed to ignore him while she dug deeper into the soft vanilla, pink with strawberry juice. Matthew figured she hadn't heard him and was going to repeat his question, but she looked up at him with tears in her eyes.

"It was an accident and it wasn't all together my fault. There were extenuating circumstances, other people were there."

"What circumstances?" Matthew questioned while she shifted her weight on the hard bench, as though she might be uncomfortable. "What's the big secret?"

"Nothing Matthew. Just eat your ice cream." She put her spoon down. "You and me, we've always been close. We always said we'd take care of each other no matter what. Growing up in a household like ours, we had to have a united front. You just have to trust me on this. It was an accident. I just don't want everybody weighing in about it."

"Another thing you need to keep in mind," Peaches went on, "it was a cheap house, and we won't be getting a lot of money from the insurance. That would really bother Pop." She shook her head at the thought. "It may even be too much trouble for the insurance company to worry about. The neighbors certainly lined up to buy the property, I mean after the house was gone. I'm glad it burned. We should have hired someone to get rid of it long ago."

"Do you mean that? Why? I would never have thought of that on my own." Matthew was such an innocent, thought Peaches. Pausing for a moment, he continued, "If we had wanted it burned down, who would we have gotten to do it?"

"Forget I said anything." Peaches regretted her statement. Matthew took things so literally.

"Who Peaches? Who do you hire to burn a house down? Who does that sort of thing?"

Peaches smiled, humoring Matthew as if they were kids. "Okay, okay." She thought for a minute. "As for someone to do the job, right off the bat I might say Clute. He's crazy enough to do something that stupid, that's why I divorced him, let me tell you."

Matthew nodded in agreement and reached into his breast pocket for a toothpick while Peaches continued, "or it could've been any one of them neighbors. They would have happily obliged. Then of course, quicker than lightning they'd of turned us in to the police."

"I don't know why they never liked us much, especially after Ma died. She was sort of the family ambassador, don't you think?"

"Probably, but Pop had no use for them. They always thought he drank too much. And I think they were scared of you. When I finally cut loose from Clute and came back home, I'll bet they were ready to bolt." Peaches smiled. "It's a funny neighborhood. Everyone is so full of advice. Remember that time Greeley offered to mow our lawn? He said he didn't appreciate the scraggly look of it and Pop told him it was especially manicured to look like a field." Peaches brushed her green hair out of her eyes. "And then there was Mrs. Boon who knocked on the door with some juice diet she'd read about and I told her she'd best use it on herself." Peaches laughed slapping the table. "Boy she left in a huff, never came back neither."

"It's been almost a month since the fire," Matthew said thoughtfully. Peaches pushed her empty ice cream cup away. Not wanting to talk about the fire again, she got up from the picnic table with some difficulty.

"Let's get outda here."

. . .

As they drove into Bucky's RV sales lot, Matthew pointed out that the motor home they intended to buy now had license plates. They found Bucky inside his cluttered office waiting and eager to finalize the deal.

"I've never signed my name so many times," Matthew flexed his right hand. Peaches gave her brother a look. She had insisted that both their names be included on the paper work because Matthew had to take more responsibility for his life. This was a small start. Whether he cared or not, he would be co-owner.

"This is the last one." Bucky smiled then leaned toward them. "Now you were going to be paying cash? I should have mentioned that I'm reluctant to take a check on such an instant delivery. Why if the thing bounces..."

"We said cash and that means cash." Peaches interrupted. "Matthew, get the man his money."

Matthew placed the small brown suitcase he had brought in with him on his lap and opened it. Bucky didn't mean to be nosey and tried not to look, but he gasped in spite of himself when he saw that under a layer of newspaper, the suitcase was filled with money.

Taking his time, Matthew counted the amount carefully. When he finished, he counted it all over again. He closed the suitcase and handed the stack of bills to his sister.

"Here you go, Mr. Bucky."

Bucky suspiciously felt one of the bills, holding it up to the single light bulb over his desk; he wasn't sure what he was actually looking for. Nobody had ever given him cash for an RV before, and he wondered how to recognize fake money. These people were a little odd, but they seemed honest. Besides, they were local. The money sounded real when he crinkled it.

Concluding that it was probably okay, he methodically counted the money, carefully made piles and separated the different denominations. Even though it came out right, he counted it all over again.

"I owe you some change." Glassy eyed, he took a dollar from his pocket and dropped it in Peaches' hand. "The Bounder is yours. The keys are in the ignition. Happy motoring." They shook hands all around.

Even though the Plymouth was stuffed with their belongings, mostly salvaged from the house fire, it didn't take long to transfer the contents to the motor home. Together, they brought the car keys to Bucky, who had been watching out the sales office window. They shook hands again before heading back to their new home.

Peaches was anxious to get going. "You sure we've got everything out of the Plymouth, Brother?"

"Yep, everything's out, we're ready to roll." He rubbed his hands together while he enthusiastically chewed a toothpick. "Let's name her."

"She's got a name," Peaches opened the door and waited for the automatic step to come out. "Didn't Bucky say it was a Bounder? I think it suits her just fine. Didn't you see that little kangaroo on the side? It's very appropriate. Kangaroos bound."

"Bounder's okay, but I was thinking of something more personal. How about Betty Elizabeth?"

"Bounder's fine." Peaches reiterated. "Having one name is biblical. I'll drive." She sat down in the driver's seat and popped two pieces of gum into her mouth. "Look at Moses and Abraham."

Matthew nodded in agreement. "Yeah, Rocky too. Of course, I know he really has two names but--"

Peaches didn't let him finish. Before he could go on and on about his hero, she hitched her seatbelt, started the engine, and joyfully yelled, "First stop Niagara Falls," and drove out of the parking lot. Matthew drummed the dash and yelled, "Yo Adrian, let's go!"

Peaches glanced over at her brother with exasperation. "I'm not Adrian and you're not Rocky. Now fasten your seatbelt."

CHAPTER THREE

It was only about two inches from Pittsburgh to Niagara Falls, not far at all. Matthew sat in the passenger seat balancing the eastern side of the United States in his lap. Using the Allegheny River as a starting point, he made a pencil line marking the road north from Pittsburgh into New York State, all the way to the Canadian border where they would find Niagara Falls.

Peaches commented that the Bounder drove just like a car and was even easier to drive than the school bus she had driven for the City of Pittsburgh early in her career. She was grateful that the motor home was automatic, she'd found shifting tricky in the bus. She also liked the big steering wheel and the enormous windshield that gave her an expansive command of the road.

"Look at those cars get out of the way," Peaches said gleefully, flooring the RV. Cars did give them a wide berth. But when an 18-wheeler passed on the left it made the Bounder sway uncomfortably. She tightened her grip on the wheel and slowed the RV down. She chewed her gum nervously.

"Why'd you pick Niagara Falls?" Matthew looked up from the map. "Why didn't you pick some place South or West, someplace nice and warm? It's almost September."

Without taking her eyes off the road, Peaches explained. "For one thing, Niagara Falls doesn't seem like too long a trip for our first time out. I figure it'll give us a chance to get used to our new living arrangements." She turned her right blinker on. "I also have fond memories of the place."

"Didn't you and Clute go to Morristown, New Jersey on your honeymoon?"

"We did. Clute thought the Ford Museum there was connected to ex- President Gerald Ford, his idol at the time. It wasn't. But that's not what I'm talking about. Don't you remember that one and only family vacation we went on when we were kids? It was supposed to be that five-day extravaganza to Niagara Falls. I remember planning it was so much fun. It was like it was really going to happen." Peaches sped up the Bounder in her enthusiasm. "We were going to stay at the Algonquin Hotel. Then after we got started, Pop kept saying he'd bitten off more than he could chew and Ma kept telling him to keep quiet."

"Sure, I remember," he looked up from the map again. "But we never got there."

"Right," she checked her mirrors. "By the time we got to Binghamton we'd had three flat tires and then the car broke down. We all agreed he'd bitten off more than he could chew so we went home. The trip was never mentioned again. This time we're going to get there. We both know that Pop didn't listen to anyone, but if he'd listened to anybody at all he would have gotten way farther than a bottle of liquor."

"Isn't Cousin Marlene somewhere around there?" Matthew asked, attempting to change the subject.

"Cousin Marlene, I haven't thought about her in years. She's probably still in jail."

Matthew shrugged his shoulders. "I suppose we could pay her a visit."

"Oh no," Peaches was emphatic. "We want new lives, new people. I don't want to get too close to a jail. Besides I won't meet anybody good in prison."

"It's the nice thing to do." Matthew spoke quietly and then had a question. "Are you going to do all the deciding from now on? That was okay when we were kids. You handled Pop better than me. And what we've done so far is okay, but sometimes I'd like to do the deciding."

"Matthew, I only make decisions when they need to be made. Jump in anytime and we'll talk about it. Hey, are you watching where we're going? I see I-79 is coming up. Better check that map."

Matthew traced the penciled line with his finger. "Exit 20. That's what we want. Then after that we stay on 79 for more than 100 miles,

I think."

"Clute had the same complaint." Peaches drove the Bounder down the entrance ramp and then eased it into traffic on the six-lane highway. "He didn't like that I was smarter than him. Of course I don't mean that I'm smarter than you," she added quickly. "Anyway, I always had to step in. He didn't make decisions much but when he did they'd be doozies." She accelerated and moved into the middle lane.

"Remember the time he bought that so-called house all by himself? He picked it out from a picture he'd seen at a realtor's office. Without telling me, mind you, he gave the guy a big down payment, all of our savings, the rent money and then some. He thought he'd surprise me." Peaches made a clicking noise with her tongue. "He blindfolded me one Sunday morning, put me in the car and then we went out looking for our new house. We rode around and around stopping every once in a while so's he could look at his map. We made a lot of turns but he never found the house. Eventually, on my suggestion, mind you, we drove to the realtor's office for some clarification but the office and the realtor were gone. So was our down payment." She paused in a meaningful way. "Yup, Clute was never very good at decisions."

"You got the money back, didn't you?"

"No, not really. I had to do some fancy foot work or we'd of been out on the street." Peaches mumbled so that Matthew had to strain to hear her, "That's when things really went bad."

"You mean between you and Clute?"

Peaches didn't answer. Instead she gripped the wheel and sent the Bounder out into the left lane. Her brother's questions were starting to irritate her. She changed the subject.

"I know everybody thinks it's a great thing to be making the decisions but honestly it's a lot of responsibility. How about we alternate. Niagara Falls is my pick, then you can have a turn."

"Okay, but Marlene isn't a turn. She's an obligation." There was a long pause while Peaches considered this. She reluctantly agreed to visit their cousin and then brightened suggesting they get something to eat.

Matthew reminded her how they had seen a sign a while back announcing an upcoming McDonald's.

Peaches nodded. "You know, we'll have to be getting some things for the kitchen. We don't need to be spending our money for outside food when we can make our own stuff. We're kind of like turtles, self-sufficient. Don't ya think?"

"Yeah, but we don't have that stuff yet so don't forget to stop." He rubbed his hands together.

"See, look at that Matthew, you're making decisions already."

"Oh shut up."

. . .

The Bounder rocked uncomfortably when Peaches drove off the highway and entered the entrance ramp for McDonald's, following the sign, RV's and Trucks-Park In Rear.

"Humph, look how far we are from the restaurant," Peaches grumbled. "This traveling in a recreational vehicle is going to take some getting used to."

The lot was crowded, but they found a space between a tanker truck and an 18-wheeler. Peaches chewed her gum furiously as she gripped the wheel and watched her mirrors, easing the RV in straight.

"There now, that was a pretty neat piece of cake." She turned the ignition key. "I think I'm getting used to this thing already."

Peaches carefully hopped out and walked around to the front of the Bounder, she admired its big headlights and huge windshield. Continuing around to join Matthew, who had started for the restaurant, she passed under the large rear-view mirror of the J.B. Hunt truck parked just to the left of their RV. To commemorate this special occasion Peaches took the gum out of her mouth and slapped it on the back of the large truck mirror.

"I've always wanted to do that." Peaches grinned as she caught up to Matthew in the parking lot.

"Do what?" asked Matthew.

"Oh, nothing."

Inside the restaurant they placed their order. While waiting they decided to 'take out' and have their first meal in the Bounder, sitting at their new dinette. But as they carried their substantial bag of fast food back to the RV, Peaches immediately noticed a problem.

"What's that?" She pointed to a large black mark and a slight dent on the side of the RV just above the left front tire. "Oh my god! Don't you see it?" She exclaimed, as if Matthew was blind to the problem. Peaches clenched her fists and narrowed her eyes, announcing, "It wasn't there before. It had to be that J.B. Hunt truck. He's the one who hit us."

"You're probably right." Matthew looked at the fender closely and ran his fingers over the black smudge. "I don't think it's a big deal," he reassured her. "There's not much damage. I thought those guys were supposed to be good drivers, professionals."

"Professional my foot. This one is a lousy hit and run nincompoop. He's trying to ruin our vacation." Her anger increased as she looked closely at the damage. Her eyes were moist as she delivered her ultimatum. "If I ever see him again--"

"What do mean? You don't even know what he looks like."

"Don't worry, I don't have to know what the creep looks like. I'll remember his truck."

"There are lots of those trucks around, all the time," Matthew opened the door to the RV. "How do you expect--"

"I'll know." She labored up the steps following her brother. "I'll know."

Their first meal went down hard. The dent was all Peaches could talk about as Matthew listened. His sister dissected the situation numerous times, speculating on how a clumsy barbarian could hit an almost new RV that was only hours old. Downheartedly Peaches pointed out that this could be a bad omen.

Matthew's seat faced the windshield, and as he was biting into the second half of his second Big Mac, he happened to notice a white piece of paper fluttering under the wiper.

"Hold on there, Peaches. It may not have been a hit and run after all." He got up and went outside. Standing at the door, still angry and waiting for her brother, Peaches tried to grab the paper from him as he came back in.

"Let me see that." But Matthew evaded her as he read it out loud.

"The guy's name is Dominick. J.B. Hunt is the company name. He says he's sorry."

Peaches grabbed the paper. "Sorry? Sorry? That's not good enough. Is that guy blind?" She went outside again waving the note. Matthew followed. "Look at all that black. The paint's crumbled. How will we ever match that beige?"

"Peaches handed the note back to Matthew while she examined the damage.

Matthew read the rest of the note. "He says we can call his company and they'll pay to get it fixed. He left a phone number."

"He did?" Peaches stopped abruptly to read the note for herself.

"Well, that's the least he can do. I still think the man needs to be taught a lesson."

As she spoke she hauled herself up the RV steps once again. "This note could have blown away," she huffed. "Couldn't he have waited around to tell us in person. Would it have been so hard to go into that restaurant and ask whose shiny almost new RV might be out in the parking lot and just happened to have been scraped by an incompetent imitation of a professional driver?"

"Let's finish lunch," Matthew coaxed, "then we'll make the call."

"I wish we had one of them mobile phones. We could do it right now, before that trucking company goes out of business or evaporates or something."

After lunch was finished, they found a pay phone. Matthew made the call with Peaches prompting his every word. It was a quick call and information was exchanged.

Back in the RV, Peaches took the wheel.

"You have to admit it sis, they were pretty nice," Matthew made himself comfortable.

"Humph, the way I see it they didn't have a choice. But don't worry, I'm still going to find that guy." The two travelers bumped back out onto I-79 in their damaged motor home. "The way I see it, some people need to be taught a lesson."

CHAPTER FOUR

"If you don't put your glasses on," Peaches warned, "we'll end up in Milwaukee." Matthew squinted hard at the New York State map. He ignored her and got up and went to the dinette, flattening the map to get a better idea of where they were.

"We need to get a fix on exactly where Marlene's prison is," Matthew reminded her. "What's the address?"

Still uncomfortable about visiting a prison, Peaches stepped on the gas. "It would be in the address book, but I'm not sure we brought it."

"We know we didn't leave it in the Plymouth," Matthew reasoned, "And it didn't get burned up in the fire because I've seen it since. It's probably in that back room somewhere. Maybe in those boxes on the side." The Bounder surged ahead and passed a van. Fighting to keep his balance, Matthew careened down the short hallway into the bedroom.

He emerged a few minutes later and waved a small black book. "I've got it here." He held on and made his way to the dinette. It never occurred to him to tell Peaches to slow down. "What would she be under anyway? Marlene or Packer?" He leafed through the pages.

"Probably C for catastrophe."

Matthew looked doubtful then brightened. "Yup you're right. She's listed in the C's." Cousin Marlene Packer, Greybottom Women's Correctional Penitentiary, Greybottom, NY. I'll check the map." He located the town and did some measuring with his pocket ruler. "Looks like it's only about half an inch from Niagara Falls, forty maybe fifty-five miles, that's not too bad."

"Which comes first?" asked Peaches.

"What?"

"Which one comes first, the Falls or the Penitentiary?"

"If we keep going on I-79, then veer off to the right, we'll hit the penitentiary. Niagara Falls is further on."

"Okay then, I've got a plan. That is, if you don't mind. I know you're a little sensitive about this decision making thing." She glanced at him in the rear-view mirror. Matthew thought he might be getting hungry again. For some reason, dealing with his sister always made him feel hungry.

"If we do that right veer up the road and get headed toward the jail, there's sure to be a Walmart's around there," Peaches said. "We can stock up on supplies, stay the night right there in the parking lot, and get started bright and early tomorrow. We'll hit the penitentiary maybe late morning. We don't even have to stay long. Won't she be surprised?" That last comment sounded more enthusiastic than she meant it to be. "What do you think?"

Matthew took a toothpick out of his pocket and held it a minute before putting it in the corner of his mouth.

"Well that's okay with me, but what makes you think Walmart's is going to like the idea of us staying the night?"

"I've seen it lots of times. Back home over on Route 25 you'd swear the store was throwing an afterhours party. Lot's of RV's park there after closing time. No skin off Walmart's teeth. After all, these are self-contained vehicles and you'd better believe that all those RV people need supplies. Paying customers right at the door." Peaches changed lanes. "A little friendly PR never hurts. Now check your map, we don't want to miss that right veer." Within 20 minutes they had found I-51.

"Terrific," Peaches said as she gleefully eased the big vehicle onto the new route. Now all we need is a Walmart's."

But half-hour later, they were still looking. Matthew was discouraged but Peaches was incredulous.

"I don't understand it. They have stores literally all over these United States and we can't find one? I don't want to spend our first night in the penitentiary parking lot. That would definitely add to that black cloud we've already experienced."

An 18-wheeler shook the Bounder as it passed on the left. They read Walmart: Nobody Sells for Less in big letters painted across the back of the truck.

"Look at that." Peaches whooped. "He'll lead us right to the door."

"Are you crazy?" Matthew cried. "What if that thing's going to some warehouse in Rochester?"

Despite his protests, Peaches stayed with the truck, braked when he did, turned and followed the truck with unwavering faith. As miles passed, Matthew sat with his arms crossed, more and more convinced that his sister's idea would lead them nowhere they would want to go.

Suddenly Peaches cried, "Look, his blinker's on!" She put their blinker on too. They exited with the truck, and sure enough, within a mile both vehicles turned into the spacious parking lot of a Walmart supercenter. Peaches triumphantly found a parking spot and turned off the engine. She was glowing.

"Now let's go shopping."

"How about a list, Peaches? Don't you think we need a list?"

"Nah. You make a list if you like, but I've got it all pretty much inside my head." She tapped her temple with her finger. "Besides, we only need a few things." As Peaches walked down the steps, she called over her shoulder, "Bring the money."

Three hours later, the shoppers were done. As they came out, each pushed a full-to-the-brim shopping cart while pulling another.

Peaches huffed, "I don't want to haul these way over there. Why don't I just drive the RV up here to the front entrance and we'll load everything in?"

"Okay," Matthew lined up the carts. "I'll go back and get the other three." It took a while, but working together they got everything crammed into their new home. Matthew had suggested that they put everything away as it went inside, which prompted an exasperated Peaches to yell, "Just get it all in. We'll put it away later."

Tired and frustrated, Matthew pleaded, "But we need to find things when we need them."

"The place is not that big. We'll find 'em." She pushed the last of their purchases in through the Bounder door, climbed the steps and crawled over the pile of new things that were spread out on the floor. Matthew shoved the food they had bought into the limited cupboard space. And after seeing how their new purchases filled the place, Peaches conceded that traveling any farther than across the parking lot would be difficult. They worked hard and eventually their tight little home seemed tighter, but more like home.

After a dinner of warmed tomato soup and a couple of Ellio's Pizzas that didn't fit in the freezer, they looked around contentedly. The friendly smell of dinner was still in the air. Peaches looked at Matthew and smiled, her hazel eyes sincere, wise. Her brother knew by that look, she was going to impart some sort of important life changing information. He knew she expected all his attention.

Peaches leaned across the dinette and spoke with gravity, "Matthew, I'm still hungry. Are you?"

Outside, night at Walmart had snuck up on them. Peaches retired to the back bedroom and called out to her brother, "Isn't this wonderful?" She made up the double bed with fresh sheets right from the package. Then she rummaged around and put things away. Matthew still had a lot to do. He hadn't reached the 'wonderful' stage yet. He wanted to go to sleep, but first he had to figure out how to make the dinette into a bed. If he were smaller, he could just lie down on that skinny couch next to it.

He fiddled with the tabletop for a while and must have hit the right button because there was a click as the brace released from beneath the dinette. After he guided it down to fit in between the benches, Matthew lay the seat backs down on the lowered table to make the mattress. He unpacked his new blue sheets and awkwardly put them around the mattress knowing he would get used to this routine eventually.

Suddenly Peaches bustled out of the bedroom. She clutched several balled up pairs of socks. "Looky here. Bucky forgot to take this stuff out of a drawer. I'll bet they'll fit you." She dumped the socks in the sink. "This was in there too." She held up her hand and displayed a ruby colored ring. "It fits me so I'm keepin' it. We finally have a good omen." Peaches yawned and then headed back to the bedroom. "I'm goin' to bed now, good night."

Matthew mumbled, "Good night." He turned out the kitchen light and climbed into his own dina-bed covering himself with his new quilt.

During their shopping spree they had seen a red queen-size quilt with chickens printed all over it. Peaches insisted they buy it. He did need a blanket and was touched that she remembered his fondness for chickens, but he missed his Rocky Balboa quilt. It had been lost in the fire, and so far, he hadn't been able to find another.

Shadows danced on the drawn curtains. Motor sounds revved, then hummed, eventually dying in the night. Matthew liked the idea that he was sleeping under a window, even though he had to sit up to actually look out. He didn't mind either that his dina-bed was just a scooch too short for his 6'2" frame. It was really quite comfortable if he lay on his side in a semi-fetal position.

Sitting up, he peeked through the curtains. In the glow of the parking lot lights, he could see three other motor homes silhouetted against the night. The RV parked closest to them displayed, *Viv and Dave* painted inside a great big heart.

Loneliness surrounded Matthew like cold fog. He lay back and pulled his quilt around him. He sighed and wondered where his daughter Mimi might be. He hadn't thought of her all day. Then he remembered that today was Friday. Tomorrow would be Saturday, his regular visiting day and he wouldn't be there. Mimi was five years old, six next month. The seventh of September, her birthday, was only two weeks away. Apprehension grabbed at his heart as he tried to snuggle into his new quilt. They were traveling north to Niagara Falls, but Mimi and her mother were back in Pittsburgh. He was going in the wrong direction.

. . .

To Matthew, it felt like Saturday. Maybe it was the noise from the Walmart parking lot, not quite a bustle, but a Saturday kind of slow drift in of early shoppers. When he looked out of his kitchen window, he was relieved that Viv and Dave's motor home was gone. Down the hall Peaches shuffled to the bathroom, mumbling good morning, much like she had done every morning at the house back in Pittsburgh. This would be their first full day in the Bounder.

Finally dressed and revved up for the day, Peaches snapped in a tape and loudly sang, *My Way* along with Frank Sinatra while she prepared breakfast for the two of them: coffee, two bowls of Frosted Flakes covered with sliced banana along with a plate full of toaster waffles smothered in maple syrup. She instructed Matthew to put his bed away so they could use the table, as she spread English muffins with a good coating of butter and jelly. Contentedly, they ate everything.

"Remember the time we formed the eating club with Marlene?" Peaches mused over coffee. "I ate five hamburgers at that picnic. You could only eat four, but Marlene couldn't let me win so she ate six burgers and an ice cream cone just to show off." Peaches giggled. "We disqualified her after she threw up."

Matthew nodded. He was not really listening. There were lots of those Marlene/Peaches/Matthew stories that didn't seem that funny anymore.

Preoccupied, Matthew murmured, "I'll be right back," and went outside to check the tire pressure. A few minutes later, forgetting to get it done, he climbed back in. Dishes in the sink, Peaches was already buckled up in the driver's seat, which signaled that she was ready to start.

Matthew thought he'd give an alternative plan one more try. "I've been thinking about it and I could miss the whole prison stop all together and go right on to Niagara Falls." He fumbled in his pocket for a toothpick and spoke with enthusiasm, "We could be at the Falls late morning and head right back home this afternoon. I'd be able to see Mimi tomorrow."

Peaches sighed and looked impatient. "Home? This is our home now. And didn't you say visiting Marlene was the right thing to do?"

"But Peaches, we've waited this long. Can't we put it off a little longer?" Matthew continued in earnest. "She'll be mad we didn't come sooner and I'll feel like a gawker." Standing, he gripped the back of the passenger seat and kept talking. "Can you imagine Marlene in a jump suit? Wouldn't you rather see her at Aunt Blossom's when she's free?"

"Frankly no." Peaches was getting impatient. "She's controlled in a prison. We can leave and she can't. Come to think of it, my old boyfriend Richie might be living there too. He was kind of a good for nothing. Why don't you just sit down? We'll talk about it while we're driving. We'll meander north and see what happens."

Matthew didn't move.

"Sit down!" Peaches ordered as she turned the key. Then she sweetened her voice and tried to be diplomatic. "Oh, come on. Let's get it over with. It's just a visit. You can see Mimi anytime."

"No. You always do this. You always get your way. You don't have any idea what we're getting into and I can't see Mimi anytime." Matthew sat down in the passenger seat so she'd stop telling him to and continued, "I can't see her now and this visit to the prison will stir up trouble. I wish I hadn't brought it up. Think, maybe they'll do a background check. They always find something wrong. Do you want trouble? I don't want trouble."

Peaches made a face. "Trouble? You're just afraid. You've always been indecisive and afraid. That's why I had to step in all the time to protect you."

Matthew's voice was controlled. "I'm not any of those things. I know what I want. I just get all tied up in what you want." He thought for a moment and added in desperation, "And besides, those guards might know about the fire. They might arrest you thinking you burned the house down deliberately."

It made him feel like he was getting somewhere when Peaches shifted in her seat. In reality, she had repositioned her foot on the gas pedal.

He continued, "And besides, I never paid that parking ticket from Pa's funeral. You told me not to. The one I got for parking by the hydrant when the car wouldn't work. They arrest people for not paying parking tickets. I don't want to go to jail!"

Peaches ignored Matthew and put the motor home in gear and pulled out of the Walmart parking lot. "Matthew, the people at the prison don't care about the fire and besides, we're just visiting, they don't care about us. Everything will be okay; be brave and trust me. And if they do arrest you, I'll visit."

Matthew hesitated for a few moments. He sensed defeat. He reluctantly pulled his seatbelt on as they headed north toward Greybottom and Cousin Marlene.

After driving in silence for a while, Peaches spoke up. "Do you think when we get there, we'll be able to walk right in and ask for Marlene?"

Matthew was still irritated and didn't even look at his sister.

She continued, "The only thing I remember about Marlene and the prison is that we're on the visitor's list. Ma mentioned that once. That makes sense since we're just about the only family she's got except for her mother."

"I think Aunt Blossom stays in Pittsburgh," Matthew said drily.

Peaches nodded in agreement. "I suspect that means we're expected."

"Oh come on, you're telling me that we've been expected for the last eight years?"

Peaches thought about what he had said, "Well, in a matter of speaking, yes. Or at least I think so." They zoomed by a signpost. "Hey, would you look at that? The jail is only 20 miles away."

Matthew was uneasy. "I'll bet they have regulations about just showing up. They might be busy with prison things."

The Bounder wound its way through the outskirts of Greybottom. The terrain became hilly as the RV rimmed fields already harvested and lumbered past orchards where red apples hung like Christmas ornaments in the sun. The air was chilly.

As they rounded a turn, layers of chain-linked fence topped with looped razor wire lined the left side of the road. This sent a chill down Matthew's spine. Peaches drove on. Eventually, they could see a large grey cement building that stood beyond the chain-link on sparse grounds, a stark contrast to the lush countryside they had just traveled through. Dark clouds appeared and blocked the bright sun. They suggested rain.

Matthew clutched the armrests of his seat and shuddered, "I can't go in there."

"Matthew, they intentionally make it bleak. If it was too appealing, everybody would want to go." To cheer things up, Peaches reached over and turned the Frank Sinatra tape over. She hummed along as '*Fools Rush In*' filled the motor home. Eventually, a small but important looking sign marked the driveway of the Greybottom Correctional Facility.

"Here we are," Peaches announced brightly as she stopped the Bounder at a small cement guardhouse. A uniformed officer holding a clipboard walked out and asked their business.

"Hi, we were in the area and thought we'd drop by. Our Cousin Marlene is here."

"She's an inmate?" The guard asked gravely. He glanced at his clipboard. "What's your name? Have you prearranged this visit?"

Peaches looked down at him from the driver's side window and kept her hands on the wheel. She expected to be waved right through.

"Well, no," Peaches said. "We were just in the area. I'm Peaches Packer and this is my brother, Matthew Packer. Of course, I used to be Peaches Nordahl, but after my divorce from Clute I took my name back and became a Packer again. Nordahl was hard to say, and besides, I certainly didn't want to be associated with Clute anymore, since he wasn't all together faithful."

The officer looked at Peaches with disinterest and ignored her attempts to be friendly.

"Wait here." He went back into the guardhouse where they could see he was using the phone. When he returned, he carried a folder. Matthew noticed that the man's crew cut was so short that the sun reflected off his scalp.

"Here's a folder of pertinent information. You can see your cousin this afternoon at two o'clock."

"Two o'clock? What are we gonna do for four hours?"

The officer ignored her question and continued, "There's a list in there that explains what you are and are not allowed to bring an inmate. It will also explain visitation guidelines. If you do not follow the guidelines, you will be asked to leave." Peaches smiled amiably as she tried to make eye contact. The guard was kind of cute.

Peaches tried to strike up a conversation. "I imagine you have to keep things buttoned up around here." The guard just walked away. A bus had pulled up beside them, wire over the windows, Greybottom Correctional painted on the side.

"Hide!" Peaches clutched the folder and hunkered down in her seat with some difficulty. "Marlene might be in there. If she sees, us it'll spoil the surprise."

"I'm not hiding," Matthew sat up straighter. "You know Marlene, even if she sees us out here, she'll still make a big deal when she sees us in there. Let's get out of here."

Still slumped as best she could, Peaches thrust the prison information at Matthew and backed them out onto Route 35 headed toward downtown Greybottom.

Peaches sat up straight in her seat. "How 'bout we get something to eat and look this stuff over? It must be brunch time and I don't feel much like cooking." She drove through town and looked for a place to eat while Matthew leafed through the packet of material.

"They emphasize plastic," he said. He squinted at the information. "We can bring her a big plastic spoon, but only if it's flexible, a flipper—"

"A flipper? What's that?"

"You know, one of those things you turn stuff with." He made an up and down motion with his hand.

"Know why they specify plastic, not metal?" Peaches offered knowingly as she turned the RV into the Princess Diner parking lot. "They don't want us bringing anything in there that can be used as a weapon."

"We can't bring ketchup," he went on. "They also don't want us to bring egg rolls or even TV dinners."

"Well, let's face it Matthew, why would we want to bring Cousin Marlene, who we haven't seen in over eight years, ketchup let alone a TV dinner?" She parked and turned in his direction. "All you've told me is what we can't bring, except for the plastic. Don't they have a 'can bring' list in there? Practical things like bedroom slippers or dominos?"

"Dominos aren't practical."

"Sure they are. They help pass the time. You'd like them if you were better at 'em."

They continued their discussion of what to bring their cousin as they walked across the Princess parking lot. They debated as they ate cheese omelets, home fries, and bagels with low fat cream cheese lathered on top.

Finally, Matthew put down his fork and thoughtfully asked, "If you were in jail, what would you like most? I mean, from a woman's point of view?"

Peaches pondered the question looking into the distance as she fingered the new ring on her finger. Suddenly her face brightened.

"If I were in jail, I'd want someone to bring me a great big fat...key. That's what I'd like most." And she slammed her hand down on the table and shook with laughter. Her Jell-O mold dessert quivered, as Matthew's root beer float slopped onto the table.

Eventually, they left the diner with a list of things they thought would please Marlene, but also fit within the prison guidelines. They drove around looking for stores.

"There," called Matthew. "That CVS will have some of this stuff."

Matthew kept the guidelines handy while Peaches grabbed a shopping basket, "You know how Marlene is. She'll be expecting us to make up for all those years. I'll get the romance novel. You get the gum. I'll meet you in the cosmetics aisle."

"Cosmetics? What do I know about cosmetics? I'll get a TV Guide."

"Matthew, you're just like Clute. He sure liked it when I made the extra effort and put on some makeup, but he was hopeless as far as helping me choose the right colors. Go ahead and pick up one of those People magazines too."

Eventually, Peaches found Matthew near the check out. He looked through a rack of postcards just to the right of the cash register.

"Hey Peaches, here are a couple of pictures of Niagara Falls. It's really pretty. I'm gettin' one for Mimi."

"Maybe we should get some of those for Marlene," Peaches suggested. "After we're gone she can pretend she's come right along with us." She surveyed the postcards for herself. "Look at this one. That's a picture of the prison. Do you think it would be in poor taste to get that one too? Maybe she'd like to see what the outside is like." They made their purchases and left to find a supermarket.

In the next hour and a half, Peaches and Matthew collected one large box of Dunkin Donut holes, one tube of Chapstick, a TV guide, two romance novels, The Big Book of Cross Word Puzzles, one pair of pink fluffy bedroom slippers, Purple Passion lipstick and matching nail polish (Peaches figured that if you couldn't bring ketchup, red lipstick and polish would be frowned upon) one carton of Lucky Strikes, postcards, an adjustable baseball cap with the New York Yankees logo on the crown, one 12 pack of Doublemint Gum and a strip of pictures taken of the two of them in a coin operated picture booth.

"Now that's all. That's enough. We're not obligated to bring a truck load," Matthew declared. Then he noticed the time. "Uh oh, we'd better hurry, we have 15 minutes to get back."

They rushed to the Bounder. Peaches forgot to wait for the automatic step to come out, she leaped up and hit her shin on the first stationery step. She banged her knee on the second, but she made it inside and fell into the driver's seat. She rubbed her bruised leg as Matthew followed with the bags.

They raced back to the prison and arrived at the guardhouse at two. The same official walked out.

"State your business," he demanded, just as before.

"Don't you remember us?" Peaches asked with surprise. "I'm Peaches Packer and this is Matthew Packer. We have an appointment to see our Cousin Marlene and here we are."

The guard pointed. "Go through the gates and follow signs to the parking lot."

As they left the guardhouse, they easily located the smallish lot and felt lucky to find a spot the RV would fit into. But after the Bounder was parked, neither of them moved. They sat and looked out the big front windshield to the scrubby farmland beyond.

"We're here." Matthew broke the silence.

"Yup, here we are," Peaches agreed, not moving.

"We never talked about this like you said we would."

"We can't talk now, we have an appointment. And besides, by the time we talk we could be in and out. Come on, let's go get it over with."

Peaches got up and headed for the door. "I've got the donut holes you get the rest."

. . .

"Are you hyperventilating?" Peaches slowed down to get a better look at her brother. Matthew's breaths were shallow, he almost panted as he and Peaches walked down the dingy corridor of the Greybottom Correctional Facility.

He whispered nervously, "Don't inhale, it smells funny in here. We could catch something."

"They don't open windows in a prison," Peaches explained. "That's so no one can escape. Of course, the air's going to smell funny. Don't worry, you can't catch incarceration."

Halfway down the hall, a uniformed guard, who sat at a small metal desk stopped them asking for their identification.

Peaches looked around for a place to set the box of donut holes down and had no choice but to balance them on top of a stack of papers in front of the guard. She leaned her green purse on a clear corner of the desk and dug down and looked for her wallet. It was a large purse with several compartments, and it took some time.

"I'm not surprised you need to see ID," Peaches commented to make conversation, "We could have been sent by one of those gangs. You know, the Bloods or those Crispies." She laughed to herself as her brother looked on in horror. "Now they'd be the ones to get Marlene outda here. You go ahead Matthew," she dug deeper into her bag without looking up, "Marlene's awaitin'. I'll be just a few minutes."

Handing his ID to the guard, Matthew nudged Peaches and whispered, "Don't say stuff like that."

"My license is in here somewhere." She took out the bicycle pump she carried in her purse and set it on the desk.

"Miss, did you come on a bike?"

"No, but you never know when somebody might need blowing up. I might to have a fix-it shop some day. As she dug even deeper she asked, "How about my Shop Rite card? My name's signed on the back."

"It has to have a picture," the Guard seemed bored as he handed Matthew's license back.

"Can't my brother vouch for me?" She nodded toward Matthew, but the guard only shook his head. She lifted out a number of other things, including a Hershey Bar, a box of Oreos and a toothbrush wrapped in a green scarf. Finally, she located her wallet at the bottom. "Luckily, I had it renewed just last year otherwise, I'd still be a Nordahl with no picture."

"A Nordahl?" The puzzled guard questioned, and then thought better of it. He directed them farther down the corridor to another officer and what looked like a metal detector.

Matthew stepped up first. He placed the bags he carried on a conveyer belt and emptied his pockets into a little basket. He walked through the detecting arch. The indicator light showed green.

"This is just like on TV," Peaches enthused and placed her handbag and the box of donut holes on the conveyer belt. She confidently strolled through the metal detector while a large red light came on above her head.

Matthew rolled his eyes and the guard looked suspicious. He gestured toward the light and cleared his throat.

"Officer, I don't have anything. I don't even have pockets." She twirled around.

"Perhaps a belt buckle?"

Peaches shook her head.

"Let's try it again."

The officer directed her through a second time. Matthew's heart sank as the red light went bright. He imagined armed guards swooping in as the dingy prison walls closed around them.

"Are you wearing a supporting undergarment?"

"A what?" Peaches cleared her throat. "You mean a bra? Well of course. I always wear one." Her tone was defensive.

"Would your supportive undergarment have metal parts?"

Peaches thought for a moment. "Yes! My Maidenform. It's underwire. Of course, that's making the thing go off."

Matthew was mortified at his sister's disclosure. His face felt hot.

"We'll find out," the officer continued. "I'd like you to step into the lady's room and remove it. Put it in this basket."

Peaches glared at him.

"But now that we know what the problem is, why?"

"Regulations," the officer said with a nod toward the lavatory.

Peaches went in and grumbled as she came out. "This is ridiculous. What if I had lots of fillings in my teeth? Would I have to put my head in the basket too? If this doesn't work out, you're not laying a frisking hand on me."

Minus her bra, the green light went on as she passed through the detector.

"See, I told ya," Peaches looked at the guard with satisfaction. Matthew felt clammy and a little nauseous but relieved.

"Boy, if I had known this was going to be such a *thing* I would have agreed to keep right on going to Niagara Falls, no stopping. I thought it would be a good idea to visit this place. Now I see it would have been better just to send postcards." Peaches went back into the lavatory.

Matthew stood inconspicuously for a few minutes then asked the guard. "Do you do this to every visitor?"

"It's random." The officer looked at his watch then added, "Usually we check first timers. After today, your pictures and your updated information will be in our data base."

"Pictures? You don't have any pictures of us," Peaches noted as she came back out.

"We will," the officer relayed. He directed first Matthew and then Peaches to stand in front of a screen as he aimed a Polaroid and took their pictures. The pictures slowly revealed themselves, on the corner of the officer's desk.

Peaches had just about had enough. Not only was she tired and exasperated from the ordeal, but her picture made her look uncharacteristically fat and out of shape.

"You'll have to leave your personal belongings in the lockers in the next room. I'll check those packages you've gotten for your cousin. I'll return any items not appropriate for the inmate when your visit is through. As Matthew lifted one of the bags onto the desk, the Yankee cap fell out.

"For example, you can't leave that hat."

"Why? Peaches asked, "It's a New York team. This is New York State isn't it?"

"It's not the team, Miss. It's the color. Weren't you provided with instructions? It explicitly says you can't bring anything blue or orange to any inmate. This hat is blue."

He took the hat and placed it on a table behind him. "What are you going to do with the hat?" asked Matthew.

"If it's still here, you can pick it up on your way out."

Matthew was shocked. "You mean someone might steal it? But this is a prison. What if I wore a blue Yankee hat in here? What would happen?"

"That's okay. You're a visitor. You're allowed to wear a blue cap."

"Let me have it." Matthew held out his hand. "We just won't give it to Marlene." He put it securely on his head.

"Do you have to, Matthew?" Peaches picked out one of the donut holes and popped it in her mouth. All the commotion was making her hungry. "You always look so silly in hats."

"Put your personal belongings in a locker then continue down the corridor through the doors at the end. By that time Miss Packer's approved items will be available. I'll let them know you're ready to see her."

Matthew pulled the hat farther down on his head and followed Peaches into the locker room. He reminded her that Rocky wore a baseball hat.

"Not all the time. Besides, he's handsome." Faced with a bank of grey metal lockers, she chose one near the door and tried to stuff her green pocketbook through the opening. "These lockers are tiny. Maybe I should take some of this stuff out to the Bounder," Peaches suggested.

"Oh no." Matthew had had it with his sister. "If you do that, you won't come back. I'll be left in here visiting Marlene by myself." It was finally decided they would put half the contents in one locker and the other half in another and use a third one for the bag.

"What a big ta-do," Peaches said as she slammed the last door. "It's getting late, we're never going to get outa this place."

Matthew glared at her. At the end of the hallway, they picked up Marlene's gift bags and pushed through double doors at the same time, their bodies got stuck briefly in the door opening.

"Look at all these people." Peaches put her hands on her hips. "We'll have to let Marlene find us."

An officer checked his clipboard and directed them to a table. He explained the rules.

"Visitors may kiss and hug at the beginning and end of each visit. You may hold hands during the visit, but no other physical contact is allowed. Stay at your assigned table. Do you understand? There will be no contact with any other inmates other than the person you have come to see. Any questions?"

"She's our cousin," explained Peaches as she sat down. "We won't be doing much hand holding."

They had had the impression that their cousin would come out right away, but that didn't happen.

"Peaches, don't do that," whispered Matthew when she nodded and smiled to an inmate who passed close to their table. "Didn't you hear what the guard said? The long wait is probably a test. I know they're watching every move."

"I'm just being friendly." Peaches checked her watch. "Do you realize we've been waiting almost an hour? That's just like Marlene."

Matthew felt uncomfortable. "Maybe they can't find her. Knowing Marlene, she probably escaped. Course, they could be checking our records. Maybe we should go."

"Or maybe this place is disorganized."

Peaches could be unpredictable when she was agitated, which put Matthew on edge.

"Look!" Peaches pointed across the room. "Those people came in after we did and their inmate is already visiting. I know that guy over by the window came in after we did. He's only been here for twenty minutes tops, and his person is already here. Something's funny about this and I'm going to find out what."

"Hey," Matthew sat up with relief. "Isn't that her?"

Peaches craned her neck. "No, that's not her." She stood up to get a better look. "Oh sure, that's her." She yelled and waved, "Marlene, over here!"

Marlene was coming toward them at a good clip. She was a monument of a woman dressed in green, her dark hair blunt cut like Buster Brown. As she approached, Matthew stood up with his sister and Marlene caught them both in an awkward bear hug.

"You two certainly took your time gettin' here," Matthew and Peaches sat back down while Marlene made herself comfortable across from her cousins. "I declare, you two are bigger and better!" With her chunky forearms on the table she asked, "Have I changed? Don't I look a little sallow in green?"

Matthew didn't think she looked sallow but she did indeed look like a big avocado. Not wasting any time, Marlene got down to business. "I'm ready." She rubbed her hands together. "Ya have to tell me the news. Once in a while, Pittsburgh makes the evening TV, but not very often and then it's never something I want to actually know about." Marlene folded her hands and waited eagerly.

"Well," Matthew started, "Pa died and the house burned down."

"No. Whew whee. You're just lettin' me have it aren't you? That's a lotta bad luck." Marlene shook her head.

Peaches picked up the conversation, "We bought one of those RV's. It's right out in the parking lot. That's where we live now."

"What about Clute? Where's he? You two have any little ones?"

"No, he's history," answered Peaches right away. "But I'm in the market for someone. I need a whole new life."

Before she could go on Marlene asked, "If you're not married to Clute than what's that fancy ring on your finger? You engaged to someone else?"

Peaches fingered the ruby ring and shook her head. She was at a loss to explain how desperate she really was for a partner, not a pretend vacation with her brother. But Marlene didn't wait on an explanation and moved the conversation along.

"Ma wrote something about a little girl. You sure you don't have a little girl? What caused the fire anyway?"

"The fire was accidental," Matthew answered quickly. "And that little girl is Mimi."

"Mimi? Mimi who?"

"Mimi Packer. She's mine," Matthew explained proudly.

"You?" Marlene was all astonishment. "I didn't think you even liked girls, let alone having one of your own."

"I like girls, just not all girls."

"So how did Mimi come about?" Marlene leaned toward them, her forearms rooted her to the table. "You're makin' me work hard for this information."

"Oh, in the regular way."

"You know what I mean. Who'd you marry?"

"Nobody." Matthew cleared his throat. "Maybe you remember Dawn? She's the girl who lived above Ziggie's Grocery. We were going out some, nothing serious. A movie once in awhile—"

"What do ya mean, nothing serious?" Marlene sat up and slapped her hand on the table.

"She tricked him," chimed in Peaches. "She threw herself at my brother and then lied and said she was on the pill and bang, she's pregnant. She did it for the money."

"What money?" Marlene tried to stay with her.

"Unemployment from when he was laid off from the bus garage or more likely to just get back at me." Peaches self-righteously sat up straight and then settled back into her chair. "My brother here had the sense not to marry her, although it took a great deal of persuading.

You might remember that I know Dawn better than most."

"Wasn't she your best friend in high school?" Marlene said.

"Exactly." Peaches went on, "that relationship fell apart about the time we left that institution although of late it's heated up a bit. Anyway, people now-a-days practice dual parenting. They don't have to get married just for the child's sake anymore. In fact, anything I've read emphasizes that if the parents aren't happy, the child isn't happy and Matthew would not have had one bit of happiness with Dawn." Matthew felt invisible. "We do love Mimi though. She's a sweet little thing."

"Well." Marlene digested the news. "Where is Mimi now? In the RV?"

"With Dawn," Matthew said. "Her sixth birthday is just two weeks away."

Marlene was quiet for a moment as she tried to make sense of it.

She took a deep breath and then changed the subject. "Did Clute die?"

"No such luck. I divorced him and took my rightful name back." Peaches shook her head. "I couldn't stand him any more."

"Why not? You thought he was pretty nifty there for a while."

"I found out that he was not all-together faithful. My mother put up with my father's goings-on until the day she died, so I just decided one day that wasn't for me. By the time Clute got home from his job at Sunoco, I had all his belongings out on the front lawn. You should have seen him, he pleaded innocence, but I knew. That was almost a year ago. So for my 42nd birthday, I gave me the gift of freedom."

"Hum," said Marlene.

They sat in silence for a little while to honor Peaches' freedom and to allow Marlene to soak up the family news.

Peaches took gum from her pocket and offered it around and then popped a stick into her mouth.

"Well, how are you?" Matthew finally asked. "I mean, um... well, how is everything?"

"I only have 258 more days in this place. It ain't been any picnic, but it ain't been that tough either. I got my GED a while back. You remember I dropped out of high school during our senior year to be with Ned," Marlene scratched her nose. "Now I'm thinking of taking a college course or two in my remaining time here. Lots of people do it although, I've heard that some of the courses can be pretty tough."

Marlene shifted her weight on the hard chair. "I'm not so sure I'm up to tough, so I thought there might something easy, birding or flower arranging, something to kind of ease me in. I want to be prepared when I get out. I'm planning to go straight and I'll need a direction." Marlene nodded and continued. "Ned'll be in the slammer for three more years, so I won't have his bad influence nudging me into anything. I'll get back on my feet before he sees the light of day. I'll be all right."

Marlene suddenly brightened with a new idea. "Course, I could forget about a career and ride around with you two in the RV. Those things are great. Wouldn't that be fun?"

Peaches and Matthew both smiled politely.

"Do you think you'll get your license back?" asked Peaches to change the subject.

"Hum, I would think so, eventually. After all, it was an accident. You know that old guy wasn't watching where he was going at all. It wasn't my fault he walked out into traffic."

"Marlene, weren't you driving kind of fast?"

"Well maybe, but we were being chased. You know that."

"Marlene," Matthew cried. "You'd just robbed a bank and those guys chasing you were the police."

"Oh, I know all that stuff. It was just an unfortunate chain of events."

"You could have killed him." Matthew felt his face grow hot.

"I know, I know. They would have tacked on a considerable number of years to my time here."

"What about the guy?" Matthew cried. "Don't you care about him?"

"Of course, I care," Marlene said. "I'm not going to jump off the deep end about some old guy who's too slow to get himself across a street and too blind to actually see traffic. But sure, I care."

Matthew rubbed the side of his face, hard.

Peaches cleared her throat and changed the subject again. "We brought you some stuff."

"I was thinking you might have," Marlene said. "All those years watching other people get presents every time visiting day came around. It's sure hard on a person's mind."

"We brought donut holes," Peaches said.

"Well, that's special." Marlene clasped her hands with enthusiasm.

"And Doublemint gum."

Marlene nodded.

"And we brought People and TV Guide and slippers and a Chap Stick." Matthew smiled.

"My, my," said Marlene with enthusiasm. "It's just like Christmas. You've outdone yourselves."

"And two novels, *Trophy Husband*, and *Tender Torment*. They're romances, the lady at the drug store said they were good." Marlene smiled and nodded.

"And we were going to give you that hat Matthew's wearing, but we couldn't because it's blue. It would have been better if you were a Pirates fan like everybody else in Pittsburgh. Black, gold, white, yes, but the rules say no blue."

"Well, I see it's blue. It doesn't even look good on Matthew." Marlene sniffed. "They'd actually extend that stupid rule to include a genuine Yankee cap? Isn't this New York State? Here let me try it on." And she reached over and took it off Matthew's head. "He's really not the baseball type anyway." She put the hat squarely on top of her head and pulled it down at the brim. "I like this. I like this a lot."

"But you can't keep it," Matthew whispered.

Marlene looked at Matthew. "You just want it for your self. You were always a little selfish. I think I should be able to keep this present even if it's not perfectly and completely legal. After all, I waited years for presents. I don't have to wear it out in public. I know I can't do that, but in the privacy of my cell, what's the harm?"

Peaches whispered, "Marlene get a grip on yourself. The regulations say you can't have that hat. We'll get in trouble if we give it to you."

The guard nearby eyed them and quietly walked over. "Is everything all right here?"

"Right as rain," Marlene said a little too loudly. They all smiled brightly to back her up.

After he had gone, Marlene hissed at Peaches, "What do you mean self-control, you frumpy, overweight blabber mouth? At least I'm not wearing a fancy ring pretending I'm engaged."

Stunned Peaches boiled up a retort as Marlene called the guard back.

"Excuse me sir, let me run this by you," Marlene started calmly. "I've just been presented with a genuine Yankee hat." She pointed to the hat on her head. "I'm planning on keeping it just as a souvenir, that's not a problem is it?"

"According to regulations inmates are not allowed to have clothing in blue. That hat is blue."

"I don't care, you make me wear this ugly green thing." Marlene raised her voice. "I like blue and I like the Yankees. It's un-American not to allow me to keep this hat." Matthew froze as Marlene went on. "That's just one example of some of the stupider rules around here. I'm simply exercising my freedom of opinion." Marlene was getting excited. She reached up holding the hat on her head. "I refuse to--"

"Sorry folks, this visit is over," the guard said quietly, but emphatically.

With difficulty, he took the hat off of Marlene's head and handed it to Matthew.

"Over? Over so soon? They just got here. It took them years to get here and you want them to leave? That's un-American too. You're un-American." Marlene gestured with her fist toward the guard as she hopped up and down.

Guards seemed to appear from nowhere. The group of relatives was surrounded. Matthew and Peaches were told to leave.

"It's been nice, Marlene," Peaches quickly got up,

"See ya now." Matthew nodded as he backed toward the door. He clutched the baseball hat.

With a guard on each side of Marlene, she was marched, with difficulty, toward a door on the other side of the room.

"Come back real soon, ya here," she yelled as Peaches and Matthew headed the other way toward the exit sign. After making a quick stop in the locker room to collect Peaches' things, they scrambled out into the late afternoon sunlight. They sprinted as best they could toward the RV. Peaches unlocked the door and, without a word, they climbed into their seats. Peaches started the RV, backed out and headed toward Route 98.

A few miles down the road, Matthew broke the silence. "That was terrible. She hasn't changed a bit."

CHAPTER FIVE

Even though August was too early to see even a splash of pretty colored leaves in the wooded hills of upstate New York, Peaches and Matthew agreed that the potential was there. As the Bounder traveled north away from Greybottom and toward Niagara Falls, Peaches and Matthew quietly recovered from their visit with Marlene.

It was a little after five in the afternoon and neither had mentioned dinner despite signs that announced that a burger restaurant was coming up ten miles away, then three and finally 500 feet on the right. In a last minute decision, Peaches turned the wheel and sent the RV swerving into a Burger King parking lot. It eventually stopped with a jolt.

"What-ja-do that for?" Matthew gasped as he righted himself. "There you go again, making all the decisions on your own." Then he thought for a moment, "It's okay though, after all that visitin', I guess I could go for a little something."

"We're not here to eat. Look at that truck over there. It's JB Hunt. It may be the one."

"The one?" Matthew was dismayed. "Haven't we had enough trouble for one day without you holding a grudge? Peaches, we don't have any real damage and I guarantee there won't be any on that truck either. Maybe a smudge of paint on his tire and that could be from anything. Besides, how would you know if it's even the right truck?"

"My gum's on his mirror," she said with a big grin.

"Your what?"

Peaches had stopped the RV not far from the 18-wheeler. She ignored him.

"I'll be right back." She rushed out the door, but came back slower. As she climbed the steps a few moments later, she reported, "Nope, that's not the one."

"You're looking for gum? What gum? Your gum? That's disgusting." Matthew made a face. "How do you know it didn't fall off?"

"It was squishy when I slapped it between the mirror and its brace. That gum will be on there long after the truck dies."

Matthew reached for the map to reassure himself that Niagara Falls wasn't too far away. He wearily said, "Let's keep going. I'll see if I can find a camp ground."

"Roger Wilco." Peaches stepped on the gas.

He was tired of his sister showing off, so he didn't even ask who Roger Wilco was.

. . .

It took them a couple of hours to find Falls View Trailer Park, but once they did, its twinkling lights announced a safe haven. Matthew went in to make arrangements, but came right out.

"We can't stay here. No room. In fact, the guy said there won't be any vacancies in any of the trailer parks around here. There's an RV rally. He suggested Walmart's."

Disappointed, but with no other choice, they followed the clerk's directions to the local big box store's roomy parking lot. Peaches chose a spot far away from the vehicles already there. She didn't want to take a chance that their RV might get hit again.

Exhausted, they went to bed right away. But before climbing under the covers, Peaches sat on the edge of her bed and thought about what Marlene had said. She held up her hand and admired her ring. Marlene was right. Anyone interested in her might take one look and assume she was spoken for. It could be mistaken for an engagement ring. At 42, she couldn't afford to scare off prospects. The ring was beautiful and she loved the way it naturally reflected her sparkling personality and style. She decided to leave it on for now and just slip it into her pocket if Mr. Right showed up.

Something else bothered her. Marlene had called her frumpy and overweight. That hit a nerve. Peaches looked at herself in the mirror that hung on the back of her bedroom door. She turned around and looked from a different angle. It might be possible that underneath her roomy new sweat suit there were some extra pounds, certainly not more than a hundred. But frumpy? Marlene was the queen of frumpy and it horrified Peaches to think she was in that category. Of course, Peaches recalled, Dawn had mentioned 'frumpy' more than once. Or was it dumpy? But not Marlene, she's family.

Maybe, Peaches thought, she's simply jealous because of that ugly green thing she has to wear or maybe Marlene's mad because of her silly haircut. Peaches regarded her favorite muumuu that lay in a beige heap in the corner. It worried her that if she really was frumpy, how long had that been going on? Wouldn't Matthew have mentioned it? She thought for a moment, probably not. It was true that for some reason, there hadn't been any interest in her of late, so if she was going to find a man, perhaps she should make a few adjustments.

After mulling over the situation for a while, Peaches made the only decision she could. She would change. She didn't know how, but she'd have to figure it out. Wrapped in her robe, she went to the kitchen for some potato chips and a diet soda. She said good night to Matthew and added, "Let's get going early. I feel a transformation coming on."

But when Peaches and Matthew got up late the next morning, the transformation had to be put on hold. Without breakfast, they scrambled into action and drove toward Niagara Falls. They hoped to beat members of the RV rally and possible hoards of late summer tourists.

The rain should have discouraged everyone, but there were no spaces left large enough to accommodate the Bounder in the first three parking lots, at least in Peaches' opinion. Frustrated, she drove by all the others not finding any place she wanted to put their RV.

"I'm not ready to do that one either."

Matthew sighed loudly. "I could drive."

"Be patient. Let's drive through town. You look, I'll drive."

"Look for what?"

"At least six spots in a row."

"Six? We're not that big."

"I'm not ready to parallel park. I need room to maneuver."

"I could drive," Matthew repeated.

Peaches was offended. "Is something wrong with my driving? I'm just being extra careful. You never know who might be out there. Stop complaining. Something will free up."

"When? We haven't even had breakfast yet."

"You know, you're right." With a grunt, Peaches took a sharp right into a small strip mall; the Bounder almost filled the parking lot.

"Oh come on, we can't park here. See that sign: No Falls Parking."

"This is the best I can do right now." Peaches turned off the engine. "How do they know we don't have business here? Anyway, we're having breakfast, not visiting the Falls. We're not even ready for the Falls."

"Don't get snippy. I'm simply pointing out that we're not customers so we'll get a ticket and this thing's so big we'll get a big ticket."

"We'll buy some gum." Peaches solved the problem as she got eggs and bacon out of the fridge. "Besides, nobody's here so our RV makes it look like they're busy."

"There are no customers here because they aren't opened yet and when they do open, they won't have any customers because we're taking up all the parking spaces. How 'bout we try one of those valet places."

"Oh no, we're not paying to park this boat." Peaches thought for a moment then got an idea. "This is what we're going to do. After we eat, I'll stay in the motor home and you go look at the Falls. If it's still raining when you come back you can tell me all about it, but if it's sunny, I'll go."

"That's stupid." Matthew was incensed. "You want me to go by myself, in the rain, to look at water falling over some rocks, while you stay here dry and happy, babysitting the Bounder?"

"Matthew, we don't have a choice." They bickered while they ate breakfast, but in the end Matthew left, trudging through puddles to find Niagara Falls. He hadn't gone half a block when Peaches cranked open the louvered window and yelled, "The other way, Matthew."

. . .

Four hours later, the rain had stopped. Matthew, exhausted and soaked to the skin, finally found the small strip mall on Pine, but the parking lot was empty. Peaches and the Bounder were gone. He could be at the wrong place, but no, there was Wu's Chinese and the barbershop his sister had suggested he go to. Even the CVS was over there at the end. His heart raced and a wave of panic took his breath away. He wrapped his flapping Cave of the Winds poncho close around him.

He tried the easy solution. He looked up and down the rain soaked street. He expected to see the Bounder barreling toward him, headlights flashing. It wasn't. A flock of geese in perfect V formation flew overhead. They honked wildly as they headed southeast. Confused, he became aware of another honking. It persisted until he noticed it came from the IGA parking lot across the street. Was that their RV tucked in the back of the lot? It was. His sister waved.

With both arms in the air, Matthew waved back. He crossed the street enthusiastically. He dodged cars, as the brochures in his hand flapped like captured birds. Still some distance away, Peaches was a blur of red and there was something on her head. Matthew didn't once remember his sister ever wearing a hat. No matter, he was glad to see her. He walked briskly across the lot dripping water. By the time he reached the Bounder, Peaches had gone inside. Matthew opened the door and gratefully waited for the automatic step to come out. He went on in, happy to be home.

A small puddle collected on the carpeted floor as Matthew looked at his sister. Peaches had not been wearing a hat at all. She had done something to her hair and she had a dress on he was sure he had never seen before.

Peaches giggled under his gaze. "The morning was serendipitous. I learned that word in *Glamour*." She twirled and knocked a bag of Cheez Doodles off the counter. "It's the new me. What do you think?" When he said nothing, she spoke louder as if her brother was hard of hearing. "What do you think? Say something."

Matthew looked closer and blinked. "What happened?" Smiling she smoothed her form fitted red dress. The V of her neckline showed modest cleavage. The sleeves were stylishly pushed up to the elbow, as yellow stars of all sizes danced in and around the material.

"That's quite a dress."

"Walmart. I got it the other day on a whim. I was saving it."

Matthew nodded. He realized he was on shaky ground.

She continued in a deep voice. "Before you is the new, passionate me. No more frumpy muumuus. No more trying to make me into something I'm not. I'm a fire breathing female."

Matthew took a step back.

"See this hair?"

He blinked. "Is it real?"

"It's mine, all right. I got it in a box at CVS just after you left. I must admit it's not exactly how I thought it would turn out, but I'm getting used to it." Peaches picked up the Clairol box from the counter and showed him the woman on the front panel. "First, I cut it to look like the girl's in the picture. It's called a blunt cut. Anyone can do it."

Matthew nodded and noticed that one side of Peaches' hair was longer than the other. When she twirled, the two sides formed an unnatural ridge at the back. He wanted to sit down, but didn't dare.

"You probably think it started when Marlene called me frumpy." Peaches sat down at the dinette. "She's one to talk. But it really started with Dawn. You know how difficult and opinionated she can be."

Matthew opened his mouth to object, but Peaches went on.

"Remember when she criticized my dress at Mimi's birthday party last year? At the time, I disregarded her for Mimi's sake. But she's the one that first used the word frumpy and it's been eatin' on me ever since, even though I know she wouldn't even remember."

Matthew sneezed.

"But having great big, prison inmate Marlene remind me about that word at the jail was just too much. I knew I had to do a little something. So I went into the drugstore for *Glamour* magazine. I figured it would guide me. I also got some gum like I said and, wouldn't you know, but right next to the gum was the hair coloring section. I knew immediately that that was the answer. I particularly liked the frosting look so I got this Frost and Tip stuff."

Matthew shifted his weight and sneezed again.

"Anyway, when I came back, I said to myself, why wait? Just do it. It's the neatest stuff and it doesn't take any time at all." She picked up a badly stained piece of rubber. "Look they have this little cap."

"But you have orange patches on your green head." Matthew moved back another step in case Peaches took this information badly.

She seemed to not hear him and went on. "You put this rubber hat on. See it has holes." She showed him how her finger could poke right through and explained, "They provide you with a little crochet hook to pull the part of your hair you want to color right through." She demonstrated with a pulling action. "But the crochet hook fell down the sink so I used a fork. It worked even better. It made the holes a little bigger and that meant it was easier to pull the hair through." She paused for a moment as Matthew's comment sank in. "What patches?"

"Orange patches. You've got 'em all over your head."

She plumped her hair with her free hand. "What do you know about hair? Of course, it's possible that a little too much of that color cream went down through the holes onto the other hair, but it'll blend with the first washing. Don't-cha-think?" She checked the box again. "I was a little surprised that the color wasn't exactly like the picture, but that might have happened when I got busy reading this article about attitudes and forgot about the processing time. I think *Glamour* has given me new direction." Peaches held the frost and tip box up again. "Don't you think we look just like sisters?"

Matthew smiled and changed the subject. "I saw the Falls, and speaking of misreading, I walked down a path that was closed down. I slipped where the pavement was torn up and almost fell into the water, but I held onto the broken fence and yelled and yelled until the men that had been working there came back from a break. Five guys dragged me out. They said I could have died. They called an ambulance and when the paramedics came they wanted me to get checked out at the hospital, but I slipped out the side door and ran. They only chased me for a block or two. I guess they figured I was okay if I could run."

Not really listening, Peaches was busy making a sandwich, "Let's face it I'm never going to run. I'll probably never be small either but with the new me comes the attitude that what you see is what you get, and with me you get a lot." Matthew opened his mouth to say something but Peaches went on, "I think this color goes better with my personality; I wanted to make a statement."

Matthew coughed and his Cave of the Winds poncho rustled a bit. "Orange is a statement, Peaches."

Matthew sneezed with more force than any of the other times. He was chilled to the bone and still dripping wet. Peaches finally noticed.

"Good god, you look half drowned. How come?" She had not heard the account of his brush with death. "It stopped raining hours ago." She thought for a moment. "I know why. I heard on the radio this morning that there's more rain here because of the waterfalls than in regular places. Maybe that baseball hat you like to wear brings you bad luck. It didn't do Marlene much good. You and I had better stick together from now on." She was in a benevolent mood. "The sun's coming out. Let's leave the Bounder right here for the afternoon and go look at the Falls." Matthew opened his mouth to protest, but she continued. "There's plenty of room. They won't mind. We should have thought of it before. Now go get changed." Matthew gave her a weary look. "You don't mind going again, do you? You can be my guide."

After Matthew put on dry clothes and they had a bit to eat, he felt better so they headed out toward the Falls. Peaches walked tall as she felt gentle breezes tussle her new hair. The IGA parking lot was half-full. She suddenly had second thoughts about leaving the Bounder.

"Matthew, let's go to the supermarket first."

"Why? You said it would be okay for us to stay here."

"I think it is." Peaches waited for Matthew to open the market door for her. "I just think it would be smart to let them know we're serious customers. This won't take any time at all."

"Why are you making everything so complicated? We don't need anything."

Peaches whispered, "We're establishing a presence in the store." With determination, they walked up and down the aisles and pushed a shopping cart to play the part of serious shoppers. At frozen foods, Peaches considered a bag of peas, but put them back. She added red shoe polish and a package of household sponges to their cart.

"Do you even have red shoes?"

"No," Peaches looked down at her sandals. "But I'm looking for some to go with this dress." People noticed her. In the candy aisle, she chose several packs of Doublemint Gum.

"You can never have too much gum." She smiled at Matthew. "You go look at the fruit." Peaches noticed a nice looking man while she looked at paper towels in aisle eight. He had walked passed her while he checked out some cleaning products, but she felt he was really looking at her.

She thought she heard him say "wow" under his breath. He smiled nicely and apologized when he got in her way. With warm enthusiasm Peaches smiled back. Her admirer was well dressed. She was about to say something clever when Matthew interrupted with a bag of grapefruit. As she turned back to speak to the man, he was gone, his green jacket slipped out of sight around the corner into the next aisle.

"Oh Matthew, look what you've done." Peaches was exasperated. "When there's a man near me pretend you don't know me. How am I supposed to meet anyone if you keep scaring them off?" The shopping experience was over in about 15 minutes.

Depositing the grocery bag inside the Bounder, they turned to go.

"Now what are you doing?" Matthew was tired and had lost patience with his sister.

"If there's any doubt that we're paying customers this will prove it." Peaches taped the register slip to the front windshield. They locked the door and walked across the parking lot again, ready to be tourists. A brisk walk brought them to the park entrance.

"Hey look, this is the oldest National Park in the United States," Matthew read the sign. They followed a wide walkway bordered by a riot of opulent geraniums that gracefully arched and bent on either side. Vibrant roses perfumed the air as couples strolled hand in hand. The path ended on a bluff that overlooked turbulent waters that misted the onlookers. The noise was deafening. Matthew nudged Peaches and pointed to a couple with their arms around each other kissing.

Then he shouted so he could be heard over the roar. "This is the honeymoon capital of the world. A place of new beginnings." He quoted a sign he had seen that morning.

Peaches nodded and felt forlorn as she watched the white foamy cascades of sparkling water. She wiped the spray from her cheek.

"Don't cha like it Peaches?" Matthew shouted.

"I do," Peaches shouted back. She nodded her head. She looked up at him; her orange streaks, blew wildly and glowed in the sun.

Renewed, Matthew was caught up in the moment and threw his arms out in an expansive motion. He almost hit Peaches in the head.

"It's romantic and wonderful and beautiful all at the same time."

Peaches had tears in her eyes that blurred the spectacular scene. "But Matthew, I'm here with you and you're here with me."

Matthew smiled knowingly. "I'm glad to be here with you too, Peaches," he yelled.

A desperate loneliness seized Peaches and she stared at the water. She said, mostly to herself, "In all the millions and billions of people in the world, there must be one person out there for me." But her words missed Matthew's ears. They were snatched away by the roaring water. Visiting the honeymoon capital of the world with her brother took all the zip out of the trip for Peaches.

They were both pooped with all the walking. They stopped frequently to rest on the convenient park benches and snacked when the opportunity presented itself.

Eventually, Matthew complained that he had had enough and was ready to go back to the motor home. He hoped that they would head back to Pittsburgh that afternoon. Peaches rebuffed him and pointed out that since they were finally here at the Falls, they might as well do something.

"Where's that boat we saw in the brochure?"

Matthew pulled a crumpled map from his back pocket and studied it to get his bearings. After some bickering, and much consternation, they made their way to the The Maid of the Mist pay booth. Matthew complained that he had already gotten drenched that morning and was not at all excited about a medium-sized boat that took you right to the base of tremendous plummeting water.

"You can't help but get wet."

As they viewed the waiting boat, Peaches had a solution. "Maybe you can just watch from underneath that top tier there and you won't get wet." They were a little early for the cruise so Matthew purchased coffee for himself and tea for his sister from a vendor close by. With great delight, Peaches noticed that her teabag string had a special message just like the Chinese tea bags back in Pittsburgh.

"*By putting others first, you will always win.*" Peaches thought about that. I've certainly been putting others first. Didn't I let Matthew go first this morning when I decided we'd take turns coming to the Falls? My transformation had nothing to do with that, of course and I'm certainly not winning anything hanging around with my brother. What would I win anyway, more tea? I want someone to love and cherish and take care of me.

The line was moving as people filled up Boat II. It rocked gently with the wind.

"A lot of people on board," Matthew said. "I'll stay out here in front with you until we get close. Then I'll duck in under the overhang."

It was a wonderful, exciting ride that took them to the very base of the thundering falls. When they got close to the raging water, and the deck started to get wet, Matthew left Peaches to take shelter. The loud speaker blared out garbled facts that Peaches couldn't really understand. She was content to just lean over the rail and get a close up view of the swirling water, getting misted made her feel a part of it all.

Out of the corner of her eye, she thought she saw something green. Peaches turned her head quickly. Was that the man from the supermarket? Yes. Incredible. He was standing at the rail not ten feet away. Had he seen her? Had he followed her here? Peaches quickly looked away. Then without turning her head, she moved only her eyeballs to the extreme right. He was looking at her as he steadied himself at the rail. Peaches took a chance and turned. She looked at him. He *was* looking at her and he kept looking at her and smiled a wonderful smile. Peaches smiled too, and was about to say hi, but the boat lurched and a group of people came between them. Amidst the confusion, he was gone, again. Had she imagined him? No, but it must be an omen that she saw him twice in one day. She was unsure whether she should stay where he could find her or go in search of this mystery man in the green jacket.

The boat motored back to the dock. Matthew joined her, filled with the excitement of the ride, but Peaches didn't want to stand next to her brother just then.

"Matthew you stay here, I'm going to find the ladies room."

"Good idea, Peaches. I could go too," he said and he tagged along. Peaches frantically watched for the man with the green jacket, but never saw him again.

On shore, Peaches purchased another cup of tea. She quickly read the tag: *I dream a thousand new paths. I woke and walked my old one.*

Not this time, she determined and threw the tea and the tag away and bought another. The next one Peaches read with delight. *What would you do if you knew you could not fail?* "Now we're getting the hang of it," she declared to no one.

Because neither of them thought much of strolling, they mostly sat on the handy little park benches and ate. They thought it important to sample as much of the Niagara Falls cuisine as possible. They ate Subway sandwiches and then some tasty Italian wrap that had some curiously smooth meat inside, drowned in mustard. After that, they topped it all off with Good Humor ice cream pops. Peaches got more tea. This time the tag read: *Be kind to others.* She threw that one away too and bought another that read: *Romance is right around the corner.* Peaches joyfully tore it off and stuffed it down the front of her dress as she led the way home.

. . .

"Okay, Matthew, it's your turn. You get to pick where we go next." Peaches' magnanimous mood soared with the tea tag's promise of new romance. She offered to make dinner and slipped in a Frank Sinatra tape and hummed *Strangers in the Night* as she worked. She set the table around her brother as Matthew chewed a toothpick and studied the map of New York State. In no time at all, the pizza was out of the microwave and the peas boiled. Dinner was served.

"Well, what do you think? Where shall we go next?" Peaches sat down opposite her brother. Matthew had no appetite and braced himself for what was to come.

"I'm homesick."

"You want us to go back to Pittsburgh? What's the matter with you? We've only been gone three days. We can go anywhere in the country. What's the point of going back where we came from?"

"Mimi and Dawn," Matthew sighed.

Peaches slapped her pizza slice back down on her plate, as she ranted, "I can understand how you might want to see Mimi, but Dawn? How many times do I have to say it? She's not good for you. Who was her best friend for years? Me. And don't I know her better than anyone?" Her eyes narrowed as she leaned across the table. "I've said it before, she just wants to get married. and she'll use Mimi like a carrot until you say yes." Peaches sat up straight for emphasis. "You'll have to go through me. There would be nothing worse than having Dawn Brown as a sister-in-law. Nothing worse than having her lording over me with her accusations and lies."

"What lording over you? It's only natural she'd like some permanence in her life." His sister made a face at that. "I might like to get married, and why not Dawn? You were married. You didn't ask me about Clute. What happened between you and Dawn? You'd think you owed her money or something."

"What money?" Peaches shifted in her seat, suddenly uncomfortable, but then she continued. "I know Dawn. She has a big mouth. You'd work like a slave for that girl keeping her in cigarettes and potato chips." Peaches took a second slice of pizza. "We're at the doorstep of the whole world. But you want us to go all the way back to Pittsburgh, drive aimlessly around to find those two? You don't even know where they are. That note on the door of her empty apartment with her post office box said it all. She's after child support all right. She's conniving."

"She should get child support. You don't understand. It's nice when it's just the three of us." Peaches put her hand to her chest offended but ignoring her, Matthew went on, "What happened between you two? Something bad happened that nobody's telling me."

"See she's turning you against me. I'm just trying to protect you."

"What are you protecting? I'm a grown-up," Matthew had had enough. "A turn is a turn and we're going to Pittsburgh." He grabbed for a piece of pizza.

"Why don't you think about it for awhile? Maybe you can come up with a better plan because I don't want to go," Peaches picked up her third slice. The sun was almost down. The IGA parking lot was empty except for their vehicle tucked in the back corner.

Matthew glanced out the window, "Supermarket's closed. We should get going." But over apple pie, it was decided that they would stay the night. With no more talk about where they would go the next day, they both dozed off; Peaches, while reading *Glamour* magazine and Matthew, while writing postcards to Mimi.

Eventually, Peaches woke up and stretched. She stumbled her way down the hall. "I'm turning in." After preparing his bed, Matthew curled up under his comforter and went to sleep too. Almost immediately a dream wormed its way into his thoughts and surrounded him like fog.

It started with familiar music he might have heard before in an elevator or at the movies. In front of him, Mimi waved and went round and round on an old-time carousel astride a white horse, its hooves in the air. Dawn sat cross-legged, close beside her daughter, on a carved swan seat. Matthew could see that Dawn had left enough room on that seat so that he could join her. He ran along the edge of the carousel, ready to leap on. But he couldn't keep up. Matthew breathed hard and was wet with sweat, he hated sweating; his foot caught a root and made him fall. He rolled over and over but he jumped up. There would be another chance when they came around again. He would be ready, ready to run. But it was taking too long. Finally, the horse and swan seat came around, but they were empty. Matthew was stunned, his breath caught in his throat. The music irritated him as he frantically ran to the other side. He checked up and down and underneath the platform. There was banging, and after a few turns of the empty carousel, it wasn't empty any longer. Peaches was on it and rode a carved goat. She seemed to appear out of nowhere and waved at him. With a sinking feeling, he reluctantly waved back. Peaches was the only person on the carousel. Mimi and Dawn were gone.

Matthew woke. He heard the same banging noise. He breathed hard, his sweaty pajamas sticking to him. It took a few moments before he realized that someone was knocking at the Bounder door.

"What's that?" Peaches hollered from her bedroom.

In his slippers and robe, Matthew peeked out the window.

"It's the police."

"What do they want?" Peaches came down the hall while she tied her robe tight at the waist.

"What do you want?" Matthew yelled through the door.

"Matthew, let them in." He opened the door to two uniformed officers who stood in the dim outside light.

"This supermarket is closed. You people need to move."

"Oh okay," Matthew was embarrassed.

"Why?" His sister's big frame pushed Matthew aside and filled up the doorway. "Walmart lets us stay in their parking lot."

"This is private property owned by the IGA corporation and besides, there's a sign."

"What sign? We didn't see any sign. Did you see a sign?" Matthew shook his head.

"That's probably because your vehicle is blocking it. It says no overnight parking." The taller officer seemed to be in charge. "You'll have to move."

"We were in bed already," Peaches informed them. "Couldn't you have come earlier?"

Matthew winced, but Peaches kept on going. She held her ground. "With all the people you have visiting Niagara Falls, where do you expect us to go? We couldn't even park in a regular parking lot with this thing during the day and we've already sustained damage to our vehicle. It's a dangerous situation for people who don't know the area."

Matthew looked at his sister and rolled his eyes.

"This is private property. We're just enforcing the law."

At that moment, Peaches thought of her most recent tea bag prophecy, about love being around some corner. She smiled and fluffed her blotchy orange hair, she stood up a little straighter, stuck her chest out and softened her approach. In the dim light she couldn't see if the officers were wearing rings but she would worry about that later.

"I'm Miss Peaches Packer." She extended her hand. "My brother and I are newcomers to the RV world, so we don't know all the rules." She took in a slow deep breath like they said to do in *Glamour*. She clasped her hands together at her bosom and cocked her head to the side. "It's such a long way back to that Walmart's parking lot and it's already..." she glanced at the clock over the sink, "...ten o'clock." Peaches opened her eyes wide. "Maybe you officers could suggest other alternatives. This motor-homing is great fun, but we're just getting use to it all. You understand, I'm sure." She batted her eyes.

The two men stepped into the shadows. When they returned to the RV doorway the taller officer spoke, "Normally, our hands would be tied, but we're sympathetic to your predicament."

Peaches smiled sweetly. The officer already seemed friendlier. "If you promise to be gone by daybreak, we'll let you stay the night. But you have to remember never to do this again."

"Oh thank you. Thank you officers." Her eyes fluttered. "We'll be gone by morning." Clapping her hands with enthusiasm she made a suggestion. "Now that we're up, let me put some coffee on for us all. What a hard job you have working all night. Have you been patrolmen for long?"

"Tonight is his last night. We've had this job, maybe eight years between us."

"Then we need a celebration." Peaches moved to the kitchen and switched on the coffeemaker. She lifted the pot to fill with water. As they came up the steps, Matthew moved toward the front to make room.

Peaches asked the shorter officer, who was more her type, "retiring are you?"

The patrolman laughed. "No, no. Just moving to another division."

"Oh, will you be one of those undercover agents? The ones whose stories they make into movies?"

"No, just arson."

The other officer chimed in. "He's pretty amazing. He can tell a pyromaniac just by looking them in the eyes."

Matthew bent down to study his slipper as Peaches let the metal coffee pot drop to the floor. It bounced, splashing water. "Oops. I guess we won't be having any coffee until I clean this mess up."

"Ya want us to do something?"

"No, no. Nothing to do but get a mop. The pot may be dented, but it's still under warranty and no one but a factory-trained specialist is allowed to touch it. Oh well, you gentlemen are busy. We have to watch our time if we're going to leave here bright and early in the morning." Peaches moved toward them and forced them down the steps. "It's been such a nice chat. Good night," she called pleasantly and firmly shut the door.

"Peaches what are ya doin'?" Matthew whispered frantically when they were alone. She let out a heavy sigh and whispered back.

"He investigates fires. We don't need any magical arson specialist staring into our eyes. I don't think he suspected a thing."

. . .

It was just after dawn on Monday morning when the Bounder rolled out of the IGA parking lot.

"Watch it!" Peaches clutched the armrests on the passenger seat, "Do you want me to drive?"

"I'll drive." Matthew was adamant. "When I get into an accident, you can drive."

She studied Matthew and relaxed her grip, then sat back. "Well, did you decide? You never told me where we're going."

"Florida."

"Florida?" Surprised, she listened as Matthew pointed out all the nice sandy beaches, flat country and palm trees they would see in the Sunshine State, after they stopped in their home city for a brief visit. Pittsburgh was on their way.

Matthew didn't particularly want to go to Florida, but it was the only destination he could think of beyond Pittsburgh that his sister wouldn't object to. He would figure out how they'd find his daughter so they could stop without too much hoo-ha, see Mimi and maybe even Dawn, and then go on to Florida. He didn't really care. This motor home adventure Peaches had engineered wasn't all that much fun.

Matthew quickly got the hang of how to handle the large vehicle. Like Peaches, he had driven a bus for the city; a brief experience that was curtailed shortly after he had made an unfortunate route choice a number of years ago. He had taken what he believed was a short cut, and driven down a one-way street the wrong way, and then managed a difficult right turn onto a dead end side street. Several buildings were damaged when he tried to turn around. But on the open road, Matthew felt confident. If he got into a little trouble in the city, he could always ask his sister to drive.

Peaches was annoyed. "Do we have to stop? Why waste time? Florida's a good choice."

"Pittsburgh is less than a day away."

"I know that. We just came from there," his sister said drily. "Where exactly are you planning to stop in Pittsburgh? You still don't know where to find those two."

"The P.O. box address Dawn gave me had the same zip code as our house did on Mury Brook Road. Even though I don't know exactly where they live, Mimi has to be going to the only elementary school in that area. If we stop to get gas and have something to eat once or twice we can make it by three when school lets out."

Peaches was going to point out how his idea was insane, and that the afternoon would end up a disappointment. But the determined look on her brother's face kept her quiet. Besides, there was Florida at the other end of the trip. She had always wanted to visit Florida.

"Mimi will love the motor home, don't cha think?" Matthew asked the question without needing an answer. As he drove on toward their home city, he thought of his little butterfly. Mimi was small and fragile, but tough for an almost six-year-old. She seemed to move all the time. Her brown hair was long enough to put in little braids. She liked dump trucks and pink dresses and cats.

"We probably won't find her," Peaches predicted.

Matthew sighed. She was right. He thought of the note taped to the door after Dawn and Mimi moved out of the apartment over the grocery store. Peaches had made it very clear that it was no fit place to bring up a child. Dawn had been angry at what she called his wimpishness in not standing up to his sister.

"But Dawn was brought up over a grocery store." Matthew had timidly reminded her.

"My point exactly." Peaches threw back. In the end, Matthew knew Dawn had been shamed into finding another place. Now she wouldn't even tell him where they were living. Dawn was like that. Sometimes she would call and arrange for them to meet in the park, always asking that he not bring his sister. But ever since Peaches stopped working at Best Deals Used Cars, a business owned by Dawn's father, she would insist upon coming anyway. "Someone has to protect you," she would say and remind him over and over again that no matter what, Dawn was trying to manipulate him into marriage. She would go on to point out how Dawn and Matthew were opposites and always ended every speech with, everybody knows you can't believe a word Dawn says.

The Bounder seemed to know the way home as they rolled down

the wide highway. Matthew mused about how different he and Dawn really were. He was fat. She was skinny. He was proud that she had gone across the state to a fancy four-year art school and was disappointed when she couldn't find a job in her field right away. He had stayed in Pittsburgh and gone to Allegheny Community studying liberal arts, which really hadn't given him much of a life direction. Dawn liked to travel, Matthew not so much. He liked that Dawn had strong opinions while he was willing to be flexible.

He sighed and thought about the very beginning of their romance. It had been his birthday. His father was asleep upstairs and he and Dawn waited for Peaches and Clute to come over so they could all go out for some dinner. The two of them laughed together in the living room and reminisced about when they'd been in high school, when they fell into each other's arms on a Friday afternoon. Matthew remembered feeling awkward but thrilled, like an ice cube melting in a swirling sea of warm water. The affair lasted an amazing three years and ended around the time Peaches moved back home. Almost immediately, his sister had another falling out with Dawn. They had been best friends in high school, but a misunderstanding back then had pushed them apart. Now, since Peaches was back in the picture on a daily basis something big had happened to power their smoldering feud. He was left stuck in the middle and couldn't persuade either of them to tell him what they were fighting about.

As for not being trustworthy, that just wasn't true. If anything, his sister could be creative about the truth, not Dawn. Why didn't Peaches have that job at the used car lot anymore? She said it was the two-mile commute. Who could believe that? And even though he tried his best to be horrified when he contemplated what a permanent situation with Dawn would look like, he actually thought he might like it. Just for a moment, he tried to imagine what might happen if Peaches did not stand squarely in the way, but he couldn't.

CHAPTER SIX

They moved right along on I-90, and it seemed to Matthew that the trip home was faster than the trip going. It was only 11 o'clock and they were halfway to Pittsburgh. They saw a sign for a truck stop coming up in five miles.

"Hey, let's stop and get a little something to eat? We've got plenty of time." Matthew thought food might cheer Peaches up. It usually worked when his sister was grumpy.

"I suppose I could force something down."

The truck stop came up fast. Matthew slowed and guided the Bounder down the entrance ramp. He watched the signs, *RVs and trucks to the right, cars to the left*. It gave him a thrill to think that he drove something comparable to a truck.

"Can't we get closer?" Peaches complained. "We always have to park in the boondocks. I'm not suited to all this walking."

They found a parking spot between a fifth wheeler and a pickup. Before Matthew had his seat belt unbuckled, Peaches got up and headed down the hall, towards her bedroom.

"I'll just freshen up. It won't take any time at all." When she reappeared thirty-five minutes later, he could see that her blotchy orange hair was fluffy and her cheeks pink. She had changed her sweats and put on the red dress she wore at the Falls. Her finger twinkled with the ruby ring she had found in the sock drawer.

"I'm ready."

Peaches smoothed her outfit. She loved this dress. It transformed her into something she could only define as date bait and she intended to wear it until it fell apart.

The area for truck parking, in reality, was only a short walk to a large attached restaurant and thrifty mart. They sat down at a booth with worn vinyl benches and a phone right at the table. Peaches wished she had someone to call and mentioned it to her brother.

"I suppose we could call Aunt Blossom to tell her we saw Marlene and that we're back in the area," Matthew suggested.

Peaches agreed it would be a good idea but they forgot about it and studied the menu instead. A waitress took their order. After only a short wait, Matthew slurped up his meatballs and spaghetti while Peaches launched into a pile of barbecued ribs. She used her paper napkin as a bib to protect her dress. She was ravenous and the ribs were delicious. She noticed a burly but handsome man in a black leather jacket watching her. He sat alone about three booths away with a plate filled with food in front of him.

She snatched off her bib and used it to try to clean up. She commented to Matthew, "Boy, it's hard to eat ribs neat."

The man caught her eye and smiled. And even though she was embarrassed, she got the feeling that he smiled at her in a friendly, interested way, not a critical *why can't you be neater with your sloppy ribs way*. Even though Matthew was only across the table, he was oblivious to Peaches' expanding world.

The man finished, paid his bill and got up to leave. Peaches panicked.

He headed down the aisle away from her. One man had gotten away when the boat lurched, she didn't want to see this one walk out of her life too.

She stood abruptly. "I'll be right back."

Peaches tried not to run but kept the leather jacket in sight. All she wanted was to casually say hello. She pushed down the aisle, and was almost up to him, when he yanked open the men's room door and went in.

Peaches pulled up and caught her breath. Now what? She could go into the ladies' room and bump into him on the way out but she would probably miss him. Instead she fingered through a nearby rack of potato chips and positioned herself to keep watch through the hanging bags. She had a good view of the lavatory entrance.

"Whatcha doin'?" Matthew came up behind her. "I finished off your ribs and paid the bill. Let's get going."

Defeated, Peaches looked at Matthew and then through the rack at the man leaving the lavatory. Crushed, she decided it was just too hard. But in a rush of determination, she stamped her foot.

"Hurry, get to the Bounder now. I left my curling iron on. Wait for me there. I'll be right behind you."

It worked. Instantly, Matthew was gone. He ran up the aisle and out the door. But when Peaches looked around for the man, he was gone too. He couldn't have gotten away that fast. She frantically rushed down the candy and snack food aisle and then back up paper goods.

Where was he? Desperately, she weaved into and out of the soda aisle and then rounded the corner and tripped. She landed face first in a candy display. Unhurt but shocked, she pulled herself out of the fallen rack. She felt lucky her eye wasn't poked out.

As if out of a dream, he was suddenly there. He had bent down to tie his shoe and sprawled with the display, but jumped up and was hovering over her. As she collected herself, his deep voice apologized in a valiant effort to help.

"Are you hurt?" He hunkered down by her side. "I'm so sorry. Let me help you." Peaches took a deep breath and tilted her head. Several people stopped to stare. The man's hand was warm on her arm as he led her to a table. He smelled like soap. A waiter came to see what the commotion was about and the man asked him for water.

"I'm Dominick. Let me help you. Does anything hurt?" He had asked this question ten times and acted as awkward and embarrassed as she should have felt. Dominick's face reddened when he almost spilled her water. Peaches recovered nicely, and fluffed the hair around her face. She covered the ruby ring with her other hand. Nervous, Dominick kept talking. He was from Pittsburgh and on his way home.

"I've got a little apartment over on Grand," he leaned toward her from across the table. Peaches daintily sipped water. After finding out that she lived in Pittsburgh too, he listened intently as she told him the sad story of the fire and how she was forced to travel with her brother for a time.

"Oh, your brother."

Was that relief in his face? She glanced at Dominick's left hand. It was naked. Out of the corner of her eye, Peaches saw Matthew. He fervently searched the aisles for her. She scooted down in her seat while Dominick told her he had just driven to Ohio with a delivery of paper goods, and had returned with a load of mattresses. He would be going out again in two days with clothes for a large store across the state. Peaches smiled and remembered to bat her eye lids. Dominick asked if there was something in her eye.

Matthew was gone. He looked for her down an aisle toward the back of the store. Shyly, the trucker explained how he had always found it difficult to meet people and had noticed her right away. She nodded with understanding and eventually remembered to tell him her name.

Things were going along nicely when Matthew reappeared. Over Dominick's shoulder, Peaches noticed her brother. He stood in the aisle and wildly waved both arms at her. Then he pointed at his watch. She tried not to look at him. He was attracting a crowd. Eventually, Dominick turned around to see the commotion.

"My brother wants us to get to Pittsburgh before his little girl gets out of school. I guess we'll have to go."

But before Peaches could say a proper goodbye, Matthew not being able to wait any longer, rushed over to their booth, nodded to Dominick and took Peaches' arm to help her up. He escorted her toward the door.

"I'm glad we got to talk," Dominick called after them. He sounded forlorn. He scribbled his phone number on a napkin and called after them, "Wait, take my number!"

He caught up to Peaches in the parking lot and pressed the paper into her hand. "Call me sometime."

Matthew hustled Peaches into the RV and Dominick headed toward a long line of trucks.

Peaches watched for her man from the RV window. She glowed and was too dazed to be angry at her brother. Matthew heaved himself into the driver's seat and started the engine. He pulled the Bounder out at the same time Dominick pulled his truck out of the line, both headed toward the wide exit. Now they were side by side. Peaches smiled and waved. But her smile faded when she noticed it was a JB Hunt truck. Dominick motioned them on ahead. Peaches gripped the dinette and forced herself to look away. Nothing was going to spoil this moment. But she couldn't help herself. As they drove past the big truck, she looked. There on the back of the passenger side mirror, was a big wad of gum.

• • •

"I had to do it." Matthew eased the Bounder onto I-79 south. "I had no choice Peaches. We have to get to the school before three." When they were out on the road, he felt better and kept talking. "At least you've got his number. I wouldn't let that guy get away. He actually likes you." There was a little more surprise in his voice than he had intended.

They were picking up speed.

"I think you should call him." He glanced at Peaches through the rear-view-mirror. "What's the matter with you?"

She stared ahead wide-eyed with a queer look on her face.

"I saw it. I saw my gum."

"Your gum? What gum?"

"Dominick's the nincompoop," she wailed. "He's the one that hit us in the parking lot, I can't call him."

"Oh, come on, Peaches. That could be anybody's gum."

"No, I could tell."

Matthew glanced at Peaches. She looked like she might cry.

"It's not about one little call, Matt. It's about the rest of my life. I think I'm in love. Why do I always find the nincompoops?"

"Don't call him." Matthew was problem solving. He could see through his side mirrors that Dominick and his big truck were staying with them.

"What-do-ya-mean don't call him?" Peaches cried. "I have to call him. He likes me."

When Matthew pulled out to pass a car, Dominick pulled his truck out and passed the car too. When Matthew slowed to read a sign, Dominick slowed too.

"This Dominick seems like a pretty good driver to me," Matthew commented. "Think about it this way, we know that truck probably hit us, but we don't know if this guy was driving. I mean, maybe they switch off or maybe his friend was driving and Dominick left the note. Or maybe there are two Dominicks that drive that truck. We don't know anything about trucking."

"I think you're right." Peaches had moved to the passenger seat and looked over at her brother with amazed relief. "If you'd hit a motor home just a few days ago, would you be out romancing one of the owners of that vehicle? You wouldn't forget a thing like that, would ya?"

The 18-wheeler followed the motor home for another half-hour. Peaches watched Dominick drive his truck from the large side view mirror and sighed from time to time.

"It must make him pretty happy having you keep an eye on him."

"What? He can see me?" She quickly moved from the passenger seat to the floor. She used the stairwell for her feet. "I don't want him to think I'm too interested. Why didn't you say something before?" She adjusted herself then asked, "What's he doing now?"

"Just driving."

And as Matthew drove, Peaches was content to sit on the floor. She held on to the handrail for support and scooted down just a bit to make sure she couldn't be seen.

"Is he still there?"

"He's waving. Maybe he wants to remind us that he's back there. He's probably wondering where you went."

"You think so?"

"Uh oh, now he's flashing his lights. I know what that means. Those professional drivers don't like slow pokes." Matthew held on to the wheel and pushed down hard on the accelerator. "Hold on." The Bounder leaped ahead and passed everyone on the right. It fishtailed a little and something crashed in the back bedroom. Dominick stayed with them. Peaches braced herself and gripped the handrail with both hands. She hoped the door wouldn't fly open.

"What'r ya doin? Slow down!" Peaches hollered over the roar of the engine.

"He's professional. Probably got some info from his CB." Matthew yelled back. He tried to control the shuddering motor home. "There's a reason he's speeding us up. It must be big." Matthew tore around a van. He's still flashing. I can't go any faster."

"Slow down! You'll kill us! Slow down!"

Matthew sped up for a few more horrible minutes and then took his foot off the pedal. He braked in jerks.

"I can't do it. This thing can't do 85."

"Good god, that was awful." Peaches adjusted herself on the stairs. "What's he doing now?"

"Pulling up beside us." Ruefully, he added, "He probably thinks I'm a wimp." Now Dominick's truck was alongside the motor home, his passenger side window was down. The closeness was uncomfortable, but to show there were no hard feelings Matthew made a thumbs-up sign, smiled and waved. When the Bounder fishtailed again Matthew grabbed the wheel with both hands. He took a quick look over at Dominick and realized the trucker was trying to tell him something. Matthew wanted to roll down his window, but didn't dare take his hands off the wheel.

He worked at the window with his left elbow and mistakenly put on the seat heater as the side mirror swiveled. It was distracting to have to look at himself at a time like this. Still trying to get the window down, he hit the left directional and finally the brakes, sending Dominick and his truck out ahead. Matthew had had enough.

"I'm pullin' over." He clenched his jaw and eased the RV off, bobbling onto the shoulder. Even after coming to a complete stop, he still held the wheel tight. His mirror image stared back at him. He sweated. Peaches was gripping the handrail. Her feet planted wide, her dress above her knees.

The 18-wheeler slipped in front of the motor home and lumbered to a stop. Before Peaches could get herself up and back into the passenger's seat, Dominick had jumped out of his truck and run over to the Bounder. He yanked open the motor home door.

"How about tonight? Could I see you tonight?"

With her head tilted Peaches nodded and smiled.

. . .

Miry Brook Elementary was quiet when the RV stopped in front.

Caustically Peaches pointed out, "See, we're too early, nothing's happening here." Then more gently, she urged Matthew to drive down the road to where their house used to be so they could see what was happening with the old property. "It's just a few blocks, we'll be back in plenty of time."

"We're here and we're staying." Matthew felt lucky to find four parking spaces in a row right across the street from the school. "It's almost three and these spaces'll fill up faster than a hobo on a sandwich." As he rolled down his window, fresh air came in. It was cool and autumny. "Remember, it's my turn. I'm here to see Mimi and I'm not going to miss her."

Peaches regarded her brother. "What's gotten in to you? You dragged me away from a romantic rendezvous on a hunch. You haven't seen Mimi in awhile, what makes you think Dawn's going to let you see her now?"

"I don't know. Maybe she won't."

Peaches continued, "Mimi's my niece. I like being an aunt, but I certainly don't want to see Dawn. Don't draw this out. Let's have a nice visit with Mimi and then leave."

Matthew turned in his seat to face his sister. "You don't understand anything. You're giving all the orders. Why can't you leave me alone?"

"Because we're a partnership, but mostly we're family. You've always listened to me."

Matthew ignored her and went on. "When Pop was alive and you were working everything was fine. You and Dawn were not exactly friends but okay with each other. So when Pop got sick things got a little crazy. I didn't mind staying home, taking care of him. But when he died, I thought, you know, I could really do something with my life. But then you got that divorce and you stopped working and things got crazier. Dawn thinks I'm wimpy for listening to you, but mostly she's mad at you Peaches. I don't know why, but she's mad at you."

"Wimpy for listening to me? Humph. You're my only family, except for Aunt Blossom and Marlene and Mimi of course, and that second cousin out in Detroit and I think there's another one over there in Peekskill. Anyway, I'm here to protect you." Peaches used the armrests to hoist herself up. "Sometimes, a person has to do certain things in life that may not appear conventional. And then other people like Dawn have a complete lack of understanding and blow that thing out of proportion." She headed toward the back and ended the conversation.

• • •

In no time at all, a blue Suburban squeezed into the space in front of the Bounder. A black car parallel parked in back of them. Then a little red car double-parked and blocked them in.

Matthew thought he saw Dawn. Tall and skinny her gliding steps made her stand out.

"I think I see her," he yelled to his sister who was rummaging around in the bedroom. Now she was closer and from a block away he recognized Dawn and felt relieved and happy.

"Who? Mimi?" Peaches came back with her hands full. "Good, we could leave now." She arranged her nail products on the dash. She took her ring off and tossed it up by the polish and started to work on her nails. Then she paused to look out the window.

"Oh it's Dawn," she sounded disappointed. "Why doesn't that girl pick up her feet? In my opinion, we're wasting our time."

Matthew was going to protest but decided not to, he was tired of trying to change her mind. For him, seeing Dawn like this from the motor home's big front windshield was comforting, and he didn't want Peaches to spoil it. At least they had the right school and apparently the right time.

Imagining the surprise this would be to Mimi, and Dawn too, Matthew's heart beat more rapidly and his palms were wet. In a moment, they would all be together.

Dawn glided closer. The smell of nail polish remover was strong as Peaches worked at her nails. Suddenly, hoards of small children ran through the double doors across the street as if escaping a prison. They all looked like Mimi.

"Is that her?" He said out loud. "There?" But he wasn't sure. "Mimi?"

Peaches looked up and shook her bottle of polish. Matthew didn't wait for his sister's response. He put on his baseball cap and went for the door.

"Matthew, don't do anything stupid."

"What does that mean? I'm going to see my daughter."

"And Dawn." Peaches worked with her file. "Remember, watch

yourself around that woman, and don't believe a word she says."

"Oh, lighten up, Peaches. Are you coming or not?"

"I'm sympathetic. I know about the homecoming feeling." Peaches finished one hand and moved to work on the other.

Matthew was down the stairs.

"She'll turn you against me." The door slammed, but Peaches barely noticed and, even though he was gone, she talked as she concentrated on her left hand. "Mimi will see me when she sees the motor home." She held one hand up admiringly and then reached for the polish saying with a giggle, "I have a lot to do to get ready for my date."

. . .

From the Bounder, Peaches watched her brother dodge traffic and head toward the front of the elementary school. When he reached the sidewalk, Mimi rushed at her father with outstretched arms. The little girl was lost in Matthew's size when they hugged, and even from across the street, her delighted laugh danced through the Bounder's open window.

Peaches sniffed the air. Apparently, Dawn wasn't mad anymore because she seemed glad to see Matthew too, and pranced around him as he fussed over Mimi. Peaches eyes narrowed as Dawn hugged her brother.

"The child doesn't even look like him," Peaches murmured under her breath. She blew on her fingernails and even though they were still a little sticky, she got up for a couple of Oreo cookies.

Matthew gestured toward the motor home. Peaches thought about hiding in the bathroom but instead, retrieved her ring from the vent area in back of the dash. It would be nice to see Mimi. Maybe Dawn would wait at the curb. She touched her thumb to the nail of her middle finger and left a slight imprint in the glossy red polish. Maybe she needed another cookie.

Peaches grimaced and watched her brother take Mimi's hand and start across the street. Dawn followed but hung back a bit. Resigned to being invaded, Peaches bit down into her third chocolaty biscuit and sat down at the dinette like a presiding judge. She was ready.

"The steps move, Daddy," The child's voice squealed. Mimi laughed as she climbed up into the motor home.

"Aunt Peaches."

Peaches smiled and opened her arms to her niece and engulfed the little girl in a big hug. As Mimi sat next to her, Peaches asked her about school.

"I'm in kindergarten. We play a lot," Mimi reported. She wiggled in her seat. "Sometimes a boy pulls my hair."

"You give his hair a yank right back."

"Come on Mimi. Let me show you around," her father interrupted.

Matthew walked and Mimi skipped behind him toward Peaches' room in the back.

"Don't mind the mess back there," Peaches called, airily waving her hand. "I'm getting ready for a date."

"Do you drive this Daddy? Does it move when you're sleeping?"

"Hello Peaches," Dawn spoke softly from the stairwell. She took in the compact home with one glance. "Nice place," she said congenially. "It must be economical."

Peaches felt a tightening in her chest. Dawn's familiar perfume, Shalimar, filled the air. As she gave the woman a forced smile Peaches thought, nice indeed, I'll bet you'd like it for yourself, but said out loud, "Mimi says a boy pulls her hair."

"They've only been in school a couple days." Dawn moved further into the motor home. "I could say something, but I'll wait and see how it goes. What's up with your hair?"

Peaches smiled, "You like it?" and sat up a little straighter. She was about to make a clever comment when Dawn spoke again.

"It amazes me that you two would buy a thing like this after that fire. I knew you had to do something, but a motor home? Isn't it a little tight?"

"It's perfect for the two of us." Peaches' smile was sugary. "I suppose compared to your palatial apartment this can't hold a candle but for now, it's good enough for the Packers." Dawn glanced toward the back. Mimi jumped off the bed and was headed back up the aisle.

"Aunt Peaches, we're coming for supper. We're having McDonald's right here in the kitchen. Daddy said so." Matthew lumbered behind, a big smile on his face.

"Really? Oh darn, I can't come." Peaches made a sarcastic face at Dawn but smiled when Mimi passed on her way toward the front. "Did I mention I have a date?" Then she addressed Dawn. "The Bounder fits our needs. We're moving on with our lives." Peaches readjusted herself on the bench. "Everyone says the house burning was such a tragedy, but I've come to think of it as a blessing." She sounded a little defensive. "As you know, our father let the house go and the neighborhood was certainly going downhill, definitely not what it used to be."

"Probably because you moved back into it."

Peaches ignored Dawn's comment and continued, "My biggest regret is that Mimi was there that afternoon. She's such a little thing. It's good that Matthew had her outside."

"Did anyone figure out what really happened?"

"Well, as you know, it was an unavoidable accident."

"So you're admitting you burned it down?" Dawn leaned on the kitchen counter. "Maybe you wanted to live in a motor home with your brother until your Prince Charming arrived? Or was it the money?" Dawn smiled innocently. She was being particularly catty. "You didn't get quite enough from the used car lot so you thought you'd add to it with some insurance money? Matthew said you two would eventually collect. You do have a thing about money."

Peaches ignored Dawn's acid comments and tried to explain. "He's probably right. We should eventually collect, but it really depends on the investigation, you know, what they find. And Dawn, you know very well that accidents happen. Meanwhile, we're living thriftily in our Bounder."

"Which investigation?"

Peaches smiled sweetly. "Why the fire of course. Is there another investigation?"

"You know there is. There's an investigation about some lost money at my father's car lot. You remember, the car lot where you kept the books."

"There was money lost?" Matthew had caught some of their conversation. But now Mimi wanted to know about the console between the front seats.

Peaches paled, but held her ground. "The truth lies somewhere in the facts."

There was an uncomfortable pause before Dawn spoke.

"So why'd ya do it?" This question surprised and flustered Peaches.

"What? Me? I--"

"Why do you have that carrot top? It's not exactly natural."

"This? Dye. Dye of course." Peaches said with a gush of relief, a little friendlier than she had intended. They heard Mimi laugh from the front.

"What'd ja' think I meant?"

Shaken by Dawn's question, Peaches let herself be distracted by something out the window and the conversation lagged again. So as Dawn watched Mimi, Peaches turned to watch Dawn and studied her former friend with a critical eye. There was a blotch of blue eye shadow smoothed over each eyelid and her dark brown hair was annoyingly shiny. She was skinny, her multicolored tie-died shirt hung from bony shoulders and faintly emphasized small breasts. Peaches found that the sweet scent of her perfume wasn't quite as pleasing now as when they had been friends.

Then Peaches asked in a soft voice, "Dawn, I've been worried about something. How does Mimi feel about fires?"

"Probably the same way you should feel about theft."

But Peaches didn't seem to hear.

"I'm concerned that Mimi might turn to arson in an attempt to bring the family closer. Dawn, you do nothing to relieve the animosity between us. I'm just doing what's right for my family."

"Peaches, why don't you get a real life? Leave us alone. Mimi, sweetheart, time to go."

"I wanta see Daddy's bed first." The little girl looked up at her mother with Matthew's brown eyes.

"Okay. Try to be quick. I'll be outside."

"I think I'll go too," piped up Peaches. Dawn gave her a disgusted look then headed toward the door. The bottom step extended.

"Can't you get that stupid step to stay out? I need someplace to sit," Dawn complained as she pulled out a cigarette. She lit up and continued, "Peaches Packer, I don't know whether to be horrified or embarrassed by our conversations. What's the matter with you? You never used to be like this. Strange things happen when you're around. And you're around a lot."

Peaches put her hands on her hips. "Fires happen. Mistakes happen and they're not necessarily my fault."

Mimi leaped from the RV to the grass and tried to beat the step.

Matthew came outside just behind his daughter, oblivious to the tension that crowded the air.

"What'cha doin' out here?" Dawn and Peaches glared at each other and ignored him. Mimi did a cartwheel. Abruptly, Peaches announced she had things to do and hurried back inside and closed the door behind her.

"We'll meet back here at 6 o'clock?" Matthew eagerly made plans with Dawn.

Dawn took Mimi's hand and replied sweetly, "Six will be just fine as long as your sister's not here."

Inside, Peaches made her own plans over a small ice cream sundae. She was famished from the confrontation with Dawn. She was also nervous about tonight and food calmed her and eased her into a dating frame of mind.

"You can drive me over to the diner at 5:30." She announced to Matthew as he climbed back into the motor home. "That will give us plenty of time."

"But I have to be here at six o'clock, and if I leave for the diner at 5:30, I can't be back here in time."

"Don't be selfish, Matthew. You know this is an important date, my big chance. You can see Mimi any time and who cares about Dawn? My date is at six o'clock across town and I need to be there."

"But this is where they're coming to meet me." There was a desperate edge to his voice. "I can't move."

Peaches looked up, her spoon filled with the last of the double fudge sauce. "You can move, you just have to be sure you move back here after you've moved me over there. They'll wait."

Matthew thought for a moment. "You're right. I do have to move. I'm picking up food and then I'll have just enough time to get back here."

"That's very nice," she said pointedly. "Now where do I fit in?"

"I'll leave you off a little early," Matthew said amiably. "I'll drop you off first, swing by McDonald's, and be back here in plenty of time."

"I guess that might work," Peaches agreed. She didn't realize how late in the afternoon it already was.

"I'll get you there about 5:15. Will that be all right?" Matthew looked in the cupboard for some comfort food for himself.

"Five fifteen? What am I going to do for forty-five minutes?"

"I don't know, but I can't take the chance I might miss Mimi and Dawn."

"You don't seem to mind taking the chance that I'll be wandering around the parking lot of a diner. Anyone could pick me up."

"Nobody's going to pick you up. This'll work." Matthew glanced at the clock, "Geez, look at the time, we need to leave in about 15 minutes."

"Fifteen minutes?" Peaches came to life. "I can't get ready in fifteen minutes." But she charged down the hall to her bedroom nonetheless. A few moments later, she bustled out wrapped in her fluffy white robe and slammed the bathroom door. "If I'm not out of here, don't you dare move this thing."

Peaches showered fast and toweled off in record time. But she got caught up examining her hair color in the mirror. It might have faded a little. But, mindful of the time, she awkwardly manipulated her new round brush with her right hand, while trying to blow dry her hair into curls with the left.

"Time to go." Matthew called pleasantly. She studied her hair color again and was aware that it was a little odd, but she liked it. It looked alive and interesting. Peaches realized that she had never felt particularly interesting until recently, and now even her hair was interesting.

Suddenly she heard Matthew, "Peaches we've got to go." His voice was intense, "You'll have to get ready on the way." Peaches charged out of the bathroom leaving the blow dryer hanging.

"At least let me get my clothes on."

Matthew impatiently fidgeted in the driver's seat. A few minutes later, she posed at the bedroom doorway, a vision in a purple dress that flowed to the floor with a scoop neck, capped sleeves and yellow belt.

Matthew took it all in and glanced at the clock, "We're leaving now."

He eased the Bounder out of its parking space while Peaches teetered toward the bathroom, her makeup bag dangled from her arm.

She called, "Just watch the turns."

Peaches pulled the stopper and dumped the contents of the plastic bag into the sink. Luckily she had picked up a brochure about applying makeup from the CVS back in Niagara Falls.

She balanced the instructions on the edge of the sink and planted her feet wide. She was ready to start. The RV swayed and the light was poor. This would be a challenge. Peaches didn't even notice the Bounder's movement. Her spirits soared because she knew that her new love would be waiting for her at the diner, eventually.

Step one: start with a clean face. She considered washing again, but since her makeup was heaped in the sink, she went on to step two: moisturizing. Unfortunately, she had forgotten to get moisturizer so she went on to step three: foundation.

According to the instructions, she was to put a dab of the tan cream on her forehead, chin and each cheek but even in the picture the dab looked so small it couldn't possibly do the trick so she dabbed a little more. After all, Peaches reasoned, her face was much bigger than the illustration and she wanted her makeup to be perfect, so she wouldn't skimp. Two fingers was all she needed to smooth it around, careful to blend at the jaw line, just like the illustration. She checked her reflection in the mirror, her face looked like it was coated in tan cement. So that's why they call it foundation, she thought knowingly.

Step four, eyes: Peaches' eyes were hazel so she chose green eye shadow from the collection of colors in the little case. At least she thought it was green. It might be gray or beige, it was hard to tell. The light in the bathroom wasn't what you would call bright. Whatever the color, it went on nicely.

The motor home lurched. "Watch the corners, Matthew, the corners!" she yelled.

As she held onto the sink with her left hand, Peaches used the other to add a hint of shimmering white just below each eyebrow. The brochure suggested this for eveningwear. She tilted her head to see the result. Not bad. She looked closely at her eyebrows, she decided that they really needed plucking.

"We're almost there," called Matthew.

Her stomach lurched with the motor home and she forgot about her eyebrows, she had better finish up. The brochure suggested black mascara for a 'maximum dark lash effect' but CVS had been out of black and the lady behind the counter thought blue would probably work okay. Still braced with one hand, Peaches approached her eye with the little brush wand cautiously. Suddenly, the RV zigzagged to the left and then the right.

"Stop swerving, Matthew. I almost poked my eye out." The RV stopped moving.

"We're at a light." Matthew yelled.

Peaches quickly spread the mascara on the lashes above and below each eye. Now just the blush, concealer, eyeliner, lip liner and lipstick and she would be done. She wanted to keep it simple. The Bounder moved again.

"The diner's right in front of us. I don't see any big trucks yet."

"That's because we're forty-five minutes early," Peaches yelled back. "I'm almost done." She opened her new peaches and cream blush. She had always liked the sound of a peaches and cream complexion and thought this might be just perfect. It went on with a special brush that was included. It looked a little orange so she rubbed it gently with her fingers to blend it in. She noticed that some of the mascara she had just put on her lashes was smudged above and below her eyes and she wondered what the brochure would say about that, but the brochure was on the floor.

Peaches grabbed some toilet tissue and rubbed away the blue smudges.

Her right eye looked red and the eye shadow was smeared. The hint of shimmering white was gone but she kept on going.

When she couldn't find the lip liner, she thought it might have gone down the drain. She had steadied herself with the sink stopper handle awhile back. But there it was, amongst everything else in the bottom of the sink bowl. She used the little pencil to add a good quarter inch to her lip line. She checked her image in the mirror and could see that her lips were on their way to being more sensuous.

The Bounder had stopped and Matthew was yelling. "We're here. Come on, I have to get back."

"I'm almost ready." She filled in her new lip line with Pink Seduction as a final touch. She threw the makeup back into the bag and decided to bring it along. She charged out of the bathroom. "I'm just going to get my pocketbook and my earrings and maybe some other shoes. I'm so excited!"

"It's already 5:30. As it is I'm going barely make it back in time. You've got to get out."

Despite Matthew's glare, Peaches grabbed her purse from the kitchen counter and then rushed back to her bedroom for the rest of the stuff. She felt wonderful and wanted to arrive at the diner looking like a queen, not an afterthought.

The RV door clicked closed, Peaches stood in the parking lot alone.

Matthew had turned the Bounder around and glanced at his sister. She was a large, anxious woman with orange and green hair, wearing a purple dress. She clutched an oversized green bag and an extra pair of shoes.

"How are you getting home?" he yelled out the window.

"Oh." Surprised at the question, she bit her lower lip in thought. Then she yelled, "If I'm not there by nine o'clock, come and get me." Matthew waved and left.

She slowly turned and walked toward the diner entrance. The Starlight marquee was outlined with pink blinking bulbs. Her bag was heavy with makeup and her sneakers dangled at her side. Her thong sandals were new and that stylish leather part that runs between the big and second toe was already almost unbearable on her left foot. Dominick wouldn't show up for thirty minutes and it crossed Peaches' mind as she hauled the door opened that he might not show up at all.

• • •

An oversized goldfish languidly swam in a large tank of green water just inside the entrance to the Starlight Diner. Peaches decided that this might be a good place to wait for Dominick. She fluttered her finger in the water trying to pet the curious fish, when she noticed an 18-wheeler go by one of the big diner windows heading toward the back parking area. He's here and he's early, she thought. She felt light and bubbly, but mostly nervous as she rushed toward the front doors to meet him. Peaches caught herself and changed her plan. It would spoil everything if her date thought she was too eager. Quickly, she slipped out the front door and started walking toward the road to hide in the front bushes.

She would arrive at the diner after Dominick was already inside. That would create just a little anxiety for him. The latest issue of *Glamour* had recommended anxiety to spice up a relationship or was it was unavailability. She couldn't remember.

He walked around the corner.

"Peaches?" Dominick called. "Peaches where ya goin?" He crossed the parking lot quickly. Peaches swayed a little when he came close; the smell of Old Spice aftershave was intoxicating.

"I'm glad you came." Dominick smiled. His teeth were white, his lips inviting. He had changed into a red plaid shirt that peeked out from under his leather bomber jacket. His dark brown hair seemed wavier than when she had first met him. Did he get a haircut? Together they walked to the entrance of the restaurant.

Dominick held the glass door open and cupped her elbow as they looked around for a table. Someone yelled for more coffee as the couple walked by the fish tank.

Now this is a date, thought Peaches, as they moved past a big display case of pies and cakes toward seats in the back. Peaches noticed their handsome image reflected in the wall mirror. She could hardly breathe as they sat down at a booth in a secluded corner.

The setting was perfect except for the sticky floor and a dome light that hung over their booth. It annihilated any romantic glow Peaches might have hoped for. But so far things were going great.

With her elbow on the table, Peaches contentedly rested her chin in the palm of her hand and watched Dominick take off his jacket. She smiled as he folded it neatly and placed it beside him on the red vinyl.

A few chest hairs danced seductively at the neckline of his undershirt.

Then Peaches remembered her plan to be quiet, shy, and mysterious.

She quickly took her elbow off the table, sat up straight, and clasped her hands in her lap.

"You have beautiful eyes." Dominick broke the ice right away and caused Peaches to blush and smile shyly. "How was your afternoon?"

Peaches grimaced. Her afternoon was the last thing she wanted to talk about.

"What did I say?" Dominick was genuinely concerned. He ran his fingers through his hair. "Did I say something wrong?"

The conversation stalled as two glasses of ice water were set on the table. Dominick thanked the waitress and Peaches grabbed for a glass and drained it. Dominick tried again.

"Peaches, I want to tell you why I asked you out tonight." He looked directly at her. "You're different. In some ways you kind of remind me...of me." Peaches looked surprised, this was not what she expected. Dominick continued, "With people like us, things don't always go our way. You know what I mean. Like this afternoon, when your brother kept showing up. The same kind of stuff happens to me all the time. A lot of people would have gotten angry and told him off, but you didn't. I think you're very kind."

Dominick thought she was kind. Nobody had ever said that before. Peaches wondered what she should talk about now that she knew she was kind. She couldn't talk about Dawn. And how could she kindly explain her embarrassment about the fire or her objections to her brother and Dawn getting married? But he had asked her. Maybe she should risk telling him her version right off before Dawn had a chance to spoil things. Twisting the ring on her finger she looked into his wide dark eyes. He was waiting. She had to say something. She had to make it count.

"I had a terrible afternoon," Peaches blurted out. "Ever since I left her father's used car business we haven't been able to get along at all." Peaches' face felt instantly hot and her eyes became moist. Dominick looked surprised and sat up a little as if to distance himself from the terrible afternoon. He handed her his napkin. "I had no other choice. And now every time I see her, she's difficult. She wants to marry my brother. How could I let that happen? Doesn't she realize that he's the only one I have? Nobody understands me," Peaches took a breath, "like you do."

"Who's she? What happened?"

"It's too painful to go into now." She blew her nose and continued, "Dawn was sort of my friend, now we're enemies. We were almost like sisters before she called me a thief. She even was questioning me about the fire." She wiped her eyes, blew her nose again and glanced at Dominick who rubbed his jaw thoughtfully, a vague, puzzled look on his face.

"There was a fire?"

Peaches reached for her empty glass just to have something to hold. Maybe this was too much for Dominick, after all he'd seen her only once before, twice if you counted flagging down the motor home so he could ask her out. This was all wrong. Peaches had wanted to keep their conversation light and amusing, she even had jokes.

"And you saw Dawn? Is that why you're upset?"

Peaches nodded. Interrupted by the waitress, they ordered hamburgers and French fries without looking at the menu. Dominick asked for more napkins and water. He turned back to Peaches and gave her his full attention.

"There was a fire?" He asked again.

"We were all home. Matthew and me and even little Mimi, that's Matthew's little girl. We lost almost everything. It was an accident, but it was because Dawn showed up unannounced for Matthew's birthday. But she's giving me a terribly hard time, even accusing me of arson."

"Why?"

Peaches sat up and clutched the edge of the table. She leaned toward Dominick. "I let slip that I thought that burning the house down was a blessing. And I meant it, but not in the way Dawn took it. Now she thinks I'm a frivolous idiot. Then I had the idea that maybe little Mimi might try starting a fire to bring us all closer."

"The little girl?" Dominick looked surprised again.

Peaches cringed, and was vaguely aware that what she was saying might not be making much sense so she tried to be clearer. "I realize that that might not have been the smartest thing to do. She's really a wonderful little girl, but you know how children are. I was just making conversation, really." The waitress brought their food. "Of course, Dawn took all this completely wrong and reacted badly." Peaches paused for a breath and reached for the ketchup. "When I had the idea that little Mimi could start a fire and mentioned it to Dawn," Peaches dabbed at her eyes and Dominick nodded, "it made her very angry. Not that I care of course." She watched Dominick's face. " I love Mimi and she loves me, but Dawn is so judgmental she may prevent me from seeing the child. She may even turn you against me."

"Hmm," Dominick nodded his head thoughtfully and ignored his food. Peaches waited, she had never known a man to just listen, not even Matthew, certainly not Clute. He would have identified the problem incorrectly and then flown into a tirade and pointed out what she really should have done about it.

Three women sat down in the booth behind Dominick, their loud voices made it hard to hear. They leaned in toward each other. This made Peaches' stomach flutter with the intimacy. She thought she might cry again.

"I don't have any answers." Dominick smiled at her with real concern. She felt better now and reached for her hamburger. Then it occurred to her that she might be monopolizing the conversation.

"Do you have a dog?"

"No, no dog." Dominick smiled again. "I had a dog named Pilot when I was a boy. Do you have a dog?" Peaches shook her head. "Any other pets?" Peaches shook her head again.

As they picked at their French fries he revealed that he had an iguana and a brother named Al who was also a truck driver. Like Dominick, he lived in Pittsburgh.

"You'd like my brother, he makes people laugh."

She felt better and told this to Dominick. He smiled back at her and then shook his head and said, "Families can be hard to figure out."

Peaches was comforted. See, I'm not crazy. He agrees with me. The date continued going great. Peaches meant to ask Dominick about the truck and the Bounder accident, but the waitress interrupted when she came to check on them. Peaches also wanted to explain about the gum that was on his mirror, but there was never a good time. There were so many other things to talk about.

Peaches mentioned that she wanted to do something extraordinary in her life. Something she could call her very own. He listened as she told him how she needed someone to lean on. The glow in her heart grew. She was really getting to know this wonderful, exceptional man. She bit into her hamburger which was still warm, rare, and juicy, just like she liked it.

It was 8:45. Their shoulders softly touched as Peaches and Dominick walked out of the diner into the night. Peaches glanced back at the blinking pink sign because she wanted to remember every detail, forever.

. . .

"There's no way," Peaches murmured. She looked up at the passenger door of Dominick's eighteen-wheeler. She glanced over at her date and was trying to figure out a way to handle the situation.

"Should I call a cab?" Dominick asked, a little nervous.

"A cab?" She was incredulous as she changed into her sneakers. If this stupid truck was part of Dominick's life, damn it, it would be part of her life too.

Her eyes narrowed at the high door as she hiked up her dress. She put one foot on the running board and grabbed the edge of the diamond plate and hauled herself up. But her weight wasn't distributed correctly and she had to jump back to the ground.

"Can I help?" Dominick stood close.

"Prop me up when I start. Keep me against the truck while I climb, but if I start falling, you'd better move."

"Why? I'm not going to let you fall. You could get hurt."

"Dominick, I'll be fine. We can't take the chance that I might land on you, you're the only one who knows how to drive this thing."

She stepped on the running board and held on first to the mirror brace, then to the handle that was screwed to the side of the cab. For as long as he could, Dominick stood, his hands on her back, shoring her up. Slowly, carefully, Peaches climbed the small diamond plate steps all the way up to the high passenger door.

"I don't think we'll be needing that taxi," she called down cheerfully as she settled into the passenger's seat. Dominick hurried around to the driver's side as Peaches looked around the cab. The brown leather bench seat was worn where Dominick sat. Her side was smooth and virtually unused. The smell of aftershave mingled with a vague smell of salami and something else, maybe sweat. There were personal things around too, like a used Dunkin Donuts coffee cup and a silver cross that hung from the knob on the radio. A comb peeked out from the ashtray and a bobble-headed baseball player nodded his greeting from the dash. It was an intimate experience, almost like peeking into her new love's closet or even his diary.

Dominick clicked his seatbelt and welcomed her aboard. His smile was warm as his gaze lingered on her face. And as he slid the key into the ignition, Peaches slid across the leather bench seat until her thigh felt the warmth of his thigh. In a bold move, Dominick's hand left the key and, being taller than Peaches, easily put his arm around her shoulders. He pulled her close while her fingers gently rested on his pant leg. Her head inclined to the left and let his muscular shoulder support her. Her brain raced as she planned her next move. Silently, they looked straight ahead and treasured this first real intimate moment.

As he bent toward her, Peaches was sure he was going to kiss her, but Dominick's seat belt held him secure and it made them both laugh nervously. He released it. Now his breath was on her cheek as she tilted her face upward toward that first breathless kiss. This time, this first time, she wanted to keep her eyes open so she could watch.

Suddenly, the cab filled with light. Peaches screamed, her fingers dug into Dominick's leg. Dominick screamed. They jumped apart as if they were teenagers caught making out on a back road. All they could see were two bright lights coming straight at them. Just when it seemed like the lights would crash right through the truck, they went out. It took a moment or two before their eyes adjusted. When they did, there, right in front of them, was the Bounder. Dawn and Matthew laughed together inside.

It took a while for Peaches to compose herself. Her instinct was to leap out of the truck, run to the Bounder and strangle Dawn. But she figured that was exactly what Dawn would expect her to do.

As usual, Peaches' good sense took over. First of all, Dominick would think she was a crazy woman and secondly, her seat was a good distance off the ground and she might kill herself on the way down.

If she were sent to jail for the murder of Dawn Brown, Dominick might not want to see her again and she would have to endure the unthinkable, a shared cell with Marlene. Instead, Peaches popped some gum into her mouth to give it something to do and carefully opened her door. Dominick, sensing her departure, opened his door, got out and ran around to help her descend. In the meantime, Dawn sent Matthew out to greet them.

Matthew, oblivious to Peaches' contemptuous stare said, "Hi, how're you doing? Dawn suggested we come a little early in case things weren't working out." Peaches chewed furiously. Now Dawn had come out and walked over to Dominick.

She held out her hand. "Hi, I'm Dawn. Did you two have a good time?"

But before he could react, Peaches ignored everyone else and took Dominick's arm. She led him to the other side of the JB Hunt truck so they could be alone. A full moon had come out from behind the clouds and created a glow befitting the Starlight Diner.

"I've had a wonderful time." Dominick spoke softly and stood very close to Peaches as she tried to think of something clever to say. With a smile, Peaches asked if she would see him again.

"Two weeks. As soon as I'm back, we'll meet at the Starlight again. Two weeks. Same time, same place. Okay?"

Dominick kissed her gently as Peaches murmured, "Perfect."

CHAPTER SEVEN

After Dominick left, Peaches closed herself off in the back bedroom while Matthew drove the motor home to Dawn's apartment. The garden apartment complex was nice enough, and Peaches remembered passing it on her way to work. She watched from the window as Dawn left the RV, followed by Matthew who carried their sleeping child. When he came back alone, both Packers were quiet, neither wanted to ruin their own personal thoughts of the evening by tapping into the passion and frustration that sat on the edge of their memories. Eventually, Matthew broke the silence.

"Now what should we do? We can't stay here in the street and we can't go back to the school." He suggested they spend the night at the old house. "There's not much there but the driveway. Dawn and I saw it. We won't be bothering anybody." Peaches made a face and called his idea tacky.

"How about Aunt Blossom's?" Matthew suggested.

Cousin Marlene's mother Blossom was a welcoming, motherly woman.

Peaches agreed, adding, "We can update her on Marlene. She'll be happy to see us." They hadn't seen Blossom since the fire a month before. Even after all these years, she was still angry with her daughter for getting mixed up with Ned and the bank robbery, and refused to see her in prison. She did regularly send packages with various things she imagined Marlene might need.

They drove west. Blossom's house was right off I-79. She had lived in that house with Uncle Morton for years and years and refused to sell when the Interstate was expanded into its present configuration. Uncle Morton died shortly after the freeway expansion was completed, but Blossom had stayed in the house in his honor, a commemoration of their love. She was a little hard of hearing so the constant traffic noise didn't bother her, although she liked to complain about it to family and friends. When Peaches and Matthew arrived at #2021 off I-79's service road it was after midnight. There were no lights on in the small Cape Cod style house.

"Do you think we should knock on the door to let her know we're here?" Matthew killed the engine. The Bounder filled the small driveway and blocked in the Ford that was tucked under the carport. The whole area was quiet and dark except for traffic on the freeway. Just then, a light came on in an upstairs window and Aunt Blossom looked down on them calling, "Yoo-hoo. Who's there?"

"This might be a mistake," Matthew murmured as he waved from the RV door. "Aunt Blossom, it's us." It had started raining.

"Looky who's here. And in a mo-bi-le home to boot, how fancy. I'm awake. You know I never sleep. Come on in. I'm coming down."

A few minutes later, the front door opened. Blossom shook her head saying, "Your Uncle Mort always wanted a motor home." Peaches and Matthew walked in to the overheated, overstuffed living room. Peaches noted that Blossom was herself overstuffed, a short plump woman wrapped in a white terry cloth robe tied at the waist. Pink brocade slippers peeked from beneath the hem.

"What are you two doing here? Peaches, what have you done? Who did that to your hair? I have never seen anything quite like it." This made Peaches smile with pride, until she noticed Blossom's perfectly dyed red hair.

It was the exact color she'd wanted. And, in fact, Blossom's hair was styled almost exactly as it had been on Peaches' Clairol box. It made her own droopy blotchy orange hair seem less like a statement and more like a mistake. They were ushered into the small kitchen where the smell of stale oil surrounded them.

Despite her size, Blossom moved quickly and placed a bottle of blackberry wine on the yellow Formica counter and pulled three juice glasses from the cabinet.

"Just a cup of tea for me," Peaches spoke up.

"Tea? That's not going to help you sleep, dear. It has caffeine. Here, have some blackberry wine. It's sweet. Some for you too Matthew?" Without waiting for answers, she handed him a full glass and continued. "If you're going to sleep here, you need something against the interstate." She went on, "It's intuitively thoughtful that you've come today, profoundly intuitive." Blossom passed a glass of wine to Peaches and kept one for herself. "You know what today is, don't you?" Peaches and Matthew shook their heads. "Of course, you do. Otherwise, you wouldn't have come." While their Aunt pulled crackers from the cabinet and got cheese from the refrigerator, they both assured Blossom that they didn't know what she was talking about.

"It's Mort's birthday. He would have been 76. We'll make a party. I would have done it myself, but it wouldn't be much fun all alone." Blossom sighed and drained her juice glass. "If that good for nothing daughter of ours hadn't gone and gotten herself locked up I know she'd be here." She poured more wine for herself and went on, thoughtfully gaining momentum.

"Too bad Mort's not here either. He loved birthdays." Aunt Blossom shook her head, her eyes started to tear. Peaches suspected that Blossom might have had some of the wine before they'd gotten there.

Matthew sipped his wine quietly.

"But now with you two here, my prayers are answered. It will be a day of joyful celebration." Blossom raised her glass. "We could even take that motor home of yours to the cemetery and have the party there." She passed the crackers and cheese.

"We weren't really going to stay for very long, Aunt Blossom." Matthew's empty glass was filled again.

"Nonsense. You certainly have time for a party."

"We only have two weeks." The moment she spoke Peaches realized she had said too much and tried to explain. "We don't really have two weeks to stay--"

"We were thinking of going to Florida," Matthew interrupted. The wine made him feel good. "We're toying with the idea," he said, smiling like an excited child.

"Florida? Mort was always going to take me to Florida. But all our dreams died that afternoon he fell off the roof."

Her loud sigh hung in the kitchen as she pulled a crumpled Kleenex from her pocket and dabbed at her eyes. Peaches finished her wine and said nothing as Blossom pulled herself together, and Matthew looked sad.

"We should get some sleep." Peaches experienced a vague trapped feeling and wanted to leave.

"We do have a big day ahead of us. I've got it all planned. More wine?" Blossom clasped her hands to her big bosom and sighed again. "I think I'd like just a bit more, we are celebrating. I can't tell you how glad I am you're here." Blossom paused for a moment before she filled her juice glass. "Matthew dear, while you're here, there are a few things around that could use some fixing. You wouldn't mind would you? You know, a little painting and a few nails here and there. And Thanksgiving will be coming. No one should be alone on Thanksgiving. We'll have a traditional family get together. That's only a few months away." Matthew started to speak, but Peaches kicked him under the table hard.

After another round of blackberry wine for everyone, Aunt Blossom went back upstairs and the brother and sister returned to the motor home. Inside, Matthew sat on the couch and yawned as Peaches sat down at the dinette.

"Matthew we need to talk." The wine made her sleepy. "Are we going to Florida or not? We need a plan. Otherwise Aunt Blossom is going to take over." She shook her head. "I can't believe she's still celebrating Uncle Mort's birthday. Hasn't it been about ten years?"

"Florida?" Matthew said with a chuckle. "What a great idea. Whose idea was that anyway?"

"It was your idea!"

"Oh yeah. I remember now." He scratched his head. "I just wanted to come home to Pittsburgh. I made up the Florida part. I figured you could swallow Florida." Matthew nodded firmly, now he knew what he was talking about. "Well, we can do that right after the party. I'm glad we're taking the Bounder." Matthew hiccupped. "Just think, if it's still raining, we can park close to Uncle Mort so the awning can stretch right over the grave. Course we might get stuck, and you know, have to spend the night with all the ghosts." He laughed as Peaches rolled her eyes and got up to go to bed.

"Say, wait a minute," Matthew had a clear moment, "you gonna see Dominick again? I want to see Mimi and Dawn. How can we do that if we're in Florida?" Matthew shrugged his shoulders and pushed his dark wavy hair out of his eyes. "Peaches, I don't want to leave Pittsburgh. Is there a reason we have to leave? Why do we have to leave if all the people we care about are right here?"

"Because we're supposed to be on vacation," Peaches said loudly, her frustration building. "We're sampling possibilities and we're supposed to be having fun." Peaches sat down. "Truthfully, I don't care about Florida, but it was your turn and you wanted to go." Peaches stood again, "Dominick will be gone for two weeks, then we have another date at the diner and this time I don't want your help. So if we do go to Florida, we have to be back in two weeks." She headed toward her room. "As for now," she turned around, we cannot stay. We have to tell Aunt Blossom that we cannot stay. Do you understand? We both have to say, we cannot stay."

It was six in the morning when Peaches looked out her bedroom window. The rain had stopped, but the ground was still wet. Lights were on downstairs at Blossom's so Peaches turned over and went back to sleep. But by nine, Peaches and Matthew knocked on the back door of their Aunt's house, eager to get the day's festivities underway so they could be on their way.

"About time you two showed up. Sit down, sit down. I'll whip up some eggs after I finish this." Blossom was enthusiastically stirring potato salad. She shoved the bowl into the refrigerator and searched the shelves for eggs, and kept on talking.

"It's a god sent that you two are here for the party. Family is so important," she said in earnest as she cracked several eggs. "Mort will be so surprised." She poured coffee in waiting mugs. "We'll have such a good time, and then Matthew, when we get back, remember I mentioned that I have a few small things around the house to repair. You know, with Mort gone, it's hard to keep up. It's a blessing having a man around the house. Don't you think, Peaches?" She paused and smiled at her nephew.

"We can't stay," Peaches broke in.

"Oh, I understand." Blossom put toast with a pat of butter on each plate. "Where you going, again? Florida?"

"Maybe, but probably not," Peaches answered. She looked at Matthew for support.

"I love Florida!" Blossom finished scrambling and dished out the eggs roughly. "You mean the state of Florida, don't you? Vacation capital Florida?" She sat down next to Peaches. "It amazes me that my loving family is going on vacation. I haven't been on vacation for years and years. The last time I was away, Morton and I went up to northern Pennsylvania. I think it was Venuvia. We went to my ninety-three- year-old Aunt's funeral. Morton hardly knew her, but he was a good sport to go. We called it a vacation because we stayed in a motel."

She served more coffee. "You know, he was always going to take me," she sighed meaningfully, "to Florida I mean. And how smart you are to be going in a motor home." She sat down again. "How many does that thing sleep? At least three, I'll bet. What a wonderful, inexpensive way to travel."

Matthew finally sensed where she was going. "Aunt Blossom--"

But Blossom continued, "Why, I hear at some of those parks you can stay right next to the water. Vacationing is a wonderful thing. Did I mention that?"

"You did," Peaches interrupted. "But Matthew and I need to be by ourselves. If we go it will be a real fast trip. You wouldn't have any fun at all." Matthew nodded in agreement.

"By yourselves?" Blossom raised her eyebrows as she took Peaches' plate away. "Hmm, that's very odd, dear. Seems to me all you'll do is bicker and fight like you always do." She smiled sweetly as she sipped her coffee. "Maybe you could use a referee."

. . .

Lilly Lawn Cemetery was crowded with head stones lined up like soldiers. The RV inched along in first gear and went up and down the narrow roadways as Blossom sat in the passenger's seat trying to find Morton's grave. Peaches drove as Matthew stood in back of Blossom's seat trying to help.

"I'm pretty sure it's over there." The widow pointed vaguely toward the right. The motor home slowly turned onto Lane M. "No, this doesn't look familiar at all."

"We could go to the gate house. It's at the entrance," suggested

Matthew.

"I know where my Morty's buried, I just got confused. I've never been here in a motor home." They drove around for 15 more minutes.

"They've definitely added stones since the last time I was here. You don't suppose they moved him do you?" Blossom looked worried.

Peaches stopped the motor home and looked over at Blossom. The woman continued to scan the cemetery as she ignored her niece. Her brow was furrowed, her hand covering her mouth in concentration. Peaches was about to insist they ask at the entrance when Blossom perked up. "There, see those two pointy stones? Morton is right there between them."

They snaked toward the protruding headstones and finally stopped in front of Morton George Packer's grave. Peaches positioned the Bounder so that the large window above the dinette faced the gravesite. They would be able to sit and have lunch while contemplating their deceased uncle's demise. The headstone read: 1910-1981, Beloved H, B, F, F, S.

"What do those letters mean?"

"Husband, brother, father, friend, son. That's how he'd wanted it. My Morty was thrifty to the end," Blossom explained and then she bit deep into a baloney sandwich, chewed and swallowed. Blossom recounted how in the beginning, she had admired Mort from afar. "There I was, a beautician-ette, you know, in training. He'd come to the school for a cheap haircut. Even then he watched his pennies."

Peaches nodded, trying to look interested while she moved her potato salad around her plate.

"One day, I was walking out of the academy toward my Ford and miraculously there he was. He'd noticed me too." Blossom smiled as she reminisced.

"That's a nice story, but maybe we should move things along," Peaches stood up.

"You're right. Morton doesn't even know we're here. We need to pay our respects." Blossom wiped her mouth.

After they filed out of the motor home, Peaches and Matthew stood respectfully around the grave while Blossom spoke to the dirt where she imagined her husband's head might be. Matthew was sent back into the Bounder for the cake.

Keeping the candles lit was a trick, but they sang Happy Birthday loudly and meaningfully. Blossom's arms flailed as she led them in song. Out of respect, Blossom didn't want them to eat in front of her husband, so Peaches, Matthew, and the cake were shooed back inside. Blossom wanted to speak with her husband privately.

Fragments of Blossom's conversation floated into the RV through the open window.

"Going well. Peaches and Matthew. Good children. Won't be coming for awhile. Florida."

. . .

That night, after a supper of lasagna, green beans and chocolate pie, Peaches and Matthew left Blossom's small house to turn in.

"That was a great meal." Matthew stretched and rubbed his stomach.

"I think we're out of the woods. She didn't mention coming with us once at dinner. We had the birthday and now that the basement door doesn't squeak and the vacuum cleaner isn't clogged, she'll be happy to stay home and get ready for Marlene to be paroled."

"We'll see." Peaches pulled the shades and noticed that Blossom's lights were still on. "Let's not go to Florida, Matt. It's too far. I need to be back in less than two weeks."

"That's fine with me," Matthew yawned. "Let's talk about it in the morning."

When the alarm buzzed at six am, Matthew had the distinct feeling that something was about to happen. He looked out the front windshield and saw a small travel bag in the middle of the driveway. Before he'd gotten his bed put away, there was a quiet knock.

Blossom stood at the door with a conspiratorial look and an apron. A number of travel bags were stacked on the ground in back of her.

"Wait, Peaches is still sleeping and--"

"Good. We'll just get my things inside and surprise her with a whopping big breakfast. Don't forget that little one in front. That was to keep you from leaving without me."

"What do ya mean, Aunt Blossom?"

"Florida. I've decided to come."

"But…but we're not going to Florida."

"Nonsense. Everybody loves Florida and I've never been. Now get those bags. I'll start breakfast. I love having people to cook for."

The smell of bacon and general commotion woke Peaches. She rubbed her eyes as she came out of her room.

"What's going on?"

"Eggs over easy, honey?" Aunt Blossom cracked one opened. "I'm making breakfast."

"What are you doing here?" Peaches questioned Blossom.

Matthew looked helpless. She suspected that her brother had inadvertently invited their aunt to join them. Peaches suggested he come outside to talk with her. Bewildered, Matthew followed her down the steps.

"What have you done? Didn't you tell her we weren't going?"

"I didn't do anything," Matthew was defensive. "She just invited herself and walked in and took over everything. It's not my fault!"

"Okay, let's not panic. We'll think of something." Peaches already had a headache.

"But what do we do with her?" Matthew was frantic. "We can't ask her to sleep on the couch."

"She wouldn't fit there anyway. But I won't fit on the couch either. She can't stay, there's no room for her."

Matthew scratched his head. "It baffles me as to how they can say this thing sleeps six people. Could there be a secret room or something? Maybe we should have taken that tour Bucky offered." But when the two of them confronted Blossom, she wouldn't budge.

"Two weeks' vacation is nothing. It'll go by fast. You'll make your old aunty happy and you'll get back to Pittsburgh in plenty of time. Trust me."

Eventually, it was decided that Blossom and Peaches would share the back bedroom. And it was only after Aunt Blossom's big breakfast that they finally got out of the driveway and headed south on Route 109.

"I'm so happy. Your father would be proud of you for opening your home to me. Just how long will it take us to get to Florida?" asked Blossom. She sat on the skinny couch knitting.

"It's about 1,000 miles," said Matthew from the driver's seat.

"Whew, that far," Blossom exclaimed.

"Yup," Matthew continued. "About that, and if we move right along, that's about 20 hours of driving."

"Why that's less than a day. We can be in Florida by tomorrow morning. What a wonderful idea."

"Well sure, if we drive straight through."

"Just think, Matthew," Peaches joined in, "if we did drive straight through, we'd get there, see Florida and then be able to get back to Pittsburgh in just a couple of days."

"Oh," Blossom spoke up, "You don't have to rush back on my account. I'm just a poor widow, trying to be helpful to my nearest and dearest. I can be away for weeks and weeks. I've arranged for perpetual care for Uncle Morton's grave. He'll never miss me."

After an hour of driving, they pulled off the highway and into a rest stop. Peaches checked the oil while Matthew strolled the parking lot. When they came back to the RV Blossom had taken over the kitchen. She called out, "Wipe your feet" when they opened the side door to come in. Matthew and Peaches winced. But Matthew's irritation evaporated when he smelled fresh cookies. Peaches mumbled something about dieting. As they came up the steps they could see that Blossom had rearranged items in the kitchen.

"How'd you make the cookies so fast Aunt Blossom?" Matthew asked as he took one from the paper toweling. "The motor home has never smelled so good."

"I brought the dough from home. It was in the freezer. I just wanted you both to know that I'm pulling my weight. I can do things just like the rest."

In an orchestrated move, Blossom squeezed past her nephew who had moved into the dinette area. She continued toward the front and left room so that everyone else could sit at the table.

"Are you enjoying the cookies? It's so nice to have someone to cook for again. I may be a little rusty, but practice makes perfect. I'll be in charge of the cooking and that will free you two up to take care of other things around the motor home. By the way, it would be nice if we could pick up a small TV so I don't get too far behind on my programs." Blossom glanced at the clock above the sink. "If we're going to make it to Florida by tomorrow morning, I guess we'd better stop resting at the rest stop," she chuckled. "I'm so excited. God bless you."

They all took their seats. Matthew drove. Peaches sat in the passenger seat, and Blossom sat down at the dinette and picked up her knitting. She was working on black and white striped socks for Marlene, and wanted them to match what she thought must be a typical prison uniform.

"This is what Laurel and Hardy always wore in their prison scenes," she said, countering Peaches' objection that Marlene wore unflattering green. As she knit, Blossom kept up a running commentary of suggestions. "Matthew, do you ever take that baseball cap off? It's not good for your hair, you know. You don't want to go bald like your father and certainly not like your grandfather. Eventually he didn't have any hair at all. Luckily Morton had a full head of hair until the day he died. And Peaches dear, next time we stop at a pharmacy, we'll get something to fix your hair."

"What's wrong with it?" Peaches swiveled her chair around so she could face her aunt.

Blossom put down her needles and looked back at her niece over the top of her glasses. "It's unnatural. You can't mean that you actually meant it to be that color?"

"No, but--"

"See I told you. Don't be afraid, we'll fix it. I don't know if you remember but I'm a professional beautician."

Peaches just nodded. She felt something tighten in her chest.

"Have you been dating?" Blossom asked. "Probably not, I'm afraid that hair color would scare away any prospective suitor, unless of course, there was something wrong with him." Peaches kept her mouth shut and swiveled back toward the front. Blossom's statement worried her.

Just then Matthew, entered into the conversation. "Peaches why don't you tell her about Dominick? He's a truck driver. She went out with him a couple nights ago."

Peaches cringed as Blossom said, "Dominick's a truck driver? Oh dear, they're never home. He's not a drinker is he? Your father was a drinker. Of course, the drinking problem was not totally your father's fault."

"Whose fault was it?" asked Peaches.

Blossom took a deep breath and then sighed. "Why your mother's of course. She drove him to drink. Everybody knows that."

Peaches thought that their living space was starting to feel claustrophobic. Silence settled on the motor home as the little group of big people traveled south. Aunt Blossom dozed at the dinette. Peaches sat in the passenger's seat and wondered about her life. Why was it that her family made her feel bad about almost everything she did? Maybe Blossom was right. It didn't work out with Clute. Why should anything work out with Dominick? He seemed to like her but maybe there is something wrong with a man who wants to go out with a woman with orange and green hair. Peaches glanced over at Matthew who seemed to be absorbed in driving. He got a toothpick from his shirt pocket to chew on.

"Would ja look at the map and see where we're supposed to get off this road? This is taking us east. Do we want to go east? I don't think we're right."

Reluctantly Peaches got up to get the map. It was laid out flat on the table with Aunt Blossom leaning on top sleeping. When Peaches tried to gently pull it out from underneath her chubby arms, the woman woke up. Wide-awake now, Blossom took up where she left off.

"Matthew, how's that adorable little girl of yours? She's five? And what's happening with her mother? Isn't she the one that can't cook?"

"You mean Dawn? She has a nose problem," Peaches said matter-of-factly.

"A what?" asked Blossom.

"She can't smell right. Her mother is the same way. There's something wrong with her sense of smell. When she tries to cook, she can't season things right, so it tastes funny."

"Always?" asked Blossom.

"Almost always," replied Peaches as she sat down across from Blossom, and spread the map out. "Pizza and frozen vegetables usually come out okay."

"You know dear," confided Blossom. "If Matthew married Dawn, he might lose some weight. Wasn't Dawn the girl that was your best friend? In high school you two were inseparable, don't you remember?

You remember, don't you Matthew?"

"Aunt Blossom, she wasn't so great," Peaches grumbled and studied the map. "I could have had lots of friends." Road signs passed as they traveled along I -70.

"Did you see that? We're going to be near Washington, D.C.," declared Blossom. "We're so close, why don't we stop and take a look around before we go on to Florida? I don't think it would take much time at all. We're right here. My Morton always said he'd take me to Washington. He said we could see the White House where the President lives and the Lincoln Memorial and even the Smithsonian. Don't they have a wax museum too? I've always wanted to go to a wax museum. I hear the people there look like they're real. I think they have a big mall too. What d-ya think? This may be my only chance."

"Oh, I don't know Aunt Blossom, it'll take a lot of time. We have to get back to Pittsburgh soon," responded Peaches.

Matthew chimed in, "We could go to Washington, D.C. for a couple days instead of Florida, especially since we're right here."

Smelling some kind of victory, Blossom kept on talking, her voice rose enthusiastically, "But can't we do both? I've never been so close to visiting two places that I've wanted to visit all my life. Every time I'd see the President on TV, I would say to myself, "Oh would I love to go to Washington." But Morton, God rest his soul, would always make an excuse, it's too far, or it's not the right time of year or he wasn't feeling well, and we never went anywhere and now he's dead. Oh, what can I do to convince you two that this is the chance of a lifetime?" Blossom put down her knitting. "It's educational and I can't wait any longer."

"Aunt Blossom, Washington and Florida are not going anywhere. I mean if we don't go to both now, maybe we can go another time," Matthew said.

"No!" yelled Blossom. She struck the dinette. "There won't be another time. I haven't seen you two in a month, not since the fire, and before that it was your father's funeral, and before that I hadn't seen you since Morton's funeral. I don't want to wait until we have another funeral because it will probably be mine. I want to go now."

"Aunt Blossom, you need to be reasonable," Peaches said in a soothing, but firm voice.

"Reasonable?" Blossom said. "I am reasonable. I've agreed to travel with you, even though you don't have a TV. I've offered to cook and to come out of retirement to help you with your dreadful hair. Here I am a professional, ready to step in. And Matthew, I have all kinds of child rearing advice. Just ask me. I'm like a mother to you two and this is how you treat me? All I ask is that we take a short side trip to a place that I have always wanted to go. We're on vacation for god's sake." Blossom stood up, red faced with her hands out in a hopeless gesture. "I'm desperate. Are we going or not?"

Finally, Blossom was silent. Peaches and Matthew were silent. A few moments passed and Matthew cleared his throat. He spoke over his shoulder as he drove, "Well Aunt Blossom, gee, if it means that much to you, I don't see why we can't take a short side trip. That okay with you Peaches?"

Peaches glared at the side of Matthew's head and didn't say anything. She felt trapped in an airless tin box with a woman whose mission it was to be on vacation and a brother who was hopelessly kind and unable to stand up for himself.

Peaches set her jaw and narrowed her eyes. She opened her mouth to insist that Matthew stop so she could get out. The two of them could go off to Washington without her. Aunt Blossom's twinkling eyes were fixed on her. She waited for an answer.

Peaches looked away from this woman who was trying to ruin her life. But in desperation, she thought, truthfully, maybe my life isn't so great. And with that revelation Peaches caved in and very quietly said, "Sure, I guess so."

. . .

"Matthew, how could you miss the Welcome Center?" Blossom asked with exasperation. "Don't you understand, we're about to embark on unchartered waters, so to speak, and we need a map."

Matthew glanced at the gas gauge. "We'll stop to fill up at this gas station up ahead. They'll have one."

While Matthew pumped in 35 gallons at the Sunoco station, Blossom went inside. She came back quickly and grumbled as she hoisted herself inside.

"Now, what's wrong?" Peaches had no patience for her aunt.

"Morton must be rolling in his grave. This is the first time I've paid for one of these things." She waved the new map in the air. "I'll bet this would be free at the Welcome Center. The heart of a great nation rolls out the red carpet for patriotic citizens and that greedy gas station charges for maps." She sat down at the dinette and spread the *Guide to Washington* on the table. "Now let's see what we want to do."

"I'll drive," Peaches insisted as Matthew came up the stairs. Something in her voice made Blossom look up and was a warning to Matthew not to challenge her. Stuffing several pieces of Doublemint in her mouth, Peaches took the wheel and chewed furiously. If she didn't keep busy, she might strangle her relatives. They bounced and swayed back onto I-495 South, and joined hundreds of other cars jamming the roadway.

"Look at this traffic," Blossom exclaimed, a touch of admiration in her voice. "These are the people that keep our government running. It's so exciting to be a part of it. From what I can see, dear, we need an exit that takes us to E Street."

"What's that, the White House?" asked Matthew from the passenger seat.

"No. It's another Welcome Center. I think we all agree, it's important to do this trip right and the first step is the Center." Blossom spoke in a conciliatory tone. "Don't worry Peaches. We'll ask where we can buy the equipment to get that hair of yours fixed up."

Peaches' face burned. Equipment? What equipment? Did Aunt Blossom need a machine to fix her hair? She was going to say that her hair was fine and that other things needed fixing, but Blossom suddenly announced in an irritatingly loud voice, "Look at that brush fire." There was a lot of smoke and a small battalion of firefighters along the road.

"That happens all the time at my house. Smokers just throw cigarettes out the window and poof you have a brush fire."

"It could have been lots of things, Aunt Blossom," said Matthew.

"Oh no, you don't know cigarettes. They're deadly," continued Blossom. "Why, look at your house. Those foolish arson squad people are fixated on some problem in the closet, but when the day is done, I'll bet you dollars to donuts it was started by a cigarette. Maybe a match, but probably a cigarette. You'll see."

Traffic didn't move so Peaches turned around to face her aunt. "Aunt Blossom, how do you know they think it started in the closet?"

"What closet?" asked Matthew.

"I can't imagine why they're thinking the closet," Blossom speculated. "It's a poor theory that any fire would start there. After all, we were in the kitchen, not the closet and they weren't."

"But how do you know about the closet?" Peaches asked again.

Blossom thought for a moment. "I think I heard it from Herpa. You know, my friend who lives near the cemetery. She probably heard it from her daughter who's dating a young man on the arson squad. I think they're planning to get married."

Traffic was still slow as drivers gawked at the brush fire, but then moved on.

Peaches' attention went back to driving, but she couldn't help thinking about what Aunt Blossom had just said. There might be some truth to Blossom's theory about cigarettes. Dawn arriving at the scene at the time of the fire was oddly coincidental. Peaches remembered that Dawn had come from work and threw away her cigarette. Of course there's the consideration of the spilt bottle of cognac, but that wouldn't have started the fire. In fact, she was quite sure that spilling a little cognac would not have produced such a disaster. Peaches drove robotically and accelerated with traffic. But something else gnawed at her. Why would Dawn do something so dumb as to start a fire at their house? Peaches remembered how gentle and caring Dawn was toward little Mimi. She had to conclude that it was inconceivable that Dawn had started the fire. She would never have put Mimi in danger. Peaches wondered if that meant that it was her. Maybe she had done it all. Peaches shuddered imagining that if Dawn wanted to get at her she only had to start pointing out the facts to that snoopy detective that contacted them occasionally. It was only a matter of time.

"But I didn't mean to do it," Peaches said out loud.

Matthew looked her way.

"Did you say something dear?" asked Blossom.

"No." Peaches' answer was sharp. But her mind followed what she considered the logical path of events. If all the evidence points to me it wouldn't make any difference how I denied it. I'd be convicted and good lord I'll end up in prison with Marlene. Peaches felt frantic, she could feel her underarms perspiring.

Suddenly, Blossom yelled.

"Here it is. Go right. Go right." Blossom stood and pointed the way. "This is the George Washington Memorial Parkway. Isn't that a wonderful name for a road?"

No one spoke as they drove down the exit ramp and entered an area that could only be described as depressed and run down.

"This is Washington?" Blossom looked around in disbelief as they followed the parkway. "Maybe the government isn't doing as well as I thought. This looks like a war zone. Lock the door. Peaches, are you sure we're right?"

"Check the map again," Matthew suggested.

"This is the exit you told me to take." Peaches defended herself. "Maybe you read the map wrong. It's not my fault it looks this way."

"Wait a minute," Matthew said with alarm. "This a parkway. Buses can't go on parkways. That means we can't either. Peaches we've got to get off."

"Why? I can't. Do you see any place I can get off? I'm just the driver and I can't get off. What am I supposed to do?" Peaches had not grasped the problem.

"Oh my goodness, it's not my fault," Blossom was alarmed. She stood and patted her chest. "I've never been to Washington before. I was only trying to help." She sounded like she might cry. "I did the best I could."

"Better take the first exit you come to," Matthew warned. "If there's a tunnel, we're in trouble."

"What? Why?" Peaches' right blinker was on in anticipation of an exit road. "What's wrong with a tunnel? Will something happen in a tunnel?"

"We might hit," Matthew replied. He stayed surprisingly cool.

"Hit what?"

"The roof." Blossom answered the question. "The roof will hit in the tunnel and we won't be able to get out. We'll be stuck there forever and I'm claustrophobic."

Eventually, they were able to get off the George Washington

Parkway without mishap. Peaches wanted to scrap the idea of even trying to find the Welcome Center but Blossom insisted they needed it more than ever. After driving around and asking at numerous gas stations eventually they found it.

"Come on in," Blossom urged her niece. "All is forgiven. Your driving skills just need more practice."

Peaches looked at her aunt in disbelief.

"Visiting the Welcome Center is the only way to start a trip like this. You have to come in."

When they were finally inside Blossom collected pamphlets and spoke with the representative behind the counter about the Washington area while Matthew purchased a few postcards. Peaches bought some more gum.

"Wasn't that a nice young man? He was very helpful." Blossom led the way out. "I noticed he wasn't wearing a wedding ring, dear. We'll find someone to take care of you. I'll bet there are lots of nice, smart unattached men in Washington. It's always wise to go with someone who's connected." Then she looked up at Peaches and added, "We really must make your hair a priority."

Until Blossom was able to transform Peaches' hair she would try to transform her niece and nephew's attitudes about being tourists.

"To be fair, we should all have input on what we see." Blossom insisted they all study the brochures while still parked at the Welcome Center. Gathered around the dinette they pored over information about the White House, the Lincoln Memorial, and the Vietnam Memorial as Blossom made a list.

"There's so much to see," Matthew commented. Then without thinking he said, "Too bad we don't have more time." Peaches side kicked him under the table and accidentally swallowed her gum.

"I see they have a big mall here." exclaimed Blossom. "I love malls. It must be great shopping if it's in the capital. White House first then the mall." Blossom noticed Peaches roll her eyes.

"I'm sorry dear, CVS first, then the others."

Peaches didn't trust herself to say anything. She certainly wasn't going to play along with Aunt Blossom's enthusiasm. The faster they got through Washington, the better. One, maybe two days, that's all, and Florida was out as far as Peaches was concerned. She wouldn't go.

If she had to, she would hitchhike back to Pittsburgh. Their motor home adventure was less than a week old and she felt different about almost everything.

. . .

With her pocketbook slung over her shoulder, Blossom took Peaches' arm firmly and walked her toward the pharmacy.

"This is for your own good. You'll be beautiful and I can't wait. It will be so much fun to play beautician after all these years. We'll get a good color."

"Oh come on Aunt Blossom, what do you mean, all these years. You do your own hair don't you?"

"Oh no, Muriel does it. I've had a standing appointment at Kim's Bob and Curl for over thirty years. I wouldn't dare do my own hair." She patted her own dyed hair and went on enthusiastically. "After we get your hair out of the way, maybe we can find some decent clothes for you when we shop at the mall."

"Hold it! You won't touch your own hair, but you expect to color mine?" Peaches pulled her arm from Blossom's grasp. "Why would I want you to do that? And incidentally, the Mall's not for shopping, it's full of memorials." Peaches opened the pharmacy door for her aunt. "Look on the map if you don't believe me."

"Nonsense. It would be called a park if that's all it was. Malls are for shopping, and what better place to have a fabulous shopping mall than in the capitol. You're wrong. I'll bet all the good stores are there, Sears, Target, you know, maybe even Bloomies. And as for your hair, almost anyone can read directions on a box of color. I bring maturity and beauty intelligence to the experience."

The hair coloring section was in aisle three. Before Peaches could choose a color she liked, Blossom had picked up a box of Clairol featuring an auburn shade.

"Isn't this lovely? This is exactly like your natural color, only better." Blossom held the box up to the side of her niece's head. "See, it even matches your eyebrows. It's definitely very Katherine Hepburn."

"No, it isn't."

"No, it isn't what?" Blossom was losing her patience.

"It isn't exactly like my real color and why would I want to look like Katherine Hepburn anyway?"

Blossom mused, "I remember Katherine Hepburn in The Philadelphia Story. Her hair was beautiful." Then she confided, "I've always wanted to be an auburn."

"Then you get it. Maybe I'll be blond."

"But dear, you don't want to look trashy and blond won't cover the orange. I can't be responsible--"

"Aunt Blossom, I'm an adult, I'll be responsible. And I haven't decided anything. I might just leave it orange. How do you know what color Katherine Hepburn's hair was, the Philadelphia Story was in black and white?"

At the cash register, Blossom purchased two boxes of coloring, one auburn and one blond. Peaches bought some aspirin.

It was already midday and the atmosphere in the RV was tense. Peaches had a bad feeling about the whole hair project. To avoid what seemed like the inevitable, Peaches decided it would be best to keep moving. By traveling around a city her aunt had always wanted to see, it was possible that the woman might forget completely about her niece's hair. Peaches suggested they see at least one area of interest in the city before the tedious chore of finding a place to park for the night was upon them again. Everyone liked the idea, so Blossom suggested something simple like The White House.

"We can put your hair off on condition you put this on," Blossom held out a flowered scarf as Peaches glared. "The orangeie red grates on my professional sensitivities."

They hadn't left the pharmacy parking lot so to get things moving Matthew climbed behind the wheel and prepared to find The White House.

"Do you think we'll be able to park around there?" Blossom asked hopefully. "They may ask us to come in."

"Probably not." Matthew turned on the engine. "But we'll drive over and take a look. At least we'll be able to see the place." So the Bounder headed out for the home of the President. Blossom insisted that she would be best with the map, so Peaches acted as spotter.

After forty-five minutes, Matthew was confused. Blossom would call out street names and Peaches would watch for them, but most times the right street just didn't appear. Sometimes the same street showed up twice and gave them an inkling that they were going around in circles.

Finally, Blossom announced, "We have a problem."

"What?" called Matthew from the driver's seat.

"I've been studying this map, and I have yet to figure out where we are. I'm not even sure we're in Washington."

Suddenly, a flashing light on top of a vehicle leading two shiny black limousines going in the opposite direction caught Matthew's attention.

"Wow, pretty fancy cars."

"Those aren't just cars." Blossom craned her neck. "Those are the President's limousines. He always travels with two or more. I read that in *Reader's Digest*. It throws off assassins. That's how he gets around Washington. Pretty smart don't you think? I say we follow them. They're going to The White House. Matthew, you can get his autograph for Mimi."

Matthew looked at Peaches who shrugged and pushed the scarf back from her forehead.

Matthew negotiated a fairly neat U-turn at a gas station only half block up the street. They got going in the right direction just in time to see the limousines turn two blocks ahead. Blossom stood now to keep the limousines in sight

"Look," she said excitedly. "That's why we couldn't find the White House. This bridge wasn't even on the map. This must be a special route."

Matthew shrugged his shoulders and looked over at his sister.

"Maybe this was a smart move. Look at the line of cars. I guess everybody wants to meet the guy."

But something wasn't making sense to Matthew. At red traffic lights all the cars in front of the RV would go through the light and when the RV stopped the cars in back of the motor home would honk. They all seemed to be part of the same procession.

"What's-a-matter with those people? It's a red light. Can't they see it's red? You watch, these guys in front of me, they're gonna all get tickets."

They followed for another ten minutes. Sometimes, the limousines would drive out of sight, but the height of the motor home and the flashing light on the lead car helped keep the procession in sight. Eventually, the entire line slowed and turned right under a metal arch.

"Boy, this is some back entrance," exclaimed Matthew enthusiastically.

Blossom scanned the horizon. "Is that the White House up there on the hill? It's so small."

"I think it's a cemetery," Peaches commented. "That's a mausoleum."

"Arlington?" Blossom asked, somewhat surprised.

"Nope," announced Matthew. He read the archway over the entrance. "Heaven's Gate." The procession stopped, hemming the RV in. People started getting out of their cars.

"What's this?" Blossom was dismayed. Then she understood. "Somebody died and the President's going to the funeral."

As people walked past, some looked curiously up at the RV's windows.

Blossom spoke, "We can't just sit here. Maybe we'd better get out and pay our respects. At least we'll get to see the President."

Reluctantly, Matthew opened the door and climbed out to join the mourners. Peaches shook her head as her aunt pushed her out the door.

It was a large crowd. The doors of both limousines were opened and then closed. Blossom strained trying to see the President as the congregation grew quiet.

"We've all come to speed Bob on his journey home, to wish him well. We've come to bury a friend," the minister stated in a loud clear voice. "As we all know, Bob was a bowler."

"Bob?" Blossom whispered to Peaches. "Was he a cabinet member?"

"And Bob showed his compassionate humanity in small ways."

Blossom nodded and murmured, "Of course."

As Peaches pushed the scarf up from her forehead again she noticed that Matthew seemed to be moved as well. Was that a sniffle?

"Let us pray," The minister meaningfully instructed the mourners. Peaches watched as both her relatives bowed their heads.

The minister's voice went on, "Beyond death." The casket was lowered. "Ashes to ashes." The minister used a small shovel and dropped dirt into the grave. Blossom and Matthew got in line. When it was their turn, each filled the shovel with dirt and dropped it into the grave. An arm around each other, they paused in reflection, then they moved on. Finally it was over.

Matthew dabbed his eyes, while Blossom greeted the people who had stood next to her.

"Yes. We just arrived from Pittsburgh. My niece and nephew barely knew him, but insisted on bringing me. Bob was one of my dearest friends." Slowly, everyone returned to the waiting cars. The Packers returned to their motor home.

"There's a little lunch at his sister's house." Blossom pulled herself up the stairs. "Apparently it's not too far from here."

Peaches turned around from the passenger seat, "Aunt Blossom, we don't know Bob. We don't know his sister or anybody else at that funeral."

Her aunt was indignant, "I do know the President. I voted for him. And Peaches, you know yourself, people at funerals most often don't know each other. I found that out when I buried Morton. I didn't know half the people there. That's why they have these little get-togethers."

"Aunt Blossom," Matthew broke in, "the President isn't going to be there." Shocked, Blossom held her hand to her bosom as her nephew went on. "I don't think he was ever there."

"He wasn't? But we saw his cars. *Reader's Digest* said. Eventually, they'll take us to the White House, right?"

"Probably not," Matthew went on. "I think those limousines were from the funeral home. They were probably carrying Bob's family. You know, his wife and kids."

"Oh," Blossom said with a big sigh as she sat down at the dinette. "But I wanted so much to meet the President, just this one time."

"Aunt Blossom, hold on." Peaches tried to move on from this nonsense. "You wanted to see the White House, so let's go. Maybe the President will be walking his dog."

• • •

Peaches parked the motor home off to the side to let the cars in the funeral procession go. Peaches didn't look at anyone when she got up. She slipped into the bathroom and quietly closed and locked the door. She took the scarf from her head and studied herself in the mirror. She breathed deeply, then spoke quietly and firmly to her own hazel eyes.

"I can't take this. I won't be a baby-sitter for a woman who pretends to be a functioning adult. I am not a tour guide. I'm not on this trip to be insulted. I'm on vacation." Peaches continued as she shifted her weight, "I don't want to meet the President and I don't want to have lunch at Bob's sister's house. I want my family to leave me alone. All I want is someone to really love me." Peaches took another deep breath. "I like my orange hair. Dominick even likes it. I'm not the problem." Then in an emphatic whisper, "Aunt Blossom is the problem."

Matthew knocked softly. "Peaches, who you talking to? Somebody in there with you?"

Peaches regarded her hair as she ignored her brother. It was droopy, but her forehead was smooth and her nose, largish but perfectly symmetrical, overshadowed a mouth that was on the small side. She smiled at herself. She had good teeth. She liked the way she looked. The image in the mirror was her friend, possibly her only friend.

"Who could be in there with her?" Annoyed, Blossom raised her voice, "Come out of there. We want to get going."

Suddenly just as Peaches felt bombarded from all sides, Dawn popped into her thoughts, so she turned the water on. But even when she closed her eyes, Dawn's disapproving face plastered its self to the insides of her eyelids.

Peaches yelled, "Get out. This is my bathroom. I'm here and I'm doing fine without you."

Matthew's voice sounded concerned as he knocked on the door.

"Peaches?" Then to Blossom, "Somebody's in there with her.

Listen, she's talking to someone."

Peaches kept her eyes closed tight as she dealt with her former best friend, "You threw me away like a used candy wrapper calling me a thief, a pyromaniac, connecting us for life with an affair with my brother and now Mimi. Although not in that order."

Outside the door Blossom was unsettled, "It's her hair; she's depressed about her hair. It's not my fault, I would have done it." Blossom was up now wringing her hands. "It does sound like there's someone in there with her. Maybe it's someone from the funeral."

They heard Peaches' voice continue. "Not once did you listen to my side. If I was skinnier, you'd have more respect. Don't you come waltzing into my bathroom you little twit. Get out of my head. Get out." There was silence, a long silence. When Peaches opened her eyes, she felt better.

But outside in the hallway, Blossom was frantic, "Peaches, try to get out. You're scaring me. Matthew, she might be harmed."

Inside the bathroom, Peaches felt lighter and more in control. Her eyes filled with tears and her nose started to run. Her only true friend looked back from the mirror with a warm, trusting smile.

"Peaches, try to get out. Matthew, we have to do something." Blossom pulled and jiggled the door handle. "I've read how these things can get out of control. Peaches we're here. Oh my god, break it down Matthew."

"I don't think we really need to." Matthew put his hand on the knob and pushed the door gently.

"It's not a matter of need. We must." Blossom stood and wrung her hands. "Matthew put your shoulder into it. Get it opened. Hang on, Peaches we're coming."

After she wiped away the last of her tears and gave a quick swipe to her nose Peaches opened the door. Matthew, who had stepped back for more thrust, was already headed for the bathroom with full force. Blossom screamed.

He crashed into Peaches and sent her into the shower, landing on top of her.

. . .

Equipped with directions from one of the mourners, the city center was easy enough to find, but back in Washington, D.C. traffic again slowed their progress. Matthew searched for the Capitol Building as he navigated traffic. They'd been driving for an hour.

Blossom's irritation was growing until she finally cried, "I've had it. Why am I traveling with you two?" She got up. "It's a wonder we've even found the city. You're not real tourists. This is exhausting. I'm going to lie down."

"I can think of another city I'd rather be in, can't you Matts?" Peaches' remark was pointed, but Blossom didn't hear. She was already in the bedroom.

Tenaciously, Peaches and Matthew pressed on. Traffic crept as they drove along Louisiana Avenue, NW and eventually took a right onto Constitution Avenue.

"Hey, there it is." Peaches said with surprise when the stately white building came into view. "Do we have to call Blossom?" Matthew smiled and gave her a look.

"We found it." Peaches yelled. "We found the Capital Building. It's right here."

Matthew added, "Better hurry, Aunt Blossom I can't pull over."

"Come out right now." Peaches yelled again and would have gone down and knocked on the bedroom door but it opened. Blossom, a little unsteady adjusted her dress and hurried up the aisle. This caused the motor home to sway from side to side. She frantically looked out each window.

"Where is it? I've been waiting all day to see this thing." She leaned over the kitchen sink. "I don't see it. Is that it?"

"No. Over here." Peaches pointed at the big white building they had just passed. Blossom crossed the aisle and craned her neck and got a quick glimpse as they turned the corner onto Second Street.

"That wasn't such a big deal." Blossom flopped into the big side chair, disappointed.

"Ya want me to swing around the block? Traffic's moving faster now."

"No that's okay," she was uncharacteristically quiet for a long time. The side chair she clutched gently moaned as she moved it back and forth. She eventually sighed. "Everything's gone wrong." Then she lay blame. "That expensive map doesn't work and you two don't even act like real tourists. When Morton was alive, he knew how to be a tourist."

"Except he never went anyplace," Peaches pointed out.

They traveled on and caught sight of the Washington Monument, and they thought they might have seen Fort Knox. Traffic was heavy as they traveled the streets looking for the Vietnam Memorial. Peaches studied the brochure.

"Could we stop for a bite?" Blossom's voice was pleasant, almost conciliatory. Peaches wasn't fooled, her aunt was just regrouping.

"You're not supposed to be able to see it from the road." Peaches turned the brochure over.

"Maybe we could stop for some dinner." Blossom spoke louder.

"Sure, I think you'll be able to see it." Matthew spoke confidently. "We'll drive by it in a minute. I think they put everything pretty close to the road because parking is so hard."

But as Peaches knew it would, Blossom's patience evaporated.

"Excuse me. Matthew get that toothpick out've your mouth. This is awful. You're driving around aimlessly. I could do that myself. Find someplace to stop for heaven's sake. We're like sardines in here. Try to think of me for a change. I'm claustrophobic." She was up. She clutched the back of the driver's seat scanning the horizon. Her hot breath hit Matthew at the back of his neck. Peaches felt her chest tighten and inadvertently clenched her teeth. She twirled the ring on her finger and realized she was out of gum.

"There," Blossom yelled. "Right there." Blossom's arm thrust out past the right side of Matthew's head as her chubby finger pointed at a Perkins Restaurant. The parking lot was fairly big and there was a bus already there. Matthew did as he was told.

As soon as they found a parking spot, Blossom was down the steps and out the door, even before the bottom step had had a chance to roll out. She fell flat on the pavement.

"Aah." Blossom picked herself up. "Why don't you get a motor home that has real steps?" She fanned herself with a handkerchief, and added, "At least I can breathe again. Don't you two realize this trip isn't turning out anything like I thought it would?" She led the way toward the Perkins entrance and called over her shoulder, "We're going to have to have a serious discussion about the direction of this trip." Peaches and Matthew followed and eyed each other in agreement.

They were seated immediately and Peaches steeled herself for the impending conversation, but the waitress interrupted with menus. Even after ordering food, the discussion was again delayed as Blossom fluttered to the salad bar and lingered at the lettuce where she became involved in an intense conversation with a white haired man. When she returned carrying her plate of salad, she was euphoric.

"Unbelievable." Blossom sat down. "I know that man. He's from the Welcome Center. Don't you remember when I was at the counter asking directions and a man came to pay for postcards? That's him." Blossom sat down. "And the best part is that he's from Pittsburgh. He's with a church group and they're all from Pittsburgh. They're on the same trip as we are. What a coincidence. That man, George, even knows Morton's cemetery."

The waitress brought their food.

"What do you mean the same trip?" Peaches asked as she reached for the ketchup.

"Why the very same. It must be a popular route, Pittsburgh, to Washington, D.C. and then Florida. But instead of rushing around they're taking a whole three weeks. First they're sightseeing here in Washington, then going south to soak up the Florida sun." Blossom finished off her salad and put her meatloaf in front of her. "They're going to the mall tomorrow. Pass me the ketchup, would you dear. They actually know where the mall is. George says they're all mature, well-traveled adults. No offense intended, of course."

"What offense?" Peaches questioned.

"Well you know, I just mean they're focused on what's right and natural to do on vacation. For example, do you know where they're staying tonight?" Blossom went on between mouthfuls, "Motel 6, it's just out of town. The one that leaves the light on. They're watching their pocketbooks."

"We stay in our own RV, have our own lights and don't have to lay out a dime," Peaches reminded her, but Blossom didn't seem to hear.

"We'll have to find a place to park for the night," Matthew said. He reached down and picked up his napkin from the floor.

Blossom grew serious. "This is my first night. Doesn't it bother you that we don't know anything about this city?" She put her fork down. "At any moment, warring gangs could surround us. I've been told they pry open motor homes like soup cans."

"Aunt Blossom, there's nothing to worry about. We've got Matthew." Peaches went on, "Besides, you're the one who wanted to come to Washington. If we'd just kept going, we'd practically be in Florida by now."

"I'm your aunt. You know I'm not a negative person but it's my job to point out the dangers. I was inspired by the fact that the church group is staying in a civilized, safe and well-advertised motel." She leaned toward her niece, "Can Matthew keep us safe?" She looked over at her nephew who was wiping gravy from the front of his shirt.

Pausing a moment he said, "If you'd rather find a motel, we can do that."

"No. No. I think I'll be able to keep my claustrophobia under control."

They finished dinner and got up to leave at the same time as the church group. Nothing more was said about the talk they were going to have. Blossom quickly caught up to her new friend George to say good night. And as Blossom happily rejoined her relatives on their way to the Bounder, Matthew off-handedly suggested that perhaps she might want to join the tour group.

"And leave you?" They all laughed, but Peaches couldn't leave the thought alone. This could easily solve all their problems.

"Aunt Blossom, why don't you join George's group if you like them so much."

"I don't like repeating myself, but I will say it again. I'm in for the long haul." She squared her shoulders to climb the steps and continued, "You two need to see the country and it's my duty to make sure you do."

• • •

"Sure wish we could just stay here?" Matthew moaned, relieved that Blossom had gone to bed. "I'd give anything to be able to."

"Me too. But I wouldn't try it. We'd never hear the last of it from her."

Matthew wearily climbed into the driver's seat and turned the key to start the engine. Nothing happened. He repositioned himself and tried again. Nothing happened.

"I'll check under the hood." Proud that he even knew how to open the hood, he looked inside. Even though the lights in the parking lot were dim, and he'd forgotten to bring out a flashlight, Matthew moved some wires up and down. He touched a few things that were surprisingly hot. He called for Peaches to turn the key while he watched for trouble. Again, nothing happened. Maybe he had wished too hard that they spend the night where they sat. He would really prefer to have the motor home running. Suddenly, with his white hair gleaming, George was by his side.

"Got a problem?" the older man said amiably. He positioned himself beside Matthew and peered into the engine. He pulled a small flashlight out of his pocket, then fiddled around and checked things. It was immediately apparent to Matthew that George knew engines. At least he knew what not to touch. Rather quickly he pointed out how the positive terminal was not fully connected to the battery. Matthew made a mental note.

"Try it now," George called. Peaches turned the key and the engine roared. Blossom had heard the commotion and padded out in her bathrobe and fluffy slippers to join Peaches. Together they watched George stride across the parking lot to the waiting bus.

Blossom sighed, "I think God has sent him to save the trip."

Peaches murmured, "Let's hope so."

. . .

It quickly became apparent to Matthew that the responsibility of finding a place for them to park the RV for the night had fallen on his shoulders. After he'd closed the hood and climbed the Bounder steps, Blossom walked back toward the bedroom and called "Good night," followed closely by Peaches. The tour bus going to Motel 6 left a cloud of black exhaust eerily floating in the parking lot lights. The acrid smell seeped in through the RV windows. A man lazily walked his dog at the edge of the blacktop while cars moved quickly out on the street.

"They're all going home," Matthew said out loud to no one. An empty feeling churned in his gut and worked its way up to his chest, maybe even his heart. Then it crept up to his head around his eyes and temples giving him a headache. It was a familiar feeling and he knew it wouldn't go away by driving around Washington.

Eating usually helped, but he wasn't hungry, so he climbed out of the driver's seat and stretched out on the couch to relax for a couple minutes. He drifted into a restless sleep while perilously lying on his side.

Close to midnight, there was a loud knock at the door. It startled Matthew awake and he promptly fell off the couch. He expected Peaches to rush out of the bedroom, so Matthew naturally hesitated. She didn't come out, but the knocking persisted. He slowly opened the door to a uniformed police officer who stood beside a much shorter and very agitated man in a business suit.

"Grove Street," the short man spoke loud and distinctly as if Matthew were hard of hearing, "Why can't you park on Grove Street?"

Matthew tried to get his sleepy brain to work and thought that this would be a good time for his sister to charge in like she always did. But things were quiet in the back bedroom.

"I would, I will," stammered Matthew, "but something's wrong with the engine. I can't get it started."

"Get a tow truck and get this thing outa my parking lot."

"I've got some help coming," Matthew blurted out. Strengthened by his lie, he grew slightly more confident. "They said they'd be out here," Matthew looked at his watch, "anytime."

"I'm Mr. Murphy and this is my lot." The man used his pointer finger to poke the air to emphasize his words. "This is private property. The Perkins Company doesn't like overnighters. I'm tired of you vagrants parking where ever you please."

"You heard the man. Get moving," the police officer added. And they slammed the door in Matthew's face.

"What help are you expecting?" Peaches had come up behind her brother just as the door closed. This was getting to be a nightly event.

"You're going to get us arrested." He perspired even though it wasn't hot. "I thought you were going to find us a place for the night. I leave you alone and look what happens."

Matthew defended himself. "I was trying to figure out what to do." But then he sat back down on the couch and held his head in his hands and added in despair, "Peaches, this trip is turning into more work than work. I want to go home."

"I agree. It's not much fun anymore but what home do you want to go to?" Peaches knew she was being annoying and she didn't care.

Matthew was cornered. He knew she was getting testy, making him walk on eggshells again. If he wanted to go to Dawn and Mimi's apartment Peaches would be angry. And yet that's exactly where he wanted to go. He certainly would not go back to Blossom's house. His aunt would be furious for cutting her vacation short and would probably take it out on him. Then there was Uncle Mort's freakish spirit hovering in the air. Matthew crossed his arms to protect himself from the thought.

"Well, what do you want me to do?" he desperately whispered. "She acts like she's our mother but we're the ones taking care of her. Plus you'd swear she'd never been anywhere in her life and we've got the only bus. No wonder Marlene's in prison. She's probably pretty happy to be away from her mother."

"Matthew, this is serious. We need to decide on something before tomorrow, or she'll take over the whole trip and I'll never get to see Dominick again. Because of her, I'll never be able to meet anybody and I'll never have a life. I'll die taking care of our aunt. We have to figure out how to get her to go with that tour group."

"She's already taken over the whole trip as far as I'm concerned. Why would the tour group even want her?"

"Matthew, I'm the one that has to sleep with her and if something doesn't change, I'm leaving and catching a bus back to Pittsburgh and you can figure out what to do with her. I think you get along with her better than me. Besides, there's really only room for two in this thing."

Matthew looked at Peaches and spoke through clenched teeth. "That's not fair. I'm walking a tight rope over alligators for you two, and even when I'm very careful, I still get eaten alive. Everybody wants something and that something doesn't necessarily include plans to make my life easier or even happier." Matthew felt more conviction, stronger as his words came out but it was an unfamiliar feeling, uncomfortable really. Instead of feeling elated he felt on the verge of panic. To keep it under control, he sat back on the couch and hugged himself and panted just a bit. A heavy pause filled the space between them. Summoning his courage again Matthew announced to his sister, "I want to go home to Dawn."

• • •

Blossom woke up shivering. The digital clock showed 3:23 a.m. and in the dim light that seeped in through the blinds she could plainly see that Peaches had all the covers. But even after she yanked back the blankets, Blossom couldn't get back to sleep. She felt a familiar loneliness. She still missed Morton. She bounced on the thin mattress and hoped to wake Peaches who slept undisturbed with a slight snore. Blossom plumped her pillow for the eighth time and watched the clock creep towards dawn. Her mind raced while she tried to get comfortable. I try to help, but these two keep getting in my way. Blossom rolled over. I have expectations. I can't stand the thought of riding one more day in this behemoth, seeing glimpses of this and snippets of that. I want to be a real tourist. I want to do it right. Blossom turned over again, adjusting her nightgown. Two weeks is ridiculous, I've got lots of time. She punched her pillow again. It's been a good faith try but it's not working. Suddenly, the solution washed over Blossom. The Group. I need a plan.

• • •

It was almost eight a.m. Grease from yesterday's bacon and eggs coated the stovetop when Blossom went out to the kitchen. She didn't notice. She mapped out her strategy while she hunted for a frying pan. After I give them breakfast, I'll casually mention that I need to make a call. She fingered the paper in her pocket. They won't suspect that George has one of those new cellulars. She raised the shade over the sink. I'll probably have to call a cab to get to the tour bus, these two can't find their way out of a dirty sock. Blossom sniffed, it may get ugly. They suggested I go with the group but I know they want me here I'm a valuable commodity. They like my cooking and I'm easy to get along with. She got eggs out of the refrigerator and sniffed again, but they can't all have me. I have to choose. And I choose to leave these two in the dust.

She placed the frying pan on the stovetop and started cracking eggs with more force than she intended. She picked out shell fragments from the bowl with her finger.

"Good morning Aunt Blossom." Matthew's greeting made her jump. Lost in thought she hadn't noticed him sleeping on the couch. He swung his legs and stretched them across the aisle. "You might have noticed, we're still at Perkins." He defended himself, anticipating her disapproval. Blossom actually hadn't noticed.

Matthew continued. "I can explain." He threw off his quilt. "After the tour group left and there was all that hullabaloo with the policeman, I didn't know where to go so I took a nap. But now it's morning and so we can be here, no problem."

Hands on her hips, Blossom studied her nephew with his wrinkly blue striped pajamas draped around his chubby body and thought, I'm exhausted already.

His aunt's intense glare made Matthew uncomfortable. "I guess I'll get up."

"Just a minute, I have something to say." Matthew stayed down while Blossom's anger superseded her plan of action and she let him have it. "Do you realize I've been up all night? Not only am I exhausted, but I've probably caught pneumonia since your sister kept all the covers." She raised her arms desperately. "How much can I stand?" Wagging her finger at Matthew she continued, "Let me point out that this is in addition to her being oblivious to an alarming hair problem, and wanting to cut my vacation short so she can show up for some trucker date." She picked up the frying pan and took a step in his direction. "And then Matthew, there's you. Your mind is on your illegitimate daughter and her floozy mother. Where does that leave me?" Blossom stood, legs apart.

Surprised, Matthew blurted out, "Dawn's no floozy and don't you talk about my daughter like that." He sat up straight while Blossom kept on going.

"I don't think it's too much to ask to have a small amount of luxury with people my own age and the comfort of a simple bus. I would like to act like I'm on vacation. And even though you know I love malls, you've refused to find the thing despite the purchase of an expensive map and hours of riding around in this tin box. I'm claustrophobic for god's sake. It's no use. I can't do it any longer."

"But it's only been a day." Matthew tried to interject some reason.

"I'm forced to find compatibility somewhere else, with the group if they'll have me. And why wouldn't they want and appreciate an accomplished vacationer and shopper, a conversationalist extraordinaire. I have George's number." She waved the piece of paper in the air. "You can look surprised but I'm desperate. I've made a decision and no matter what you say you can't stop me. It's over!"

From the other side of the closed bedroom door they heard Peaches shout, "Yes!"

. . .

With the decision to part company heavy in the air, no one spoke at breakfast. Blossom's conviction to leave withered a bit as she watched her niece and nephew hardily eat the fried eggs and toast she had prepared. She did love feeding people and there wouldn't be much opportunity to feed anyone in the church group unless there was a Bunsen burner in the back of the bus. Her judgment was further shaken when Peaches amiably volunteered to do the dishes so Blossom could pack up her things. Matthew offered to scout out a pay phone at Perkins.

With everything covered, Blossom stood at the bedroom door with her hands on her hips. "What an understanding family I have. I know you want the best for me and I feel your pain even though you're making valiant efforts to soldier on. Maybe you could join the group too." Her statement caught everyone by surprise. "Or we could travel together in tandem following the group bus, with me of course staying in motels. It could be beneficial for everybody. I could tackle your hair Peaches, and Matthew, I could tell you how to raise that daughter of yours. I'm brimming with advice. I think I could learn to love being with the both of you if we have the buffer of others."

Matthew sensed things might turn sour and didn't know what to say to stop the possible change of events, so he left. The two women watched him walk toward the restaurant and a possible pay phone that would be the key to moving things along.

"Aunt Blossom," Peaches looked at her aunt and knew she had to go slow. Smiling her friendliest smile she approached the topic diplomatically. "Let's think this out. We're your relatives and of course we'll always be there for you. How about trying the group maybe for a day or two. You could see if you like them. Matts and I will do some sightseeing here in Washington before we head back to Pittsburgh. Try it and if the church group doesn't work out we could meet up and you could come back with us."

"You think so?" Blossom was visibly relieved. "It would be a test to see if I really like them."

"They seem nice but you never know." Peaches was reassuring.

"You two won't leave town?"

"Us? No of course not." Peaches smiled and crossed her fingers behind her back. "Now you go pack. Matthew's coming back. He'll know where to find a phone."

. . .

After several tries with the pay phone, Blossom was able to contact George. She explained the difficulty they had been having finding sights to see and a lack of comfort in their smallish motor home. She was volunteering to find another situation and could she join his group? After considerable back and forth discussion and a panicked request for Matthew to go find more coins to feed the phone, the answer was yes. George suggested that they pick Blossom up at Perkins since their bus had to pass close to the restaurant on the way to the National Mall. They would be there in an hour.

"They're coming." Blossom hugged herself. "Can you imagine? And we're going to the mall." She thought for a moment." You could follow us." Peaches and Matthew rolled their eyes as they walked across the parking lot. "There's just a little problem." Blossom waited for the automatic step to come out. "I can only bring one suitcase."

"How will you do that? You have seven." Matthew blurted out.

"I'll think of something."

. . .

One small suitcase doesn't hold much. So with limited space allowed for her belongings, Blossom packed and carefully chose from the many things she had brought.

While Peaches cleaned up the breakfast dishes she imagined her aunt frantically rushing from one side of the bedroom to the other. Even if Blossom were to groan, grunt or scream, Peaches had made the decision not to get involved. She was pleased with herself because she was already acting like Blossom's vacation was someone else's problem. What Peaches didn't know was that Blossom had a plan.

Though she was burning with curiosity, Peaches forced herself to grab a Snickers bar and go outside. She would take a walk around the parking lot, nothing too strenuous. The candy bar was not on her new diet but this was a special occasion and it would help ease the anxiety. Matthew was already outside checking the oil on the Bounder again. Before too long, they heard the bus that Blossom was waiting for cough and roar its heroic arrival from two blocks away.

"They're here." Matthew called in to his aunt as he slammed the hood.

"I know, I know," a muffled voice called back. "Tell them I'll be out."

It was a long time before Blossom appeared at the Bounder door. When she did, she carried one small suitcase. Peaches couldn't take her eyes off her aunt. She was a remarkable sight. Not only was she perspiring profusely, but she looked like she had gained at least two hundred pounds since breakfast. It seemed that Blossom had solved the one suitcase problem by layering. She had put on almost everything she owned, stretching and pulling each piece of clothing, one on top of the other, over her already ample frame.

Blossom had trouble navigating the steps. "I'll be all right. If I don't come back and I stay with the group, just drop those suitcases off when you're in Pittsburgh. You know where the key is."

"Aunt Blossom you can't--" Peaches was alarmed.

Layering several shirts wasn't so bad, but then over those tops she had slipped on sweaters and covered everything with a shawl. Her black pants could be seen peeking from beneath a pair of pink striped ones. There may have been more underneath. Over that billowed several skirts and maybe even a dress. Her jacket was tied around her already large waist.

She made it down the steps and waddled into the bus. Peaches thought the suitcase she carried looked a little familiar. Matthew was speechless. Just as the bus was leaving, Blossom opened a window.

Remembering Peaches' offer of escape she called, "We'll meet up here in three days. I'll know what I want to do by then." Peaches cringed. They would be delayed in Washington while Blossom decided whether or not she wanted to stay with the church group. But there was no time to negotiate because the bus was gone. In the back bedroom where Blossom had worked so hard, all that was left were a few pieces of clothing strewn around with her empty suitcases.

It was the first day in Washington that they had to themselves and all Peaches and Matthew could do was drive around to kill time. But they did have some success finding the Capitol Building again, and actually saw the Lincoln Memorial five times.

"Blossom must be in heaven," Matthew mused as they enjoyed BLTs at a corner deli. "She's going to love the group, don't ya think?"

"Of course she will." Peaches agreed. "She's going to love it so much it seems silly for us to stick around here. I like Washington, but we have things to do in Pittsburgh, maybe we should see if we can find the President's house and then we could just leave." Peaches held her ring up to the light then rubbed it on her sweat suit to polish it up." "Blossom won't miss us and even if she wanted to meet us back here, the group won't want to back track to Perkins just to check in day after tomorrow. If they don't come we'll know it's working out but we've wasted three days. We'll end up just leaving for Pittsburgh anyway."

"Yeah. You're probably right, but we gave our word. If we just left and she came back looking for us, she'd hate us forever. We'd better stop at the next gas station. The tank's almost empty."

In the middle of the afternoon of that first day they stopped at a Mobil station on Avenue E. Matthew hopped out to pump the twenty-five or so gallons to fill the tank.

"We'll need some money. Better get the suitcase." Matthew called up to his sister as he replaced the nozzle. He loved being able to call up for money. It made purchases so easy. And, at least right now, thanks to the life insurance redemption after their father's death, they had a lot of it.

"Coming right up." As she went to retrieve their small brown suitcase, Peaches was thinking the same thing, how handy it was to have their money tidily packed into something so convenient. It was so safe. But it wasn't under the dinette where they usually kept it so she started to look around. There it was, in Blossom's bedroom in the corner. How odd that it wound up over there. Maybe Matthew had moved it for some reason. Then she paused. No, she thought, it didn't look quite right. She knew her aunt had a similar suitcase, small and brown, with a tiger striped lining. Peaches' heart started beating hard. This suitcase was almost like their money suitcase, but not quite. Just to make sure, she opened it up. Inside, there was some of Aunt Blossom's underwear nestled against a pattern of yellow and black stripes. Gasping, Peaches immediately knew what had happened. She ran to the window and yelled out to Matthew,

"Stop the pump."

. . .

The bus was feeling hotter by the minute so Blossom shed most of her clothes and stored them in a large plastic bag provided by Eli, the nice elderly bus driver. And despite the disappointment at finding out that the Mall had no shopping, and only featured a large grass lawn and some stone-faced monuments she amiably went along with the group. Later that afternoon, the Motel 6 with a Denny's restaurant right next door was a delight to all. They would take advantage of the early bird special.

In her own private room, Blossom tingled with the thriftiness as she carefully prepared for dinner with her new found friends. She chose her blue seersucker top and her comfortable white cotton slacks, now a little wrinkled from being kept in the plastic bag. The top could be made into a tantalizing off-the-shoulder style if she pushed the scooped neck to one side. She lifted her suitcase onto the luggage holder. Her black bra would be stashed in a corner pocket if she remembered correctly. She had packed so fast, it was a wonder she had any underwear at all. She snapped the suitcase open and stood over it with her mouth opened. The suitcase held piles of money. She knew it belonged to Peaches and Matthew.

"Oh my lord." she said out loud as she slammed the top shut. She rushed to the window and yanked the drapes closed. What would happen if thieves knew she had so much money? And it wasn't even her money. She had to hide it. Frantic with worry, she grabbed her shawl and threw it across the top. Then she realized that she, 71-year-old Blossom Penelope Packer, mother of Marlene, dear Marlene who was currently doing time in prison, could be perceived as a thief. Peaches and Matthew might think she stole the money deliberately. Blossom wrung her hands. All she wanted was the chance to be a tourist and now look what had happened. Her niece and nephew would have no money until they got their suitcase back. Blossom knew she had to be at that restaurant day after tomorrow.

. . .

On the morning of the third day, Peaches and Matthew ate in the motor home to save what few dollars they had left. Nestled in a corner of the parking lot at Perkins, they watched for the big Greyhound bus that would bring Blossom and their suitcase back.

With little to no money to spend on anything, let alone more gas they had found the nearest Walmart and parked their vehicle until it was time to return to meet Blossom. Not fond of walking they spent most of their time inside their RV eating potato chips and drinking Coca-Cola.

"What if the Presbyterians don't want to come back here?" Matthew was nervous as he finished off the last bag. "What if they like Blossom enough to keep on going." He looked expectantly out the window as a truck pulled into the parking lot. "If that happens, we don't even have an address where she can send it." Then he had an idea. "Hey, she could send the whole suitcase to Dawn. Dawn's got an address."

"Listen Einstein, even if Blossom knew to do that, which she won't, we don't have enough gas money to get back to Pittsburgh to even get the suitcase."

"Dawn could drive down. She could borrow a car from the used car lot and--"

"No." Peaches cut in. "Dawn's not going to drive anywhere. I don't want her involved. My big worry is that the group is not going to listen to Blossom. She's new and she talks too much. She'll go on and on and they'll just tune her out." She took a deep breath. "No. The solution is, if they don't show up we'll have to get jobs for gas money. The Presbyterians have already checked out of their motel because they're supposed to leave for Florida today. If they don't show up here, we'll have to waste our time traveling south to find them because the money we make working for a few days is not going to last very long. And, we don't have any idea when the group with Blossom and our suitcase, will come back to Pittsburgh."

"What kind of jobs would we get?" They walked the parking lot together to get some air.

"Anything." Peaches threw up her hands. "We could wait tables. You could teach something. I could work in that hair salon we passed, remember how their sign said they needed a part-time colorist?" She patted her orange hair. "I've proven I'm pretty handy with color." But Matthew was more worried than ever as they went back inside to watch the road.

"Of course, it would only be temporary," Peaches reminded him as she twirled her ring nervously.

It wasn't until late in the afternoon when the group bus finally came back to Perkin's parking lot. The air was chilly as Peaches and Matthew went out to greet Blossom who was the first one out of the bus. She was empty handed.

"I didn't mean to take it." Blossom said right away. "Accidents happen. It was a terrible responsibility. But don't worry I took care of everything. It's in a perfectly safe place."

"Where?" Peaches asked anxiously. "Where did you put it?"

Blossom whispered so no one would hear. "It's at Motel 6, under the bed."

CHAPTER EIGHT

As Peaches and Matthew distanced themselves from Washington, D.C. their mood lightened. They had a sense of freedom as the Bounder merged on to I-91 north with a full tank of gas. Peaches quietly hummed *The Best Is Yet To Come* while Matthew drove the RV quietly and conservatively toward Pittsburgh. He still felt unhinged by the suitcase incident.

The suitcase had finally been returned first to Blossom and then to Peaches and Matthew after the manager of Blossom's motel had persuaded a member of the cleaning staff to return the valise she had found under the bed. A surveillance video clearly showed the petite woman leaving what had been Blossom's room carrying a small suitcase. Vindicated, Blossom was happily on her way to Florida with the church group.

"I think we're finally on the same page." Peaches was in a good mood.

"What page?" Matthew was startled out of his thoughts.

"It's a figure of speech. We both want to go to Pittsburgh. And even though we're going for different reasons, we're both going in the same direction. I'm going to meet the love of my life and you're going to visit your little girl." Her comment left Matthew with an odd empty feeling.

They spoke very little as the miles flew by. Matthew thought about Mimi and Dawn. He was the man in his carousel dream, never quite fast enough, never quite there for anyone. I'm a hovering helicopter and I never get to land. His mind mulled over all the facts. He had to admit that what Blossom said was true. Mimi needed a whole family. Matthew glanced at Peaches. She was studying the map again. He thought about talking it over with her, but knew that that wouldn't work.

Matthew drove on. Funny how things are, he thought. If I'd been married to Dawn when Mimi was born and then divorced later, it would be different. She wouldn't be illegitimate. But why would I divorce Dawn anyway? He held tight to the wheel while a cement truck passed on the left. What's wrong with Dawn? I like her. I think I might even love her. There's never been anybody else. Matthew looked over at Peaches. She sat in the passenger seat again, eating a sandwich. She hadn't asked him if he wanted something to eat. He turned back to the road without saying anything. Dawn is fun and she's really smart. She's a good mother and she cares about me. What's wrong with Dawn? Matthew couldn't think of a single thing. He looked over at Peaches again and then back at the road thinking, instead of Dawn, I'm married to my sister.

Peaches hummed to herself, but she came back from her thoughts to give Matthew an update.

"I figure it will take us only four or five hours to get back to Pittsburgh."

"Isn't that about how long it took us to get from Pittsburgh to Washington? Wouldn't it take about the same amount of time to go back?"

"Yes, but a few days ago the trip seemed so long and complicated. Today it doesn't seem so bad." Matthew nodded in agreement and then took a deep breath.

"Peaches, I wanted to talk to you about something," Matthew began. He did not take his eyes off the road. "You know what Aunt Blossom said is true. And I've been thinking a lot about, you know, what she said, and well, I've been thinking that, maybe I'd like to make things better."

"That's very nice of you, Matthew. But I think you're crazy to want to try." Peaches turned around in her chair and faced her brother.

He kept his eyes on the road and quickly continued, "I knew you'd have this reaction, but it won't affect you much. You could pretend it never happened."

"How exactly would I be able to avoid it, you nincompoop?"

"Peaches, this is serious."

"I am serious. There is no way, no way in the world."

"Peaches, I want to be responsible."

"And I want to be beautiful."

"Don't be sarcastic."

"Me sarcastic? I do want to be beautiful and there must be someone in Pittsburgh who can make my hair a normal color. I like orange. It's vibrant and interesting but *Glamour* thinks it might scare off, you know, men. The article said to change it, but I'd have to be pretty bad off to have my brother do my hair. Listen Matthew, I appreciate your offer but I don't want you touching it."

Matthew was stunned. He looked over at his sister who looked back at him in earnest. "Why would I have anything to do with your hair?" He shuddered. "Why is everything about you? No Peaches, I was talking about something else, something very important."

"Well my hair is important. It's very important to me. In fact my whole future depends on my hair being a normal color by this coming Wednesday. I think Dominick was being kind when he said it was different. That article said it needed to be normal." Peaches faced the front again and noticed the road signs. "Oh wait. I think we turn off here. Let me check." Peaches studied the map briefly. "Yes, here it is. Follow 141 to the next exit." She turned toward her brother. "You know, I'm still hungry. I'd like to stop for a Big Mac and maybe some fries."

"Sure," Matthew sighed, "I guess I could eat."

. . .

After stopping for a quick lunch, they were back on the road and eventually saw signs for Pittsburgh. They were almost home.

"We do have to figure out where we're going to park, Matthew," Peaches pointed out pragmatically. "We could do Walmart again, but not the one on the West Side. It's too close to Dominick's apartment. If he finishes that job early, he might be home. I don't want to take a chance he'll see me before I'm ready. You probably want to go see Mimi, don't you? Maybe we can time it so Dawn's at work. I don't want her to see my hair again. She'd want to fix it herself and I can't trust her. Matthew, didn't you have something important to tell me?"

"As a matter of fact, Peaches, I did." The Bounder went by a big green Welcome to Pittsburgh sign.

"Oh, I'm so excited to be home." Peaches clasped her hands together. "It feels like we've been away for years, doesn't it?" Then she became serious. "Matthew, I think I know what you're trying to say. I haven't wanted to talk about it. So why Aunt Blossom brought it up is beyond me. But trust me, it will all work out."

"I'm glad you feel that way Peaches. I think it will work out too," Matthew nodded. There was relief in his voice.

"The thing I don't understand is why?"

"What do you mean why? It just happened. Why do any of these things happen?"

"Oh we're calling it an accident but it may have been a group effort. And I don't mind taking some of the blame. I brought her into our lives as a friend, so I may have been a party to it in some small way, but Matthew, it had such cataclysmic results. It changed our lives."

"I think it changed our lives for the better," Matthew said.

"You do? Better? Really? I had thought that for awhile but with all the disruption and chaos that little thing has caused, I'm not so sure." Peaches looked at Matthew quizzically. "Tell me how our lives are better? I admit it wasn't the greatest house in the world but only a twisted mind would think that burning it down would be a better alternative so we could travel around in a motor home visiting our crazy relatives and having brushes with the law."

Matthew was dumbfounded. As he stared at the road he spoke in a strong even voice. "Peaches," he said without looking at her, "I'm not talking about the fire, I'm not even talking about your hair, I'm going to marry Dawn."

. . .

As he piloted the Bounder southwest toward Pittsburgh, Matthew reflected on how grueling the last few days had been. It was a comfort that they were on their way home. Now he would be one step closer to seeing Dawn and Mimi again. His planned proposal to Dawn was now out in the open, and he was surprised that his sister hadn't reacted to the news. Of course, Dawn might not accept but he'd taken that first big step, telling Peaches.

As he slowed the Bounder down, Matthew glanced sideways at his sister who seemed to be studying something across the highway. Maybe she hadn't heard him. He was about to tell her again of his intension to marry Mimi's mother, when she turned in her seat and glared at him with moist eyes.

"Oh come on, Matthew. We've been through this before." She sounded angry and desperate all at the same time. But needing to set things straight she continued, "How could you betray me like this?" Matthew's back stiffened. "I like it with just the two of us. Don't you? I've had lots of fun. Now you want to screw everything up. We just bought this thing for god's sake. And if we follow your plan, Dawn ends up with everything and I end up with nothing." She paused to dab angrily at her eyes.

Matthew would have put his hands over his ears, but since he was driving he just gripped the wheel tighter.

Peaches continued, "Pop's life insurance money is half mine and your half isn't going to last forever. If you two get married, I guarantee Dawn's father will disown her because you're related to me. She'll have to give up her apartment." She threw her arms in the air. "You don't even have a job and that means everyone will have to live here." With a touch of malice in her voice she added, "And if you think I'm giving up my bedroom, you're outda your mind." She folded her arms and nodded as she delivered the last word. "No Matthew, marriage at this time is not an option. I know you think you know what you want, but I know what's best. I'd rather you get a dog than ruin your life settling for someone like Dawn. And I don't like dogs all that much so that suggestion is coming from a desperate person."

Matthew tried to keep his attention on the road. "Peaches, forget the dog. This is serious."

"I am serious." His sister went on with a thrust of indignation. "Less than a week ago you made a commitment to me. We bought this thing agreeing we'd ride around in it for a while. Now you change your mind? Exactly what am I supposed to do?" She glanced at her brother and sensed that his resolve was weakening, so she pressed on. "Think about it. A dog isn't a bad idea." She clasped her hands. "A nice dog, not too big. It would fit perfectly in here. Of course, it could never set foot in my bedroom, but it would be a comfort to you, maybe a baby step. A loving, trusting, furry thing giving you support before we part as brother and sister. Eventually, and only when we're really ready mind you, we'll individually set our compasses and launch to follow whatever destiny this world has in store." Aghast, Matthew stared at his sister.

Undaunted, she took a deep breath. "Now this is my personal plan. After a few more dates, Dominick and I will fall in love and move in together. Then, maybe you can consider a big change for yourself. But not now." She thrust her hands out in emphasis. "It's important that we focus on getting one of us settled first. Yes Matthew, now is the perfect time for a dog."

Matthew shook his head but Peaches continued, "Trust me, a dog will be enough. Visiting Dawn and Mimi is a whole lot different than having them in our faces all the time. And another thing, a dog is always glad to see you when you come home. You can't say as much for people."

"Peaches, I don't want a dog."

"Rocky had a dog didn't he? Wasn't his name Bubba or Poochy? You could be like Rocky."

"Butkus. His name was Butkus."

"I like that name. I wouldn't mind if you wanted to name our dog, did you say Bubkiss? I'm willing to sacrifice for the sake of you and your next step."

"I don't want a dog."

"They have one at Best Deals. You remember that brown watchdog they never took care of? He needs a home."

"He has a home," Matthew said flatly, "at Best Deals."

"We might be able to buy him."

"Those guys don't let anything go for a fair price. I bet we can't."

"He may have to run away."

"Peaches. What's the matter with you? There's not enough room for us in here let alone some mutt."

"Exactly." Peaches drove home her point. "There's no room for your little family in here and by the way a used car lot is no place for a dog. The trouble is, I don't think we can just march in there and take the dog. As you know they don't like me much back there."

"Why not?" Matthew was curious. 'I thought you left working there because of the two mile commute. Now you're saying Dawn's father might disown her because of you and that they don't like you at the used car place. Did something else happen?"

"No, not really." Peaches waved her hand dismissively as her swivel chair squeaked back and forth. He sighed with exasperation as she suddenly cut their conversation short and, complaining of a headache, left to lie down in the bedroom. No one could be more maddening than his sister.

Matthew sat behind the wheel and reflected on things. He was calm now and struck with the clear realization that everything he did or wanted to do revolved around his sister. Whether it was the fire or his relationship to Dawn, or even what they would do that day, it was always her decision. And yes, she always said that she stepped in because no one else did, but had she ever given him the chance? There was that sort of promise he'd made to his father, that he would take care of her, but how much was enough?

Matthew stopped for a traffic light in the outskirts of Pittsburgh and considered his options. Dominick might marry Peaches. After all, he seemed to like her a lot. But, Matthew thought, that was probably because he didn't really know her.

It was only another few blocks to the garden apartment where Dawn and Mimi lived. The complex was fairly new and somewhat costly. Matthew was pretty sure Dawn's father was helping out with the rent. He thought about how nice it was to be back in town. For once, he felt like he knew where he was going. He smiled as he imagined Mimi running out to greet him. Now it was only two more blocks. They stopped at another light. One more block and they would all be together.

He parked the Bounder right across the street from the apartment complex and tooted the horn. Dawn's front windows overlooked his parking spot. He would watch carefully so Mimi wouldn't run into the road. But Mimi didn't come. He tooted again but still no one came. It's true they hadn't been expecting him and maybe they were at the store or coming home from Mimi's school. No, Matthew rejected that idea, it was too late in the day for that.

Where were they? Maybe Mimi was sick or maybe Dawn had

gotten tired of waiting for him to make up his mind and moved them away or back to her parent's house. His head was full of crazy ideas. But just then, the front door opened and Mimi ran out. She waved and called to him. And somehow, Matthew knew everything would be all right in the end because Dawn was right behind her.

. . .

The night was quiet and a little chilly when Matthew left Dawn's apartment alone. Peaches had stayed in the Bounder across the street. When he asked if she was coming, it was quickly pointed out that she had no intention of spending the evening with her most hated enemy and more importantly, it shocked her that Matthew would even think that she, his sister, had time to dilly dally. There were only two days left until her date with Dominick.

Matthew had had a nice time. After a dinner of leftover Chinese he and Dawn played Candyland with Mimi. But even after their daughter's 7:30 bedtime when he was alone with Dawn, he hadn't felt ready to pop the marriage question, especially since his sister was still a little resistant to the idea. He hated that Peaches might be right when she had said that marriage was a big step and that he didn't do big steps well. Besides, just in case Dawn accepted, he would want to be ready, although he wasn't clear what that actually meant.

Matthew felt shy with girls, but not so much with Dawn. He was grateful when she didn't notice how he stumbled over words or got jumbled in his thoughts. He would feel his face grow hot and clammy but Dawn ignored his change of color or she gently teased him when he blushed, which made him laugh.

As they cuddled on the couch, his arm around her slim shoulders, he told her about Blossom's need to meet the President and her desperate desire to find the famous mall, and not necessarily in that order. Dawn had nodded with understanding as he described his relief when she had finally, happily joined the tour group. It had only been a few days before but now it seemed like weeks ago. He didn't care what Peaches' problem was with Dawn, she made him feel special...maybe even loved.

He walked across Fenton Street and noticed that the light was on in the Bounder's back bedroom. Peaches must be going to bed. He felt good and was relieved that he wouldn't have to deal with his sister until morning. But before he could go to bed, he would have to deal with the familiar problem of parking. He felt confident and knew he could solve this one himself. There was no overnight RV parking on Pittsburgh streets and the Walmart on Freeport Road was resurfacing their parking lot. Maybe, he thought they could use the Mattress Factory Museum lot. After all, what better place to spend the night, even if the museum had nothing to do with mattresses. If questioned, they could always say they were eager art enthusiasts wanting to be first in line for the next day's opening. The museum was nearby and it would already be closed for the evening so there would be no guard at the entrance. Matthew was pleased with himself for coming up with the idea.

It was an easy drive to the museum lot. There was little traffic as the moon rose in the eastern sky and created a gentle glow. He tucked the motor home into a back corner and turned the headlights off. A police cruiser pulled in just after they did. It was easy to spot with its emergency lights flashing. Not up for conflict, Matthew started the engine and drove right out. Plan B was the bus garage where he used to work.

"Would you make up your mind?" Peaches yelled from the bedroom. "Should I come out and help?"

Matthew ignored her. It wasn't that far, only a mile or two, although on city streets that could take some time. Unfortunately, when they got there the gates were locked.

Now what would he do? Plans A and B had fallen flat and C wasn't in sight. It was after eleven and he was too tired to just drive around. Out of ideas and frustrated Matthew reluctantly resorted to the only alternative he knew.

"Peaches."

His sister opened her door a little too quickly. She was always eager to help. With her hair up in rollers, her face was a white mask of aloe, oatmeal, and cold cream, but Matthew barely gave her a glance. This was her third facial in as many days and from what he could see they only made her face red. Lately, when she wasn't telling him how to live his life she was trying some new beauty treatment or jabbering about her diet, which was also not working. In his opinion she hadn't lost an ounce. Instead, judging from what she ate, she was on a fast food extravaganza.

Always quick with a solution, Peaches had to repeat her suggestion twice because her facial mask was almost dry, which made it difficult to talk. "Good Deals. Let's try Good Deals." Matthew felt relieved, comforted by her suggestion. He thought, it was logical and it would probably work because Peaches used to work there. His sister was still the most annoying person he knew, but she did come up with good ideas once in a while.

They could see the bright blue Good Deals Used Cars sign as they turned onto Piedmont Avenue. Things were looking good. There was no gate. The lot was deserted and that watchdog Peaches mentioned wasn't doing any watching. As they drove past the office Matthew checked the windows just in case someone was working late, but everything was dark. The Bounder fit nicely in the back where it was partially hidden. He quickly shut off the motor and held his breath for a few moments. Then he relaxed. This place was perfect.

Even though it was late, he thought he would go out for a short walk. He was curious about the dog that lived there. He knew he didn't want it and it still irritated him that Peaches thought a dog could fill in for his whole family but he liked dogs and thought he would like to meet it. But as he walked around the lot he was disappointed. He couldn't find it.

Still determined but not knowing its name Matthew whistled a couple times. From somewhere very near, there was a low growl. Matthew froze. Suddenly in the dim light of the moon a large dog leaped from behind a car grabbing his pant leg.

. . .

Still dark, the early morning was quiet and peaceful when Peaches appeared at her bedroom door shattering the silence and waking her brother up.

"We have a problem." She energetically scratched her side. "The dog is in my room."

"Why are you waking me up?" Matthew rolled over with a groan.

"Can't you just chase him out?"

"He's on my bed." She scratched her other side. "And he's your responsibility so you've gotta get him outda there. Did you check him for fleas?"

Peaches continued to stand in the doorway glowering. Matthew realized that he had no choice but to get up so he threw his quilt aside.

"You can't blame everything on me, the dog thing was your idea." He sat on the edge of his bed and planted both feet firmly on the rug. "After you got him off my pant leg, he was pretty nice. Didn't you hear him crying outside after we went to bed? I took him out some of that sliced roast beef, but he kept whimpering. I think he's ours now. He's not a pet if he lives outside." The dog wagged his matted tail and padded down to Matthew like an old friend. He had the brown curly coat of a poodle, or maybe even an Irish water spaniel, paired with the sturdiness and stature of a pit bull, while his floppy ears and longish snout playfully suggested a beagle. Matthew greeted him warmly. "We have to give him a good name."

"He can be Bumpkin if you want but I think Revenge would be a better name. Those fleas must be all over the house by now." She furiously scratched at her arm.

Matthew abruptly snatched his hand from the dog's back, "It's Butkus! Rocky's dog was Butkus. Revenge is no name for a dog." He looked suspiciously at the dirty brown curls. "Was I supposed to check him for fleas?"

"Yes, you always check dogs for fleas. Anyone knows that but we'll be okay," his sister said with a wave of her hand. "We'll fumigate. People do it all the time. But," she emphasized, "we have to do it right away. May I remind you that I'm deep into a new relationship that would not be strengthened by the presence of bloodsucking fleas."

"I guess you're right," Matthew agreed. Then he murmured under his breath, "There's a lot for Dominick to get through here already."

The dog moved around the kitchen and sniffed intently. Matthew suddenly recognized this behavior as what their neighbor's dogs did back on Mulberry Street just before they'd lifted their leg to pee.

"Whoa there boy. Looks like you need a walk." Matthew heaved himself up.

"Nobody had to walk him before. Can't you just put him outside?"

"We need to start off on the right foot."

Shaking her head, Peaches vanished into the bathroom as Matthew reached for his clothes. She should have realized that now that her brother seemed to be convinced he needed a dog, he would take it very seriously.

Matthew used his belt as a leash and took Butkus outside into the chilly morning. The sun was just peeking over the horizon and illuminated some fluffy clouds in the west. He took frequent deep breaths and found this first walk exhilarating. He felt that he was already in better shape. When a small gray car pulled into the lot Matthew was unconcerned. The dealership would be closed for at least another hour and a half. That car was probably just turning around. But he was wrong.

The car parked not far from the motor home and a short dark-haired man got out holding a long brush. As the recently hired duster, his job was to brush the used car stock clean every morning, but Matthew didn't know this.

Matthew retreated behind the RV and peeked around the corner. To his horror, the duster walked slowly his way. Fear and guilt grabbed him. Matthew couldn't take another confrontation, especially here. He was trespassing for sure, but he was also stealing, since he was still holding onto the used car lot's dog, which he immediately released. He struggled to put his belt on while the dog trotted out to greet the man.

Matthew panicked. He needed to get inside, but the door to the RV was in full view of the intruder. He imagined the worst. The police would careen into the lot with their lights blazing and sirens screaming. Dawn's father would find out and then, the ultimate humiliation, he'd tell Dawn and then she would tell Mimi. Matthew would look like a criminal in front of the people he cared about the most. And, in the end, Peaches would hammer home some sort of lesson even though it had been her idea all along. In a low whispery voice, he called up to the window for help.

Peaches grasped the problem immediately and went into action.

As she assumed her normal air of confidence and control, she quickly went out the door to confront the man with the brush.

"What are you doing sneaking around my motor home?"

"Sneakin'? Lady I'm just the duster. What are you doin' here? The place ain't opened yet."

"A duster? When did they hire a duster? I used to work here ya know and they never had one of those when I was here." She felt she might be saying too much but she pressed on. "I'm here because I'm thinking of buying a car and maybe towing it behind my RV." She caught sight of Matthew who waited for his chance to sprint for the door. To give him that opportunity she strolled out towards the parking area as if to take a look at the cars on the other side of the lot. She kept talking and the duster followed. Matthew saw his chance and rushed inside. He didn't wait for the automatic step at all, but lept his 332 pound bulk up past the first and barely made it to the second step just as the duster turned to look.

"Who's that?"

"That's my brother," she said brightly and then continued in a confidential tone. "Honestly he's the real reason I'm here. He has fear-o-phobia. It's a rare disease that's probably incurable." Now she knew she was saying too much, but realized she had to make her story believable. "I just can't take him out any ol' time. He starts out very quiet, but then gets violent around people. Why, he can go berserk just trying to get away from them. Didn't you see him leap for the motor home? He would have rather cracked his shin than come over here. It's this," Peaches indicated the Bounder, "or the institution." She scratched her head as she continued, "The doctor suggested it. Seeing people from the safety of the RV keeps him under control."

"Can you catch somethin' like that?" The duster moved a couple steps back. "I got a family."

"I'm perfectly normal and I like people, so it's probably not contagious."

"What happens when he gets violent?"

"It's ugly. Frankly, if I were you I'd go for breakfast or at least a coffee. Maybe even take the day off. I'd mainly get out of the area. As a former employee I can vouch for you with the boss."

"Yeah, maybe I should do that." The duster warily kept his eye on the motor home as he backed up toward his car, got in and sprayed gravel as he drove away.

Overjoyed, Matthew came out as soon as the man had gone. "Boy was he scared. What'd ja tell him?"

"That you're crazy."

"Great. Nobody wants to deal with a crazy man." Matthew, scratched his leg and suddenly realized what he was saying. "You told him I was crazy? You don't think he'll tell anyone, do you?"

"No probably not. Now let's get outda here before he comes back. Maybe we should leave the dog."

"Leave Butkus? We can't!"

"Matthew it's like stealing."

"But you said it would be okay. You told me how they don't take care of him." His voice rose with emotion. "You said he's got fleas. He's thin and he needs a bath. Winter's coming. Peaches, it isn't fair. Everyone deserves a chance, even Butkus."

Peaches, Matthew and Butkus left the used car lot in the RV. The sun was up, the flea count was up and everyone's spirits seemed to be up too. Just down the street and around the corner, they found the Pretty Pooch Pet Parlor, with convenient parking right in front. They waited for the 9:00 opening with a small breakfast of eggs, bacon and toast for everyone, including the dog.

When a pleasant looking woman unlocked the parlor door, Matthew and Butkus followed her into the cramped grooming shop. Butkus fidgeted and whined, making it hard for Matthew to hold onto the dog's collar. A look of dismay washed over the woman's face when she saw the dirty, powerful looking dog but reluctantly agreed to give him a bath. Matthew thought better than to mention the fleas. But, practiced in her profession, she saw them right away and cautioned him about taking the dog back into the same environment where he would be re-infected.

"You'll need a bomb," explained the woman. "How big is your home?"

Matthew pointed to the motor home outside.

"Shouldn't be a problem. Be sure you read the directions." After leaving Butkus at the parlor he returned to the RV with two aerosol cans of flea exterminator.

"Okay Matts I see what we need to do." Peaches studied the directions printed on the can." First we bomb, then we evacuate. The fumes kill everything, right down to the eggs."

"What eggs?" Matthew was horrified. "I didn't know they were going to lay eggs."

"Apparently, right away," explained Peaches. "This says if you don't get the eggs the fleas will be back in a few days. So after we set off the bombs, we'll have to get out immediately because the fumes are lethal, even to people."

"We'll go get another breakfast," Matthew said cheerfully.

The bombs were carefully placed, one in the bedroom with Matthew, and one upfront in the kitchen area with Peaches. Simultaneously, they set them off.

"One, two, three." While the cans sprayed their poison into the air, Peaches and Matthew each held their breath and raced for the door. When they were safely outside Peaches happened to catch a glimpse of the parking restrictions. No Parking Tuesdays and Thursdays. "What day is it?"

"Tuesday, why?"

. . .

"Good thing I noticed that sign. We could have been towed."

Peaches stood at the curb, hands on her hips while Matthew shut the Bounder door for the second and hopefully last time. Coughing, while nodding in agreement, he wiped his tearing eyes. He had moved the fumigated Bounder from one side of the street to the other, holding his breath for as long as possible while using Peaches' jacket, wrapped around his head, as an air filter.

For a while, they walked along First Street just to kill time. Eventually, they stopped at the Fairway Diner.

"Everything will be finished by two," Peaches said as she enthusiastically hauled opened the door. "We've got so much time we could have brunch and lunch here." Half way down the aisle they found an empty booth. "It's been quite a morning don't ya think?"

"Bombs really scare me." Matthew sat down hard.

"I don't know what you're afraid of," chided Peaches. "Bombing is so efficient. One pull of that trigger thingie and they're all wiped out. Believe me we're doing the right thing." Then more seriously she added, "Some may say we stole the dog."

"But we're saving his life by getting him outda there, aren't we?" Matthew spoke earnestly. "I hope Dawn's father doesn't mind what we did."

Peaches sighed with disapproval as she looked at Matthew over top of her menu. She narrowed her eyes.

"Why should I worry about what Dawn's father thinks? You shouldn't either. I was loyal to that dealership once, but then Dawn's father let me go at the first sign of trouble, never taking my needs into consideration."

Matthew opened his mouth to ask a question, but she kept on going. "What choice did we have?" Abruptly she hailed the waitress. "Let's order, I'm starved."

"What if something goes wrong?" Matthew asked after the waitress left them to place their order.

"I know everything about bombing. Nothing can go wrong." Peaches assured him. "Right now, while we're having lunch, we're obliterating hundreds."

Matthew cringed and said gravely, "What about the bodies?"

"Matthew, you worry too much. Getting rid of them is not a problem."

The man in the next booth got up and almost ran down the aisle and out the door. Matthew looked around to see if there was some emergency.

"Maybe he got hair in his food." Annoyed by his statement the waitress gave him a queer look as she set down two bowls of tomato soup.

After blowing on hers to cool it, Peaches peered into her bowl and moved the croutons around with her spoon. "Hmm. There's no hair in here."

They watched through the window as the man fidgeted at the edge of the curb. When a police car came by, he frantically waved his arms and flagged it down.

"Don't we know him?" Peaches watched out the window, her brow furrowed.

"Maybe."

"Of course. He's that duster. Look at how anxious he is. I'll bet you're right. He'd be the type to complain about hair."

After an animated conversation with the two officers in the police car, the duster waited outside while one of them came into the diner and walked down the aisle toward them. When he stopped in front of their table Peaches said "Hi," as she dabbed the corners of her mouth daintily with her napkin.

"I'd like you two to step outside. I have a few questions."

"Questions? Of course. Anything we can do to help." Peaches got up quickly and whispered excitedly to her brother, "I'll bet they'll want us to sign an affidavit or something. I've always wanted to do that."

Matthew had an inkling that this had nothing to do with affidavits, hair or even the diner, but he dutifully slid out of the booth to follow his sister and the policeman. After all, they had trespassed at the used car lot and had stolen the dog. He knew for certain he'd be handcuffed and arrested. He felt sick to his stomach.

As she walked away from her soup and cheeseburger, Peaches' excitement for signing that affidavit cooled. She also wondered why they were so special. Why wasn't this policeman interested in anyone else in the diner? Just like Matthew, she had a hunch that the duster probably wasn't worried about hair at all.

As they walked out into the sunlight she gave the nervous duster a piercing look as they joined him on the sidewalk.

"I gave him a perfectly believable reason why we were at the dealership this morning." She announced as she nervously twisted the ring on her finger. Then she wondered if maybe he had spoken to Dawn's father. This guy might know about the missing money. She scowled as she thought bitterly, first they fire me and now they're going to have me hauled off to jail. She bit her lip. They should arrest Clute. He spent all our money on that house. What was I supposed to do, not eat?

With notepad in hand, the policeman addressed the duster. "Tell us what you heard."

But before he could speak Peaches jumped in, "Hold on. I can explain about that money," she glared at the duster. "It was a loan. They know me there. Dawn was my best friend in twelfth grade." Peaches' voice rose in breathless desperation. "I've been to dinner at their house lots of times. You have to believe me. It wasn't really stealing." She was frantic. Her entire life could be ruined.

"Don't listen to her," the car duster blurted out, "They killed hundreds of people." He turned to Peaches. "I heard you. You can't talk your way out of this."

"Dead people?" Peaches was stopped in her tracks.

"Oh Peaches, you know…poof." Matthew opened his hands illustrating an explosion.

Suddenly Peaches knew she had said too much as the duster went on.

"You can't trust anything she says. She keeps her brother locked up. She says he has a disease. I think she has a disease. Ask 'em what they did with the dog."

"Everybody shut up." The frustrated officer yelled. "First tell me about the bombs."

"The bombs?" Peaches switched gears instantly, gaily announcing. "Flea bombs. That's all, flea bombs."

There was a huge commotion as back up cruisers arrived with lights and sirens. Officers jumped out, guns drawn instantly surrounding the little group. Peaches and Matthew put their hands in the air as Matthew yelled. "Peaches, tell them everything or we're going to die."

. . .

The police and the Packers coughed as they filed out of the motor home. Their eyes streamed with tears. The duster waited outside and fidgeted. And while Peaches saw the wisdom in not being believable, Matthew was able to convince the officers that he and his sister were not going to bomb anyone larger than a bug. This surprised Peaches, as Matthew went on to explain how his fiancé, the daughter of Best Deals Used Cars owner would be pleased that he had taken the initiative to rescue the neglected dog. After all, their daughter Mimi, loved animals. He would be seeing the family after picking up Butkus from the pet salon. They would all appreciate the rapid response and the professionalism of the quick-witted police.

Finding the dog story believable was easy. And as the backup police started to leave, Peaches and Matthew began to relax.

Finishing up his notes, the original officer turned to Peaches,

"Why don't you tell me about that money you took."

"Did I say took?" Peaches laughed off handedly. "Not took, borrowed. I just borrowed a little money. Isn't that right Matthew?" She gave her brother a pleading look, "With all the excitement I got carried away." Then she explained to the policeman that she was a beloved, loyal ex-employee that always had the dealership's best interests at heart. They'd been there that very morning to say hello. "Unfortunately," Peaches went on, "it was too early to see anyone but that busybody duster."

Without evidence of a theft the officer had nothing to pursue. So he gave her a warning and suggested that Matthew call them if there were any further problems.

Finally, the last cruiser departed, leaving Peaches and Matthew standing on the sidewalk in front of the diner. Without saying any more the duster rapidly headed down the street, putting significant distance between him and the Packers.

With new confidence, Matthew mapped out plans for the afternoon. He was anxious to be on the road.

"First, we'll get the bugs cleaned up and then we'll go get Butkus." He went on to explain how they had to hurry because he wanted to pick up Dawn at her graphic design office when she finished for the day. It would be a surprise. After that, they would all go pick up Mimi from school. He added that he thought that both of them would be really excited about the dog.

As Matthew strolled across the street to the RV, he was thinking how well he'd handled the police. He was the one that had turned things around. If he put his mind to it, he might turn other things around too. For example, he knew that any day now he would drum up enough courage to pop the marriage question. Wasn't he already referring to Dawn as his fiancé? But then he backtracked, maybe an engagement would be enough for a long while because marriage was terrifying. The married people he knew, like his parents and his sister, both had theirs sour, leaving the marriages to deteriorate into a series of battlegrounds and infidelities. That wasn't for him. Dawn and Mimi deserved better.

As she followed her brother across Perkins Street to the RV, Peaches was not happy. "Hey super boy, what am I supposed to do this afternoon while all this stuff is going on between you and Dawn? Did you once consider what I would like to do?"

"There are lots of things you can do." Matthew stopped just before climbing the steps into the camper. "You could walk the dog. You could feed the dog. Maybe you could get something to eat yourself." Instead of waiting for her reply he took a deep breath and held it as he ran up the stairs and immediately started opening windows.

Peaches stayed outside and called through the door. "My feet hurt when I walk, you know that. And I'm on a diet, don't you remember?"

When the air inside cleared a bit, she went in, slouched in the passenger seat and wallowed in self-pity. Matthew busied himself getting rid of the flea bombs and pulling out the vacuum from the closet.

"You're right. There are lots of things I could do." She sighed deeply, "I could stay in here and play solitaire or sleep or even clean the refrigerator. There are lots of things I could do completely and utterly by myself." Then she remembered Dominick.

"What day is it today?"

. . .

"Why didn't you tell me tomorrow's Wednesday? Oh my god."

She moaned woefully as she pulled down the visor to get a good look at herself in the mirror. Her dry orange and green hair stuck out like hay and her lips were chapped. She had a particularly angry looking pimple on her chin while her glowing round cheeks filled the mirror with a childlike blush.

"Tomorrow is a do or die date and I'm not ready. You've taken so much of my time with your dog and getting your life on course I haven't had time to take care of mine." She snapped the mirror closed and gave her brother a desperate look. "I was going to lose weight. I was going to fix my hair."

Matthew nodded in agreement and continued to wipe the counter.

"You were gonna to do a lot of things." Matthew was careful to keep his voice calm.

"It's Blossom's fault, ya know. She's the one that killed my enthusiasm. If Dominick saw me like this he would never want to be involved," Peaches fretted. "What am I going to do?"

Matthew thought for a moment. "You don't have to meet him."

Peaches considered this. "You're right. I guess I don't. If I don't show up at the diner, I'll still have all the delightful memories of a love that might have been. We were compatible. I'll always remember the magic of our first kiss." Peaches sighed. "Blossom said it's downhill from there. I think I believe her. Relationships are all downhill. I could keep Dominick's number and call him when I'm ready," she said wistfully. "That is, if I'm ever ready. Instead, I'll probably find some job I hate and in my free time, I'll just live with my memories." She sighed.

"Maybe you need a pet." Matthew parroted what Peaches had suggested to him. "You could share Butkus."

"I was thinking of something that would suit me better, like maybe a bird. I like birds. There's a pet emporium over on Gifford Street. Remember, it's right next to the beauty parlor I use to go to."

"Peaches we're not very far from there why don't I leave you off and you can get your bird and maybe even get your hair fixed up. Dawn, Mimi and I will come back for you in a little while."

Peaches was stunned. "That's a great idea. I don't know why I didn't think of that myself. That makes me feel better already. Betty always did a great job. I'll be auburn again even if it was Aunt Blossom's suggestion. And it's right around the corner."

Eventually, after the RV was cleaned and aired out, they picked up the de-fleaed Butkus. The shopkeeper had added extra to the bill, given he was such a challenge, but Matthew paid the charges happily. They could just tell that the dog was feeling better although he still bucked and pulled against his collar as they walked to the motor home. Matthew turned the RV toward Gifford Street.

"Huh oh, it's one way," he announced and pulled over out of traffic. I'll go around the block."

"No, no. You can leave me off here. It's a short walk up. Just remember to pick me up in two hours. I'll watch for you. You may not recognize me."

Peaches was buoyant as she stepped out of the motor home and started up the street. She even turned to wave. Matthew waved back and drove on toward Greene where he would surprise Dawn.

As she trudged up the hill, Peaches figured that even if Betty was off, she would ask one of the other women to take care of her hair. Which day did Betty have off? Peaches couldn't remember. She hadn't used this salon for at least three years. She'd be back to her old self and maybe she would even feel good enough to meet Dominick, the heck with Aunt Blossom and her dire predictions.

Peaches pulled her blue jacket around her against the wind. She should have had Matthew take her right to the door. It was a cold walk and her feet hurt. She stopped to rest for a moment. The hill was steeper than she remembered. But of course, she had always driven over from the used car lot and parked right in front of the shop. How she would appreciate a decent head of hair although it had been fun to be green with orange highlights. Never again would she allow anyone but a professional to even touch her hair. She no longer considered Blossom a professional.

As she got closer, she was doubly sure she was doing the right thing. She reminded herself, when the hair thing was all over with she would reward herself with a pet. Peaches looked forward to starting a new life as a beautiful woman with a delicate little bird on her shoulder and a hunky guy at her side. She hoped the changes would please Dominick. He had seemed to like the orange, but then, what did he know?

As she yanked opened the door of the salon, she instantly knew that there was something terribly wrong. Right off she noticed there were no chairs. There was a large twinkling disco ball on the ceiling in the middle of a barely lit main room. She walked outside and checked the sign: Erotica. Dumbfounded, Peaches stood and held open the door, while glaring at the sign in disbelief.

"In or out Miss. Can I help you?" A man's deep voice called from somewhere inside the store.

"What?"

"The door. It's chilly and you're holding it open." A dark haired man smiled solicitously as he walked toward the front.

"You're not Betty Anne and where'd this porn shop come from?" Peaches blurted out. "I need to get my hair done."

"I can see that," the clerk agreed. "But this hasn't been a hair salon for at least a year and a half. Maybe you'd like to come in for a moment while you get your thoughts together." It had started to rain so Peaches cautiously went into the shop and closed the door behind her.

"But where's the beauty shop?"

"I don't know, really," he said, disinterested. "Can I call you a cab?"

"No." Peaches was horrified. "I don't want to be seen here. I'll run next door. I was going to get a bird anyway."

"There's no pet shop either. That's been gone for at least a year." The man came closer as if to comfort her. "Have you been away?"

Peaches took a step back. "No, not really. I used to work just a few blocks from here, bookkeeping. I hated the job. It was so tedious. All those numbers gave me a headache." She surreptitiously looked around.

"The boss was tough," she continued just to make conversation. "He could have been nicer, more sympathetic. I was his daughter's best friend in high school, but when I needed help, I was out on my ear."

"What kind of help did you need?"

"I borrowed a little money." Peaches twirled the ring on her finger. She felt a little foolish.

"Is that all? Who wouldn't let a friend borrow a little money? How little?"

"Only around $8,000." The man's eyes widened. He nodded a little less sympathetically as Peaches went on, "I have every intention of paying it all back, every penny. But it's hard without a job. And to make things worse Dawn sided with her father. Now I have no job, no beauty parlor, no bird, and no life."

"If I can be of any help my name is Oscar. I'll be back here behind the counter." The store clerk silently walked to the middle of the store and positioned himself behind a glass display case.

Not knowing what else to do, Peaches stood just to the left of the picture window and watched the rain. No one could see her there. Matthew certainly was taking his time, Peaches thought. She had an hour and forty-five minutes more to wait.

After a few minutes, Peaches was bored. She knew that any respectable young woman in this predicament would leave, rain or not. That respectable young woman would probably walk around the block a few times, get drenched, and come back just in time for her brother to pick her up. But Peaches wasn't going to do that.

Humming Sinatra's *The Lady is a Tramp* under her breath, she summoned the courage to look around. Innocently gazing at the ceiling Peaches casually walked towards the display to the right. She wondered what Frank would do in a situation like this.

It was a quiet afternoon at Erotica. Oscar settled into a chair behind the counter with what looked like *Time* magazine and ignored her. In Peaches opinion, he was a poor specimen of a clerk, leaving her to her own devices in what was obviously a store unfamiliar to her.

She casually perused the vibrators and was surprised to find that they came in different sizes. A few looked overwhelmingly painful. To cover her embarrassment she coughed, then inadvertently coughed several more times while she moved farther down the display to ladies underwear and lingerie. Aren't they pretty. Oh to be a bride again. She touched the softness of the satin and lace panties.

"Even if I'm not a bride yet, I think I could use some of these," Peaches mumbled under her breath. She examined them further and realized that the manufacturer had apparently left out the crotch. She decided that she might need two pair anyway. She particularly liked the pink and blue with contrasting trim and felt lucky to find two in her size. "I want da be sexy again," she murmured. But the bras that went with the briefs had too many holes for her to consider purchasing them. As she clutched the briefs she moved on.

When a burly man came in and slammed the door against the weather, Peaches froze, suddenly embarrassed. But the guy walked right past her and didn't even give her a glance. Did she look like a fixture in a place like this? At 260-pounds she wasn't invisible.

"Got any videos, Bud?" Oscar motioned him to the back of the store.

"What time is it now?" Peaches called to Oscar.

"Five." He indicated a woman's torso that doubled as a clock tacked on the wall. There was no head and no limbs. The belly button was the pivoting point for the clock hands that vaguely pointed in the direction of where numbers use to be and left the actual time a mystery.

After finding what he wanted, the man paid his money and left without acknowledging Peaches at all. She wondered if she was losing her edge.

Dawdling at the videos, Peaches could see why guys might like them. Curious about The Boxing Twins Get Down and Dirty, she blushed at Titillations featuring Madame Velvet and Sam the Man. There were others that captured Peaches' imagination but she couldn't figure out what all the hoopla was about or why they would be here at all. Little Red Riding Hood on a Sunday Afternoon, and Bear Claw, Indian Warrior seemed familiar, and Peaches thought she remembered watching them as a child. But she realized that she must be mistaken when she looked over the jacket cover.

After checking the clock on the wall for the tenth time, Peaches decided that it was either 4:50 or 10 minutes before six, or maybe even 10:30, but that couldn't be right. She wouldn't ask Oscar again. He had turned on a small TV behind the counter and was watching baseball. Peaches could hear the broadcaster's voice getting excited about the action.

As she moved up the left side of the store to racks of clothing, she held out a particularly bright colored shift in the softest, silkiest fabric and said half aloud, "I always wondered where to get clothes like these." She looked over at Oscar and felt self- conscious when he glanced up at her. She quickly looked away. She decided against the dress and casually continued down the line. There were soft body suits, some with leopard spots and some that were striped. Peaches had never thought of stripes as being particularly sexy, but the furry wraps and low cut dresses that she could easily envision herself in, made her think differently. Peaches kept looking back at that bright dress. It really wasn't expensive. In fact, she probably had enough to pay for it using her hair money. Who knows, she might eventually need a dress like that. The pet store was gone and she wasn't going to get her hair done, so it was only right that she come home with something special.

Peaches checked the clock again. Was it 6:00? Matthew would be here any time. This was her moment of decision. Clutching her new panties, she grabbed the dress off the hanger and hurried to check out. It might be best to meet Matthew at the corner just to avoid any misunderstanding, but with this rain he probably wouldn't even notice the name or even what kind of a store it was. She tried to act indifferent to the lineup of penises displayed in the glass case. Dodos, she thought knowingly.

She wasn't quite done at the counter when the motor home stopped in front of the store. Peaches could see it through the plate glass window so she tried to hurry Oscar along. Finally he was done and her purchases were stashed in a discreet, unmarked paper bag. She grabbed it and rushed to the door just as Matthew was walking in.

. . .

Matthew felt funny going into Erotica but he needed to pick up his sister. When they had pulled up in the motor home it looked like she was at the counter buying something. He noted that her plans had not worked out because her hair was still orange and green and it didn't look like she'd bought a bird. As he walked inside, she greeted him, and although he had lots of questions he chose not to ask them right then.

They made their way back to the motor home together as rain came down hard. Mimi and Butkus met them at the door. The little girl's face glowed with excitement and anticipation.

Mimi clapped her hands. "Is your bird in that bag?" Her aunt lumbered up the steps and sadly shook her head.

"No bird, only some underpants and a dress."

Dawn sat at the dinette and hummed a non-descript tune. She looked unusually happy and content. She off-handedly waved in Peaches' direction, but made no comment.

Drenched, disappointed and a little panicky Peaches felt weighed down with the life decisions she would have to make in the next few hours. This was Tuesday, tomorrow was D day, Dominick Day. Should she try to do something with her hair? Should she wing it and see Dominick anyway? He didn't seem to mind it the first time.

Derailed, she headed for her bedroom with flat hair and a dripping muumuu, its wet skirt clinging to her legs. Her sneakers squished a trail of rainwater all the way down the hall. She quietly closed the door and sat on the edge of the bed contemplating her next move. She had had such high expectations. How could she meet the love of her life with orange hair and a crummy attitude?

"I just can't keep up," Peaches murmured as she held her head in her hands. Things couldn't get much worse.

She abruptly sat up and said out loud. "But there's so much at stake. I have to get a grip. I have to make some plans." She sighed and slumped back. "But right now, I'm exhausted."

"We're going to eat." Dawn called through the door. "You wanna come?" Peaches was a little surprised at the invitation and didn't know what to say. She was hungry. Then it occurred to her that Dawn was asking because she pitied her. Peaches was about to yell no, when Mimi chimed in with an invitation of her own.

"Come on Aunt Peaches. We'll have fun. You could wear your new underpants."

How could Peaches say no? She wondered where they would go. McDonald's, the family favorite, would be busy, but Dawn suggested Luigi's. Not only did Peaches love Luigi's, she hadn't been there in months. Comfort food would sooth her frayed nerves.

Matthew drove them across town heading toward the restaurant.

Peaches found it tricky as she changed out of her wet clothes in the small bedroom. There was a gentle knock on the door, as she brushed through her hair. Without being asked, Dawn came in.

"What?"

"Look," Dawn started to talk right away, "I'm not trying to be your friend. You're still a thief. But I could, ya know, fix your hair before tomorrow night. You know I know how to do that." And as she left she said, "That's all. Just think about it." Peaches sat for a moment stunned, and immediately jumped to the conclusion that Dawn did pity her. Even so, an unfamiliarly warm feeling swept over her. Maybe Dawn was being nice or maybe, Peaches thought, she just wanted to make her hair fall out. There was another thing. If she used Dawn she would be breaking her professional hairdresser rule because Dawn was no hair colorist. She was some kind of a designer. But it would be nice to have it done. She wouldn't commit. She would think it over.

Matthew was sweating. He'd seen Dawn talk to his sister and this always made him nervous. Things could very rapidly get out of control.

"It's right down this street," he called, as he drove the Bounder toward the back of the restaurant where he quickly found parking.

"Boy, am I hungry," Peaches was first in line at the top of the steps.

Once outside she walked with a distinct tilt, head forward, body forward, and a surprising amount of enthusiasm, toward the restaurant door.

It was crowded, but the hostess found them a booth in a back corner right near the kitchen. Peaches liked this location because it was sort of private, but it had a good view of the place.

Peaches felt a little less anxious now that they were at a comfortable restaurant. She even had warmer feelings toward Dawn and watched as she settled into the seat opposite her. Off-handedly, Peaches confessed, "I've always wanted to start a restaurant." Mimi sat down beside her. "There's always such comfort in them. I could even have a restaurant on wheels since I like to drive."

"Do you mean like a Meals on Wheels sort of thing?" Dawn questioned, "How would you make money?"

Peaches gave Dawn a surprised look. "I don't mean Meals on Wheels, I mean the kind that prepares meals and--"

"Do you cook?" Dawn asked in disbelief.

"Like the roadside stands?" broke in Matthew. He tried to keep things from heating up. "You mean the kind that sells hotdogs and soda pop and potato chips?"

Peaches gave Matthew a bewildered look. "No, of course not. This would be more refined with healthy food like..." she tried to think, "organic. I could drive around like an ice cream truck or maybe I'd have definite locations where people would know where to find me."

"You're going to be an ice cream man?" Mimi looked at her aunt with new respect.

"You mean like a deli guy with a truck where the sides open?" Matthew clarified.

"Do you have a name in mind for this business venture?" Dawn was amused.

"Well kind of like a deli truck," conceded Peaches, ignoring Dawn's question. "But not exactly. I was really just trying to make conversation." She was sorry she'd brought it up and wasn't feeling as friendly toward Dawn as before. "What I mean is that I would like to try something totally new and courageous. Something so different that even I would be surprised."

After that no one said anything. Peaches was grateful. Maybe she could just sit here and eat her dinner without interacting with these people who had no understanding of who she was, or where she was going. Their orders were taken, after which the conversation continued to lag. Mimi made worms with straw papers.

It was nice being out of the Bounder. The restaurant was crowded and noisy and oddly enough, Peaches took pleasure in not recognizing anyone.

There was something quite delicious in anonymity. She did notice that everyone did seem to be happy, probably because they all had someone to be happy with. There was a woman with pretty blond hair at a table just beyond the bar. The length is about like mine, mused Peaches as she patted her medium length hair. And orange isn't that far from blond. She remembered how she'd told Blossom she'd wanted to be a blond. Peaches watched the woman reach her hand across the table toward her partner. I'd even keep that date tomorrow.

The waitress set a plate of warm, soft bread on the table. The pat of butter Peaches spread on her piece oozed into the grain. She took her first big delicious bite and watched the blond get up and head for the washroom. She had a nice figure. Peaches took a smaller second bite. When Peaches glanced back at the woman's table, she noticed that the blond had been sitting with... Dominick?

. . .

Harboring a distinct belief that no reaction equaled invisibility, Peaches froze. She watched Dominick, former love of her life, happily eat cake. She gripped the edge of the table with both hands and feared she might spiral out of control as she frantically considered her options. Confronting him in her condition, orange hair and a little sloppy, was out of the question. She deliberately slowed her breathing like that magazine had suggested for tension-heavy situations. But the slow breathing made her feel like she might pass out so she stopped. She realized that honestly, *Glamour* couldn't have meant such an unbelievably disastrous situation. The blond came back. Dominick looked up at the woman and smiled. Peaches gawked as he got up to pull her chair out. Matthew and Dawn had turned in their seats to try to see what she was looking at.

Matthew missed the ghostly white look of desperation on Peaches' face and said gaily, "Hey, that's--"

But Peaches was already up, whispering her decision. "I'm getting out of here."

She slipped out of the booth. Hunched over she tiptoed for the closest exit sign, the kitchen, and headed for the double doors. She parted them with more thrust than she meant. There was a loud crash as dishes broke. She had apparently run into a waiter carrying a full tray of food. Peaches picked up speed and didn't stop to apologize or even wipe the warm gravy off her back. She kept on going through the stifling kitchen, feeling the heat of the ovens on her right she smelled what might have been her dinner. She careened around the surprised cooks and workers who could have stopped her if they'd had more warning, and started to feel like she might make it outside, but unfortunately the door she chose was the manager's office. Peaches crashed into him as he came out. The big man grabbed her firmly by the arm, yelling as if she was a thief.

After only a brief pause Peaches did what anyone in her situation would do, she dragged the manager right along with her toward what she prayed would be an outside door. He struggled some, but she had momentum.

A cool September breeze had replaced the rain. Peaches was breathing hard as they faced off in the scrubby weeds at the edge of the parking lot. Infuriated, the manager railed at the impropriety and downright dumb act of running through his kitchen. "I wish I could charge double for people like you." He assumed she was running out on the check. She tried to relay an improbable story of budding love and broken dreams. In the end, he told her never to come back as he stormed inside. Peaches slumped against the building aware that, once again, she'd been betrayed.

This episode completed her day. She had achieved nothing. Her life was over, ruined forever. And what about Dominick? He had been the center of her universe for a whole two weeks. And even though she wasn't ready for her date tomorrow she knew she would have been eventually. Dominick had said she was a real woman, so what was he having dinner with?

The motor home was locked when Peaches went to go inside so

she waited near the door in the shadows where no one could see her. The night was quiet except for the breeze that rustled the leaves and Butkus' whining from inside. She could smell the exhaust from the restaurant. Her stomach rolled with hunger. As she leaned gratefully against the Bounder, she closed her eyes. Here she was, back to square one, the beginning of the beginning, and the first step of nothing.

Peaches felt trapped by a series of events not under her control. In the first place, Peaches thought, there was Dawn again, messing everything up. She had wanted to go to Luigi's. Why couldn't we have eaten at McDonald's like sensible people? And where did that woman come from? If Dominick's trucking job hadn't interrupted our romance he would have had a real chance to know me. He'd be mine forever. Two weeks is a long time to be apart. We had such a good start.

She sniffed with indignity as she thought of the manager—people like me? What does that mean? Does he think that fat people can't be in love? Does he think I really want to be big? She stood up a little straighter. Fat sneaks up on you. Everybody knows that. Disheartened, she sighed, I'm destined for nothing-ness.

Peaches wiped a tear from her eye and said out loud to no one at all, "I could meet Dominick tomorrow but should I meet him tomorrow?" She sniffed again. She answered her own question, "No, it wouldn't prove a thing."

CHAPTER NINE

When they finally met her at the Bounder, Peaches noted that for once, Dawn and Matthew had the decency to keep their mouths shut. Mimi was already asleep on Matthew's shoulder and Butkus' persistent whining had turned into loud barking from inside the RV. Surprisingly they even brought Peaches' order of chicken Parmesan with special mushroom spaghetti packed in two Styrofoam containers. Peaches confessed that she felt too depressed to eat which prompted Dawn to suggest that they give her dinner to the dog. Peaches had a change of heart and she remembered that she was always sharper on a full stomach. She sat down at the dinette, suddenly famished, while questions about Dominick and the woman gnawed at her heart.

As Matthew drove the RV through quiet Pittsburgh streets toward Dawn's apartment, Peaches mentally plodded through several scenarios. She could have been his sister or cousin or maybe an aunt. Peaches couldn't remember what he'd said about his family. But would Dominick have helped his sister with her chair? Admitting to herself that it would never occur to Matthew to help her with her chair or anything else for that matter, she continued to think. Most likely, she reasoned, the woman was a married friend. And her husband, a close personal friend of Dominick's, was away on a business trip. With nothing in the house to eat, she went to Luigi's where she ran into Dominick and they decided to eat together. This was the most logical explanation, although doubt slipped in as she thought of the candle and wine on the table. She finished off the chicken and moved on to the mushroom spaghetti. Of course, Peaches thought darkly, as a few strands of spaghetti slid from her fork onto her lap, it could have been a blind date. And he went on that date because his friends said she was a 'looker'. He stayed on that date because she was cute and not a dumpy, orange haired blimp. Peaches sniffed and wiped a few tears with her napkin. He wasn't even thinking about me.

If the blond was a girlfriend instead of just a girl friend, she'd be justified in being a little jealous, right? Unless of course he'd told the girl-friend that the crazy woman who just rammed a waiter and caused widespread confusion was actually his sister, and that it would be too embarrassing to have the woman meet her just then.

Peaches was grateful that she wasn't a jealous, controlling person and remembered something she'd read in *Glamour*, if you love someone you have to be willing to let him go. But, thought Peaches, didn't you have to have a relationship firmly in your grasp to actually be able to let it go?

. . .

Fair View Gardens was large, 150 units sprawled over several hilly acres. Dawn and Matthew had joked that the only view there was, was the view of other garden apartments that looked just like Dawn's. Matthew found the complex confusing with its maze of roads and look-alike buildings, but with Dawn's help, he finally parked the RV in front of 73A. Dawn considered Peaches state of mind and suggested that they all stay the night in her apartment. Peaches forced a smile and tried to be polite, after all, the woman was being nice, but she firmly replied that her brother and Butkus could go, but she would stay home. But it didn't take too long before Matthew convinced her to give it a try. She could use Mimi's room and look forward to a good hot shower in a large secure bathroom.

A short while later, wrapped in her slippers and robe, and carrying her nightshirt, Peaches padded down the hall of Dawn's apartment. The TV was going in the living room, but she could hear Dawn and Matthew talking. Out of sight, she stood in the hallway and listened.

"He's a moron. I should punch him out," Matthew hissed.

"You're not going to punch him out," Dawn said quickly. "He may be a jerk but he doesn't owe her a thing. They've known each other 4 hours. What does she expect?" Through her tears Peaches winced at the truth of that statement. "Your sister's a thief and maybe even a pyromaniac, so maybe she got what she deserved." Peaches quietly made it to the bathroom. Not only was her heart crushed, she hated Dawn even more.

Her thoughts raced as she leaned against the wall, she was too exhausted to move. It had been magical, those four hours. I fit so neatly into his life. I was perfect in the truck once I was inside and we had things to talk about. The path was so clear. He was my answer. I would have married him. Now she had nothing but aching memories.

It was a good shower. The water was just hot enough and came down hard. It was what she needed although it didn't wash away her feelings of worthlessness. Everyone I know has someone, Peaches realized. Even Aunt Blossom has that tour group. They couldn't possibly like her, but they're on their way to a Florida adventure together. Even oafy Marlene had all those inmates. They might be great friends if she stopped complaining, Peaches sighed. Worst of all, my own brother has Dawn and Mimi. That leaves me with the dog.

She covered her head with a towel and realized that the dog was her only friend. She cleared the foggy bathroom mirror with her hand and studied her reflection. She had never felt so unloved.

She was glad she could go right to bed. The shower made her feel rubbery and less anxious. As she lay down on Mimi's blue Sonic the Hedgehog sheets, Peaches checked the bedside clock. An illuminated Snow White smiled back at her even though her delicate arms poked out from her sides at uncomfortable angles showing that it was almost 10:30. Peaches felt a connection with the beautiful but compromised Disney figure.

The events of that evening crowded her thoughts. So much had happened. She turned over and rearranged the pillow. She watched an elf, or maybe it was a mouse, ride the second hand for halfway around the clock, and she probably dozed, but now she was awake. Peaches was careful not to fall off the small bed as she turned over and checked the clock again, 11:53 exactly. She took her pulse and then fiddled with the ring on her finger as she stared up to the splash of stars pasted on the ceiling and realized she wasn't tired anymore. She had to make a plan, but anything she considered seemed wrong. It was almost tomorrow, and she wasn't ready for tomorrow. Flinging back the covers she reached for her clothes. She'd sneak out of here and leave everyone behind. With determination, she'd make a brand new life for herself, somewhere. But before she could do anything, there was a light knock on the door.

Peaches clutched her small pile of clothes as she sat in the dark at the edge of Mimi's bed. She had been expecting Matthew or even Mimi to come in to console her, certainly not Dawn. For a moment, Peaches thought she might be dreaming. Dawn came in and sat on the edge of the bed next to her. The door was slightly ajar, so the light from the hallway filled the room with a soft glow.

"I knew you'd be up." Dawn spoke quietly, "I'm not staying long." She took a deep breath as if this were hard for her. "I know we got some things we don't agree on. You know, things we gotta work out but I wanted you to know you got a rotten deal from that guy. It wasn't right. I wanted you to know that." She leaned down and picked up a stuffed toy and set it on her lap. There was a significant pause before she continued. "So what about the date? What's gonna happen tomorrow night?"

Peaches had no earthly idea what she was going to do tomorrow night or any other night after this, but she wasn't going to tell that to Dawn.

Instead she folded the clothes on her lap, as if that was what she did every night around this time and said nothing.

Sitting together like this was comforting. She thought back to when they'd been friends. Devoted, they'd gossiped together through high school. Mostly they griped about the popular girls that seemed to have everything and about the indifferent jocks they could only dream about. Neither of them dated except for Richie. Peaches was fat and opinionated even then, a difficult combination that overpowered a shy, naïve, almost invisible Dawn.

They had gravitated together first as a defense against loneliness and then as a habit, staying together in an unlikely friendship until they'd had a falling out at the end of high school. They had drifted apart for several years and reconnected during Matthew's affair with Dawn. Now there was the business of the missing money at the used car dealership. Peaches winced at the thought. Friends were in short supply in her life.

Dawn sat silently beside Peaches for a few more minutes before getting up to leave. As she headed for the soft light of the hall,

Peaches spoke in a quiet voice, swallowing hard with the effort. "Dawn, I've got this hair. Do you think you could... could you fix it tomorrow?"

"Your hair?" Dawn blurted out. The warm feeling of friendship had touched Dawn too, but she never expected Peaches to take her up on her offer. She shrugged her shoulders in the doorway, "Yeah, I guess. Yeah, I could do it in the morning." And then she left, closing the door quietly.

Sitting in the dark, surprised that she'd asked Dawn to do anything, let alone her hair, Peaches felt oddly relieved. She tried to think realistically about Dominick. He's just a guy but right now he's the only guy. And what if that blond was a friend or a relative or even somebody else's wife and I don't show up tomorrow night. I'd lose this big opportunity. She tossed her clothes on a nearby chair. Some opportunities happen only once so I'll show up for that date.

. . .

To Peaches' astonishment, Dawn had called in sick and sipped coffee, waiting for her in the kitchen. She was ready for Peaches with towels and bowls, a brush, a blow dryer and even a mirror. It was easy to fall back into being Dawn's friend. Peaches held the two boxes of L'Oreal hair color she'd gotten with Blossom.

"Auburn or blond?" Peaches held up the boxes. "I think auburn would be the more sophisticated choice," she said to Dawn. "But honestly, I'd rather be blond. I've got fair skin. What do you think?" It was a very important decision.

"Auburn, definitely auburn. It just goes with ya better." Dawn finished her coffee. "Think about that one he was with last night. Blonds do have fair skin but they're kind of dainty. You're not dainty. Come on, I gotta go back to work when we're done. I can only be sick for part of a day, so let's get going. Take that shirt off. You know how this stuff stains anything it touches."

Peaches looked around. "Oh, don't worry about Matts," Dawn reassured. "He and Butkus took Mimi to school. They'll probably wind up at the dog park on their way home. He mentioned that."

Peaches was ready and leaned over the sink as Dawn put on the protective plastic gloves. "You're not going to change your mind, are you?" Dawn asked as she opened the two bottles included in the auburn box. She slowly poured the contents of one bottle into another.

"Wait!" Peaches stood up straight. "We could do both, auburn on the bottom and blond highlights on top. Wouldn't that be classy?"

Dawn stopped mid-pour. "I don't know. If you really don't know what you want, maybe we should wait. I mean you've got time. The date tonight is out, right? You could take a few days." She waited for Peaches to reply, then continued. "But if you did, say, want to find a job, people might take you more seriously without the streaks."

"Maybe you're right. Peaches stood at the sink ready for the application. "I'm ready. Let's just get it done."

Dawn shook the bottle and continued. "You know I'm glad that happened last night. I think it will help you focus and be somewhat normal. Maybe you'll meet someone. You'll get a job, and then you'll be on your way."

"But Dawn I've already met someone and just because I caught him at a bad time doesn't mean we can't salvage our relationship. Dominick still expects to meet me. Who knows what we saw last night? It was probably one of those flukes."

"Didn't you learn anything? That was more than a fluke that was a gigantic whale. Peaches! First there was the fire, then that money you stole and now a two timing boyfriend." Peaches was still at the sink but now she felt less cooperative.

"The trouble with you, Dawn," she countered, "you see a problem and immediately jump to the wrong conclusion. My approach is more global, sophisticated. I'm willing to be flexible. And besides, that money was a loan."

"Loan my foot! Just like that fire was an accident." Dawn shoved Peaches head down in the sink and started roughly applying the dark color liquid. "People are going to get tired of waitin' around for you to take care of business. It's been half a year and how much have you paid back? If it was a loan why'd you get fired?"

Peaches stood up. "Give me that bottle!" She could feel the hair color liquid dribble down her back as she moved toward the door to leave. "This is just like old times,' she yelled. "I can do it myself. Get out of my way."

· · ·

If Peaches hadn't been so angry she wouldn't have forgotten that she was only wearing a bra on top of her sloppy orange slacks. After she growled good morning to two wide-eyed elderly women warming the bench outside Dawn's garden apartment, she remembered.

I'm not ruining the neighborhood, Peaches wanted to shout, Dawn's already ruined it. Her frustration felt out of control, but familiar. She unlocked the Bounder and was forced to wait for the bottom step to extend. Here she was with an important life changing date coming up, and Dawn in the middle of everything messing it up. Her limbs felt heavy as she trudged up the steps. What does Dawn know about dainty?

Once inside, she reached for an opened bag of potato chips and a diet Pepsi. She sat down gratefully at the dinette and popped in a Frank Sinatra tape.

Suddenly, through her exhaustion and frustration, Peaches remembered that her head was covered with processing liquid. Staring at the clock, she wasn't sure of the timing, the directions were still in Dawn's kitchen. She vaguely recollected from the last time she'd colored her hair that it could be 20 or maybe even 40 minutes. Peaches didn't want to mess up this time and decided that that new timer they'd gotten at Walmart would be helpful. She looked but it wasn't in any of the regular places, under the kitchen window or in that new junk drawer she had started for all the things she didn't know what to do with.

After finding it in the glove compartment, she had to come up with a processing time and decided on 30 minutes, even though she knew she should add in the extra time that had already elapsed. But she figured it would be okay because the coloring agent would need a little extra time to cover the orange.

She noticed a dark bubbling area on the back of the dinette bench where she had been sitting. It appeared to be eating away the plastic.

Peaches instinctively grabbed the small tub of dishwater from the sink. It looked okay, maybe a little greasy, but nonetheless it would dilute the goo that was eating away the back of the bench. As she heaved it, the cold dishwater went from the back of the seat, to the floor and all over her shoes.

Nothing, nothing is simple, she sighed. She remembered that vinegar was a useful cleaner and after rummaging in the cupboard and finding the red wine vinegar, she poured it over the damaged area. That can sit awhile, she thought, and when my hair is done, I'll scrub that seat with Comet. That'll take those bubbly parts away.

Peaches stood in the kitchen careful not to touch anything. It was hard to wait. She fiddled with her ring and checked her nails. It worried her that if the processor could bubble up a plastic seat, what might it be doing to her scalp? Peaches looked at the timer. So far, so good, only ten more minutes and I'll be back to normal.

She decided to go stand in the shower, and then when the timer rang she would be ready. It was a dinky shower and the hot water wouldn't be so hot. Maybe she could use Dawn's shower, Peaches thought. Dawn would have gone to work by now. Matthew will be back soon with the dog and he'll let me in. In fact, she thought brightly, he might be back already.

Draping a large towel around her shoulders, Peaches grabbed her shampoo bottle and a shirt she would put on after the processor was washed away and headed out the door. The timer rang as she hurried down the RV steps.

Her heart sank when she saw that those same ladies were still sitting in front of Dawn's building. Not wanting to spark a confrontation, Peaches ducked behind the boxwoods that lined the lawn. She hadn't formulated a plan but knew she couldn't go in through the front door. The timing for the processor was important and those women might slow her down.

Peaches snuck around. She avoided the front of the building and cut in toward the side, easily locating what she assumed must be Dawn's bedroom window. She remembered the lay out of the apartment clearly and could even hear Butkus' bark.

There were venetian blinds obstructing her inside view, but the window sash worked easily. Now all she had to do was hoist herself up and into the room. Luckily, there was a hose and reel attached to the outside of the building, just to the right of the window. She soothingly spoke to Butkus while using the hose reel as a step. When her head parted the blinds, she could see that in fact, the dog was not Butkus at all but a solid black pit bull that growled and treated her like an intruder.

As she slid back to the ground, Peaches was acutely aware that her processing time was becoming alarmingly overdue. Her hair might fall out. Or even worse, it might fall out in unsightly patches. Her skin might bubble up and fall off. She had to stop it now, no matter what. Peaches was already shivering as she reached for the garden hose.

CHAPTER TEN

Peaches and Dominick had agreed to meet at the same diner where they had had their first electrifying date exactly two weeks before. Next time, she would suggest a real restaurant, something like Luigi's, but not Luigi's since it was forever spoiled for her. Even though Dominick's fidelity was in question Peaches was going to be there at seven.

As she caught another glimpse of herself in the bathroom mirror, her new hair color kept surprising her. Not quite the auburn she'd been hoping for, it was very, very dark. But she was grateful that none of her hair had fallen out and that the skin where the processing liquid had sat was a little stained, but intact and it felt okay. Her face seemed luminescent in contrast to the new color. She wished she had lost some of that weight she had been going to lose so her face didn't look like a Pittsburgh version of a full moon, but all an all she was getting use to her new look.

She had several hours before it would be time to head for the diner, and she was going to be ready. Looking through her meager wardrobe, she decided on the silk dress from Erotica, but then changed her mind. The combination of the delicate flowing gown, the harsh diner lighting, and the movement of that lazy fish through the murky water of that big tank just wouldn't work.

Instead she chose the purple version of her favorite red dress. It had been featured as a two for one special, a fabulous find at Walmart. She held the long cotton dress up and admired herself in the narrow full-length mirror conveniently located on the back of the bedroom door.

. . .

Dawn had not left for work. Matthew arrived home just as the furious woman was on her way out the door. Right away, he knew he shouldn't have left the two women alone. Dawn immediately railed at his hardheaded sister's bad behavior. She emphasized how ungrateful and mercurial she still was.

"She won't listen to anything. Not about her hair or how much trouble she's going to be in when my father finds out she took money out of the dealership. They're sending someone to check the books. She keeps saying how she'll pay everything back, but she doesn't even have a job."

"Hmm, that insurance money from Pop probably won't cover it all." Matthew interjected. "It's half gone already."

"And she still thinks there's a chance for a relationship with that two timing Romeo. I'll bet she thinks he's going to bail her out, literally," Dawn hotly declared as she grabbed her jacket. "I'm never helping her again. She's your problem. I'm going to work."

As he reluctantly climbed the RV steps, Matthew braced himself for his sister's side of the story. He was grateful that Peaches was in the back bedroom. When he noticed the damaged dinette seat, he knew things hadn't gone well in here either.

"How do you like it?" Peaches poked her head out from around the bedroom door and shook it for the proper new hairdo effect.

It was a lot to take in. Matthew stifled a surprised gulp, which Peaches took as a sign of approval. The color was darkly different and it would take some getting used to. Matthew searched for just the right words, but Peaches went on with enthusiasm.

"Oh good, I like it too. It's a lot different than I thought it would be." She was glad to have someone to talk to. "I had to figure it out on my own." Then she went on, "I want you to know, Matts. I'm proud of myself. Dawn said I'm not delicate and she's right, but I think I'm versatile. Someone like Dominick can be more himself with someone versatile than with some fruffy blond, don't you agree?" She informed him that she needed a ride to the diner, alone.

"I can't afford to have anything more go wrong." His sister went on, "I guarantee Dawn would start talking about that money thing and who knows what else.

"Ya know Peaches, I don't think it's Dawn that's gonna give you a hard time about that money. Isn't that what auditors do? They're having one of those guys come look at their books. They'll see that there's money missing, ya know. Can't they cause some trouble? I mean, if they find money missing? They'd confirm what Dawn's father already suspects and wouldn't they indict someone for that? That's what happened to Marlene. She was stealing and she never even saw any money, she just drove the getaway car for Ned."

"What do you mean? Did Dawn tell you to say that?"

"I'm saying that you could be in a lot of trouble, that's all."

"Look Matthew, I'm doing the best I can. What with the house burning down and us taking a break from stuff, trying to find a life in this RV, I haven't had a chance to address that problem. I'm busy getting some permanence back in my life and it's not a good time to be indicted."

"When is it a good time?"

"Not right now. Once Dominick and I are a couple, then I'll address the loan pay back. I'm sure Dawn and her father and even an auditor can understand that." She continued, "Matthew, when Clute lost all our money we would have been out on the street." Peaches faced Matthew with tears in her eyes. "Is that where you wanted your sister to be? Dawn's father knows me for who I am. He knows I'll pay it all back. Every penny." Peaches sniffled and went on, "The dealership was doing great and the money I borrowed amounted to a minor clerical error, and now, just because nobody's buying used cars like they use to, I have to be responsible for bailing them out."

"Peaches, you sound like Marlene," Matthew chimed in. "Didn't she tell us how innocent she was? You stole that money and you have to pay it back now."

"I can't pay it back now. I have a date." And she retreated into the bedroom and slammed the door.

Peaches sat on the edge of her bed and took a few deep breaths trying to calm her nerves. She had only two hours before it would be time for Matthew to take her over to the diner. This relationship thing with Dominick had to work out. There was so much at stake.

Being with Clute had given her some experience dealing with infidelity. She had big plans for her relationship with Dominick, so everything had to be handled very carefully. Peaches assumed the worst. That woman Dominick had been eating with at Luigi's was no sister. And Peaches realized that it was also possible that she was being presumptuous about Dominick's devotion to her. They had known each other for all of two occasions, a few moments really, but there had been magic in those moments. She was sure they'd both felt it and she couldn't let that go.

. . .

It was getting dark and Matthew, not wanting to be blamed for making Peaches late for her date, reminded her of the time more than once.

"Not yet!" She yelled. She vividly remembered the difficulties from her last trip to meet Dominick. What a disaster it was trying to get her makeup on in a moving vehicle. So this time, she insisted on being completely ready before they started driving. Last time she had been very early because of Matthew's schedule and she ended up spending a lot of time hanging around the lobby. This evening, she wanted to be a little late. Assessing her makeup one more time in the tiny bathroom mirror, she was finally satisfied. It was already seven and Dominick would be waiting. Taking a deep breath to calm herself, she yelled to Matthew, "Let's go!"

Matthew put the RV in gear and set off for the diner, while Peaches fidgeted in the passenger seat and then got up several times. Once, she changed her shoes from sneakers to glittery sandals, which were not as comfortable, but much prettier. Another time, she decided to change her pocketbook. That green bag I use all the time is functional but too large to go on a date, she thought. I'll take that little gold one I got from Walmart. It's perfect. It even matches my sandals.

She dumped the stuff from her green pocketbook out onto the dinette tabletop. She would clearly have to leave some things behind. Peaches sorted through empty candy wrappers and picked out the bare minimum: her flip-flops, several Snickers bars, extra plastic bags, these were always handy to carry home leftover food or to throw over your head if it should rain. She couldn't leave behind her lucky fish tail can opener, rescued from the house fire, her make up bag, her bicycle pump and her wallet, which was in truth bigger than the little gold purse. She could move stuff from her wallet into the little gold purse, but then she would have to leave all this other stuff at home. Eventually she threw everything back into the green bag, including the purse.

As they pulled into the almost empty parking lot of the Starlight Diner, the restaurant was bathed in the glow of its large neon sign. Peaches looked around for Dominick's truck and was surprised when it wasn't there. They were only 20 minutes late.

"Did ya ever think Peaches that he might not show up?" Matthew backed the RV into a parking space. She didn't answer because in truth she hadn't considered this.

Instead she drew herself up and announced, "He's a man of integrity and of course he'll show up. He certainly owes me an explanation for last night and he knows it. I'm ready to tell him I can't possibly pursue a relationship with him until I know with absolute certainty that he's broken up with that woman and promises never to see her again."

Matthew took a deep breath and sighed, "I know ya want this to work Peach, but you're not going steady with him. He's just a guy you met at a truck stop a couple a weeks ago."

"But he's more than just a guy," Peaches' eyes were tearing up. "Didn't you see how he looked at me? Matthew, no matter how this looks now, I'm pretty sure he's the guy."

Together they waited another 15 minutes in the motor home. They silently stared out the front windshield and hoped Dominick and his JB Hunt truck would pull into the lot.

Eventually Matthew brought up leaving. "What da ya think? We can't stay here all night. We could check inside just to make sure he's not there." Peaches thought this was a good idea and she became nervous all over again.

"I'll just be a minute." She dug around in her pocketbook for her lipstick and hairbrush.

"It might rain," Matthew stood up to go with her. "Do you want the umbrella?" She shook her head and held up her hand as she started down the stairs.

"I have my plastic bags. I'll go alone." Out the windshield he watched his sister waddle toward the entrance in her long purple dress, the green bag slung over her shoulder.

The diner door was heavy and Peaches was surprised that the restaurant was much busier than she expected. When she told the greeter she was meeting someone he brightened and pointed out that indeed there had been a man waiting for quite some time. "You must be very special," he added as he led her down an aisle of booths. She smiled when she spotted the dark haired man in a leather jacket sitting alone, his back to her. She had forgotten how broad Dominick's shoulders were and how wavy his hair was. As she nervously approached the booth she giggled with excitement and was about to call his name softly. Instead she gasped, "You're not Dominick."

Close to tears, Peaches walked back toward the front. Something's happened to him, she decided. I just know it. Her mind raced as she imagined dreadful scenarios that might have kept him from showing up. But from a booth in a corner something caught her eye. With great relief she couldn't believe her eyes. Was that him? Sure enough he sat at a table and waved at her. He got up and met her halfway.

"I was afraid you had found someone else to have dinner with," he said as he kissed her cheek warmly and gave her a hug right in the middle of the aisle.

"And I thought you had had a terrible accident." She gushed with relief adding, "And to think you were in here all the time." He escorted her to their table, his hand rested at the small of her back. Reluctantly, Peaches remembered that the man with the blond had gotten up too. But she reminded herself as she sat down as daintily as possible, all men get up like that. They have to.

As Dominick sat down opposite Peaches, he explained how the trip to the Midwest had taken him longer than it should have. She listened intently as he elaborated on the mechanical difficulties of his differential.

The inquiry she'd prepared, so she could get to the bottom of the previous night's mystery, went out of her head as Dominick spoke of everything but. When he took her hand and leaned into their conversation, she also forgot about Matthew waiting for her in the parking lot.

It was only after they had ordered that Peaches noticed her brother wandering around the diner looking for her. She hunkered down hoping he would go back outside but Dominick noticed him too and called him over, inviting him to sit down.

"I'll just have a little something." There was an awkward silence while he settled in. He sensed Peaches' displeasure, but besides being hungry, he had to find out what she wanted to do about her ride home.

"So, um, how've you been?" Matthew was grateful at being included, but felt a bit flustered. "Have you been seeing anyone? I mean anything?" He kept trying, "When'd you get back?"

"I was telling Peaches that I was afraid I wouldn't make it at all. I had trouble with the truck in Ohio."

If he was having trouble in Ohio, thought Peaches, he couldn't possibly wine and dine some little blond in Pittsburgh. That information made Peaches beam and she was sorry that she ever doubted him. Now the conversation had moved on to motor home maintenance, which she knew nothing about so she changed the subject.

"Have you ever been to that restaurant, Luigi's over on--" Dominick didn't even let her finish.

"I love that place. I stopped there last night when I got back into town. Good food, the prices are reasonable. Love it."

Horrified, Peaches watched Dominick's face as he rattled on about the ziti he had had. The glimmer of hope, that he'd gone alone, faded when he started effusing about the mushroom spaghetti his friend had had.

"You were there with a friend?" She smiled sweetly. Of course Dominick had friends, Peaches realized. Probably lots of them.

"Yeah, one of my buddies." The waiter brought their order.

"No kidding, that was you," Matthew chimed in, "We were there last night." Peaches side kicked Matthew under the table.

"Oh, then you saw Judy." Dominick looked at Peaches. "If I'd known you were there, maybe you could have met her."

"Maybe I'll wait for you outside Peach. You know, in the motor home." Matthew slid off the bench. "I'll grab something in the kitchen."

The couple was left alone. Dominick wasn't trying to hide

anything Peaches consoled herself. Imagine, he would have introduced us. Being nervous and self-conscious, she made comments about her burger and the importance of having ketchup with fries. She did want to ask about the handholding, but there was an awkwardness between them now.

Finally she asked, "Does this Judy person know about me?" She dreaded the answer. Then she thought, maybe he'll lie or maybe he'll break my heart and tell me, why no, we were too busy having a great time to talk about you. But the question sat on the table, so Peaches waited. As she looked around she couldn't help but notice the paper placemats and paper napkins on the table. She was the girl Dominick took to the diner. Of course, he barely knew her and this place, with its plastic flowers and loud clientele, had been a fun destination. They both knew how to find it. But of course, Peaches realized, they both knew how to find Luigi's too. Would he bring Judy here? For the first time in any time she could remember, she just wasn't hungry.

Dominick studied Peaches' face and then seemed to make a decision. "Judy does not know about you," he looked at her intently. "She doesn't know about you because I haven't told her and I haven't told her because she has this idea that we're sort of going together."

Peaches would have preferred that he lie. She knew what to do with a liar. And even though she didn't know what to do with this information, it did explain the handholding and it did eclipse the hair-coloring problem.

Peaches leaned her elbows on the table. "Do you think you're going with her?" Dominick gave a rueful laugh.

"No, not really," he looked at her for a long moment.

"But Dominick," Peaches pointed out, "not really isn't no."

"I know this doesn't look good but you have to give me a little time. It's complicated. I need to be out of the relationship before I can be in again. I want you to wait because frankly, I've never met anyone like you. I didn't know two people could be so comfortable with each other."

Bewildered Peaches rested her head in her hands. It hadn't been like this with Clute, she recollected. He would cheat until she found out. Like the time she had dropped in on a quiet dinner he was having with a lady friend at Burger King. His affair discovered, he pleaded for her forgiveness and promised never to see the woman again. He probably didn't, she recalled. He just found someone new. Now Dominick was asking her to wait until he was free or until he decided whether or not he wanted to be free. Why did things work out for her like this? Why were there so many people in her relationships?

Peaches felt like an elephant in a dog park. What did he expect her to do? She sadly got up. Dominick, her Dominick, was taken.

Peaches shoved the heavy diner door opened and felt as cold and dismal as the rainy evening outside. She forgot about putting a plastic bag over her head. Matthew watched for her and met her halfway. He put his arm around his sister's shoulders and gave her a squeeze.

"I'm proud of you, Peach. Let's go home."

Rushing out of the diner, Dominick caught up with them.

"Where will you be? Can I call you if, you know, things change?" Her hopes for a happy, secure future were completely gone. She was on her own. The road ahead, her road, was bleak and endless, but she said with a rueful laugh, "Sure Dominick. Maybe sometime."

CHAPTER ELEVEN

As soon as Peaches was buckled in, Matthew floored the Bounder just like a getaway car. His sister was teary and blew her nose. Occasionally, she fiddled with the ring on her finger. He was about to say something pleasant and soothing but she would have no part of it.

"Don't even try," she growled.

As they drove toward Dawn and Mimi's apartment, it occurred to Matthew that just because his sister's life was a mess, his didn't need to be. And he wished that he had already asked Dawn to marry him. They were a little farther along in their relationship than Peaches and Dominick, after all they had known each other for quite some time and they did have a six-year-old daughter together. Matthew didn't ever want to go through what Peaches was going through. He wanted Dawn to know that he was ready but it scared him to imagine himself down on one knee asking for her hand. He might not be able to get up. There had to be another way. He wanted to share his concerns with his sister and get her input but he knew this was not the time. He glanced at her quickly as she moaned and fiddled and blew her nose. He knew that at best, she would roll her eyes and say something like, leave me alone. Don't you know this is the worst day of my life? Don't be so selfish, or something like that.

The next morning at breakfast, before Peaches was awake, Matthew suggested to Dawn that they pick Mimi up from school that afternoon, go to the park, and then go out for dinner. Dawn was enthusiastic and suggested Chinese. She also reinforced his idea that they not include his sister, and commented that Peaches would be more comfortable without them in the apartment and would probably prefer Butkus' company to anyone else's.

Later that afternoon the day was still warm as Dawn and Matthew sat on a park bench and held hands. They watched Mimi and her new friend hover around the swings. When Matthew was uncharacteristically quiet, Dawn assumed he was having second thoughts about leaving Peaches out. The real truth was that he was trying to figure out just how to pop the big question and he wondered how his hero Rockie would handle it.

With his hand in his pocket, he fingered the box that held the ring he had bought that morning. He couldn't just blurt out his proposal. He wanted to make it romantic and memorable, just like the movies.

When Dawn went to check on Mimi, who had wandered past the seesaw, it struck Matthew that there were so many serendipitous events converging that things were starting to fit together. Mimi's class was learning about China. And coincidentally, that night the whole family, minus Peaches, was going to a Chinese restaurant. This was no fluke. Dawn had suggested it herself. And didn't they always have fortune cookies at those restaurants? What could be a more perfect place to hide a ring?

He smiled in giddy anticipation. This was a knockout. People would talk about this proposal for years. It might even be written up in the newspaper. After Dawn and Mimi wandered back to where Matthew sat, they decided to go for dinner.

Inside the China Pearl the atmosphere was warm and comfortable. It was probably half-full, a good number considering it was only 5:45 in the afternoon. The colorful hanging fans delighted Mimi as they were shown to a quiet booth. The bus boy brought tea. They looked at the menu briefly before their waiter came to take their order. He took a long time writing each item down and then diligently read it back in broken English. He was a little hard to understand but it seemed right. Matthew knew he would need the waiter's help to implement his plan so he made a mental note to remember him by the red carnation in his lapel. Our waiter has a red carnation, he mentally repeated several times.

Matthew was nervous. He repositioned the napkin in his lap and checked his pants pocket to make sure the ring was still there. It was a good thing that Mimi carried the conversation and chattered that her test in spelling didn't go so well and about China and her best friend, Anne, and her second best friend, Jennifer, who ate crayons and was the fastest girl runner in her class and how she couldn't wait for dinner because she was starving almost to death.

The waiter came back with their first course surprisingly fast. But everyone's soup was wrong and had to be taken back. He returned quickly with Wonton for everyone. The man was trying hard Matthew could see that.

When their main courses came, that too was a problem. Instead of spareribs the waiter brought egg rolls and he brought Lo Mien instead of Chow Mien. Mimi's drink was wrong, and he forgot their rice. Eventually, even though all the problems were rectified, Matthew was having second thoughts. He couldn't possibly entrust this waiter with the diamond ring. He would have to do it himself and he had to be smart about it so he carefully mapped out a plan.

He wouldn't be able to put the ring in the cookie while they were all at the table. And Dawn would think he was crazy if he got up and casually walked to the kitchen for no good reason. He decided instead that he would get up and leave the restaurant right after dinner as the waiter cleared the table. Maybe Dawn wouldn't notice.

Once outside he would run to the back of the building where he had seen that open window. Without attracting attention he would leap up and climb in the window. When he was in the kitchen, he would duck down, and quietly sneak past the kitchen workers. If necessary he would assume a position on the line blending in with the cooks until any suspicions passed. This was crucial and might cost him some time. In his best Chinese accent he would ask where they kept the cookies. He would also locate the waiter with the carnation and because he wouldn't want to attract attention by calling out to him, he would trip him as he passed by. He would crouch down to be face to face with him so he could explain the waiter's part in his proposal. Together, they would prepare the little dish of cookies. Matthew would deposit the ring in one of them and mark the special cookie.

When all the preparations were completed, Matthew would go back through the window, run around to the front, and return just as the waiter brought the dessert. Dawn and Mimi would be distracted by the cookies and wouldn't think to question his absence. It was tricky, but foolproof.

Matthew barely ate his dinner as he mentally rehearsed his plan.

As soon as the waiter started to clear the table, Matthew made a break for the front door. Successfully outside, he ran around the building. But the window was shut. As he panted hard, Matthew decided that the only thing he could do was to run back to the front. Desperate to get the ring in a cookie, he came back inside and immediately headed for the kitchen.

Once he was through the double doors, he was surrounded by confusion, everyone shouted in Chinese and, carrying bowls and plates, sped past him as though he were invisible. He spotted the waiter with the pink carnation by the cookies and rushed over to explain his plan. He tucked the ring into a cookie and showed it to the waiter, who smiled and seemed to understand completely. With the ring safely inside a cookie, Matthew gratefully headed out the double doors and took a right to the men's room to give himself an alibi. But, worried that he would miss the waiter and the cookie arrival, he rushed back out to the dining room and sat down with a flabbergasted Dawn and a delighted Mimi.

"Is everything all right?" Dawn questioned. Matthew nodded and tried to catch his breath, as he watched the kitchen. Sure enough, through the swinging doors came several waiters. Matthew noticed uneasily that they all had carnations in their jackets. But to Matthew's relief their waiter walked confidently over to the table and put down the little bowl. There were 4 cookies. Which one contained the ring? Maybe he should have marked the special one. What if Mimi gobbled down the cookie and swallowed the ring? That would be horrible, not to mention very bad luck.

He was about to say something when his daughter actually did grab a cookie, but her mother made her put it back and take it again, this time more slowly. Mimi broke it open and asked Matthew to read the fortune. This cookie had no ring.

"Your life is as a rosebud," read Matthew. Mimi crinkled up her nose.

"What does that mean Daddy?"

"Well honey," Matthew's palms were wet with sweat as he watched Dawn take a cookie. "I think it means that your life will smell good." Mimi crinkled up her nose again then turned her attention to Dawn who was carefully cracking her cookie in half to pull out the message. There was no ring in this one either.

"*All is not what it seems.* Hmm that's curious, now your turn Matthew."

"I'm full. Dawn, why don't you take the other two. Mimi you've probably had enough." Dawn gave him an odd look.

"I think I'll pass. Maybe I'll take them home to Peaches. She probably could use some good luck."

"You can't do that."

"Why?"

"Bad luck. Really bad luck. I think you can only have your fortune come true if you actually open the cookie in a Chinese restaurant. Go on Dawn."

"No Matthew. I'll take them with us." Dawn scooped the cookies into her napkin and put them in her bag. Meanwhile, there was a commotion across the way. Dawn got up to leave. "It's starting to get noisy in here. Let's go."

Matthew didn't see that there would be any harm as long as they were taking the cookies with them. "Wait a minute, I just need our check." Dawn sat down again as their waiter approached. Matthew looked at the waiter and wondered how much tip to add to the bill when he noticed his red carnation. Pink, wasn't the carnation pink? It had been pink in the kitchen.

"Dawn let me have those cookies!"

"I thought you were full."

"I really want them now, please. She handed him the napkin and he immediately cracked open the cookies. He found nothing but little paper messages.

"I'll be right back." He got up so quickly his chair fell backwards. Matthew rushed toward the commotion on the other side of the restaurant. Progress was fairly difficult because of his size. Several people, waiters and customers had gathered around the large round table in the corner.

"I'm keeping it," a woman screeched. Dawn's ring was partially on her finger. "It's a little small, but I'm almost sure it's real. Look at those colors."

"Excuse me, but that's my ring."

"And why is this your ring?" asked the woman with something of a snit to her voice. "If this is your ring, then what's it doing inside my cookie?"

Matthew tried to explain.

"We paid for dinner. This fortune cookie came with dinner and this was in my cookie so it's mine. What kind of a nincompoop would put a diamond ring inside a fortune cookie anyway?"

The waiter with the pink carnation stood beside the waiter with the red carnation. Matthew looked to them to sort out the problem, but they clearly didn't understand as they stood smiling and nodding and doing nothing.

Coming up behind Matthew, Dawn grasped the situation and broke in with her familiar tone of authority. She picked up the unpaid bill that lay on the table.

"Excuse me miss but it seems to me that your bill has not been paid, therefore, the fortune cookie that you claim to be yours, is in fact, not. I believe that ring belongs to this man." She reached over and with a little difficulty plucked the diamond ring from the woman's finger and put it on her own. She whirled around to face Matthew, and flashing a big smile, said, "Yes!"

. . .

With difficulty, Peaches dragged herself out of bed. She blew her nose and wiped her eyes. She was still reeling from last night's calamity. She had been hiding under the sheets all day and only came out from time to time to share little snacks with Butkus, but now she was really hungry. As she dressed she thought she heard the motor home drive up. The purple creation she had worn the night before lay at the end of the bed. The dress was no longer her favorite, although something about the yellow moons and splattered stars all over that dark background did delight her. She would probably like it again someday, but right now it represented lost love and unfulfilled dreams and she couldn't stand to look at it. She threw it under the bed. It seemed that the only thing she had going for her was tomorrow. She had just pulled on her sweatpants when Mimi came bursting through the bedroom door.

"Mommy and Daddy are getting married."

For a moment, Peaches was stunned as if she had heard that

someone had finally died after a long, long illness. In this case, that someone would probably be her. Mimi grabbed her hand and pulled her to join the others. She wanted her aunt to see the ring and hear the funny cookie story.

What could she say? This was not what she expected. Just the thought of having Dawn as her sister in-law made her stomach hurt. She was supposed to be the one celebrating, but she wasn't even in the picture.

Her brother and Dawn were giggled together in the kitchen. As she watched them, Peaches was aware that everyone had abandoned her except Butkus, who could not comprehend the jubilation in the room and sat by her side pressed against her leg. She tried to breathe in the feeling of falling in love that was thick in the air, but all she could find was empty jealousy. Her eyes welled with tears. She was supposed to be the one. Surprised at Peaches' reaction, Dawn embraced her gratefully. She mistook her tears for joy.

"Can you believe it?" Dawn glowed as she held out her left hand.

Peaches wanted to tell her that this proposal was the dumbest thing she had ever heard, but she would save that information for another time. When she looked at Dawn's ring, the diamond was awfully small. Peaches wasn't going to mention this either, especially since that stone was definitely real. It had all those twinkling colors. Only after Clute had lost all their money and she had to raise some cash had she found out that her engagement ring was zirconium instead of a real diamond, like Clute had promised. The pawnshop owner told her it was worth about $59 dollars. Matthew must have spent quite a lot of money for this one, which meant of course that their money would run out sooner than expected. They would have to stop traveling and find jobs. She was surprised that Matthew hadn't asked her advice. A zirconium ring or even glass would have been fine for Dawn. She would never know the difference. But this time, with only the dog for a friend, she kept her thoughts to herself.

• • •

Peaches sensed that she might be in for some big changes. Evenings, after the engagement announcement the happy couple sat together in either the living room or the kitchen, wherever Peaches wasn't, and talked together in low voices. Only Butkus was loyal and stayed by her side. If she had to guess, she would bet that those two were plotting to get rid of her. They had probably felt sorry for her in the beginning, but now she was in the way.

Maybe they would make her buy Matthew's half of the motor home, even though they knew there wasn't enough money in the suitcase with her name on it to do that. Or perhaps, they would send her to live with Aunt Blossom. As far as Peaches was concerned, she would rather go to prison than subject herself to Aunt Blossom's claustrophobic hospitality. If nothing else she would get fatter if she lived with her aunt. Marlene, in her present predicament might be smarter than Peaches imagined.

There was also the possibility that they wanted her to rob a bank so that the $8,000 from the dealership could get paid back. After that, she could be warehoused in prison for a few years. She had, after all, just received a letter from the accountant at Best Deals Used Cars, warning her to address the 'theft' or pay the consequences. Peaches ignored that letter. She could have sorted the problem out with Dominick. The deadline to have it paid back was only days away. More and more, she was almost positive that yes, prison might be the best alternative.

. . .

It was Friday night. Matthew and Dawn had decided to go out and left Peaches to babysit for Mimi. It was only a week after she had been dumped and slightly less than a week after Dawn and Matthew had decided to get married. Restless, Peaches could not read *Green Eggs and Ham* to Mimi one more time. Her niece suggested Slap Jacks, but Peaches had no patience for the game. Then Mimi suggested they just talk like big people do and she enthusiastically jumped in with her plans to be an astronaut because she thought she would like to fly, and she also thought the food in those little packets they carried would be pretty good.

"All you have to do is add some water," she explained.

She had seen them at school. After she'd finished flying, she would be an archeologist and find dinosaurs in tar pits. And after that, she'd be a mommy with six children.

"Six?" Peaches wondered.

Mimi explained that with six, her children would always have someone to play with.

"Now it's your turn, Aunt Peaches."

What had Peaches wanted to be at six? She had no idea. At thirteen, she wanted to be a disc jockey with a motorcycle and two butterfly tattoos. But none of that worked out. And since she had let that dream go she had been increasingly aware that her life was meandering. She had been adrift for decades. Now she was seriously considering prison as a career option. It did present itself as a worry-free environment. Look at Marlene. There would be someone, sort of like a personal assistant, directing your day. You could take courses to plan for the future. They would probably even have a weight loss program. In fact, prison might be more like a spa, thought Peaches. With Mimi's question still on the table, Peaches struggled to explain her plan.

CHAPTER TWELVE

"I'll take care of it."

"When Peaches? This says the money was due two days ago. Where are you going to get $8,000?" Peaches slammed the refrigerator shut and bustled over.

"Where did you get that?" She grabbed the accountant's letter out of her brother's hand.

"It was on the table."

"If you hadn't bought Dawn that ring we would have plenty of money left."

"I bought the ring from my half of the money, I didn't touch yours. And I'm entitled to use my half any way I want."

"Excuuuuse me. You're right. Luckily I have no life so I don't have anybody to buy an expensive ring for. I do have some money left. I'll use that. And pretty soon, we'll be getting the insurance money from the fire and I'll use that too."

Matthew shook his head, "They're going to stall for as long as they can so don't count on that money coming anytime soon. You're not gonna have enough to pay this back and I don't have much to lend you."

"Don't give me anything. You're a family man now and you can't be bothered with giving your sister money." Peaches turned her back to him.

"I don't know what's the matter with ya. You shouldn't have taken it in the first place. What if you go to jail?"

"Maybe I want to go to jail," Peaches revealed. "You'd probably like that wouldn't you. I'd be out of the way and you'd only have to think of me every eight years like Marlene."

"Peaches, don't be so angry. I didn't do anything."

"I can be angry if I want to." She started to cry. "This is just another chapter in a long list of things that have gone wrong lately or haven't you noticed, Mr. Nothing Goes Wrong In His Life?"

"Lots of things go wrong in my life." Matthew said defensively. "But at least I'm honest."

"I'm honest too. Clute messed everything up."

"Clute was swindled and you took the easy way out. You stole that money."

"It wasn't easy stealing that money. It took a lot of brainpower to fix those books."

"What kind of an aunt are you? How am I supposed to tell Mimi you're going to jail?"

"She already knows."

"Peaches, this is serious. This isn't going away. You have to do something."

"I am doing something. I was just getting lunch. Now leave me alone. Don't you have somewhere to go besides the kitchen?"

"No. And we're going figure this thing out now." Matthew sat down with emphasis. He stared hard at Peaches and gave her no alternative but to sit down too. He quickly got back up saying, "Wait, I'll get the suitcase."

Matthew spread all their money out on the kitchen table and slowly counted it out. Peaches watched intently and chewed on her fingernail. She found it comforting that someone cared enough to help her out with her problems, someone who took some kind of control, even if it was her brother.

"Okay, this isn't too bad. We've got a total of almost $7,000 left from Dad's insurance. If we pool all the money, we'll only need $1,000."

"Only $1,000?" Peaches blurted out. "It might as well be 1 million billion. Where's that money going to come from?"

"Let's look at some possibilities," Matthew said calmly. He reached for a pad and pencil. "We've got that motor home we could sell. Maybe Bucky would take it back. He probably couldn't give us what we paid for it but he'd give us something."

"But we live there."

"We can live in the apartment."

"You can live in the apartment. I can't. Honestly I think we should let things run their course. I'll go to jail. How long could it be? It would give me time to think."

Matthew considered her plan for a moment, "Listen, you can always go to jail, but maybe you could try something else first. You could get a job."

"Oh sure. What job could I get that's going to pay me $1,000 dollars?"

"Lots of jobs. You went to CCAC. You must of learned something."

"Allegheny Community College," Peaches mused. "It was so long ago. Remember, I learned how to fix bicycles and motorcycles so I could meet guys? I met Clute. But he didn't want me to get my hands dirty so I never took the second semester, but I was pretty good at it. Better than him. But then we got married and nobody fixed anything. And now, I'm not sure I'd know a piston rod from a wheel spoke, a gasket head from a cylinder head, a spark plug--"

"I get it, I get it." Matthew broke in. "Okay, so fixing motorcycles is out. What about," he thought for a moment, "child care. Or driving a bus? You know how to do that."

"Matthew, if it's a school bus, that's child care and if it's a regular bus, that's torture. I need something I can do so I don't feel pent up. That's what I liked about motorcycle maintenance. Even if I was out in the middle of nowhere on my bike and I got stuck, I could fix the problem and ride on. But, I guess I don't remember much about it now."

"You also don't have a motorcycle. Maybe you could work in a bike shop as the secretary or the accountant."

"Matthew, this is pointless. I'm going to jail and that's final."

"Peaches, let's at least try to raise the money. I'll drive over to Bucky's this afternoon and talk to him."

"No. I'll need the Bounder to live in when I get out of jail."

Matthew continued as if he hadn't heard her. "You get the newspaper and check the want ads."

"No Matthew. In jail I can learn a trade. I can lose weight. I can transform myself so I won't need the want ads."

"You can learn a trade in college. Jail is for people who are a danger to society. Is that what you are Peaches? Don't you remember when we visited Marlene, all those guards had guns? You're so outspoken and pushy they might shoot you."

"They wouldn't dare."

"They would out of complete frustration."

. . .

The part about the guards with guns bothered Peaches. She certainly wouldn't want to get on the wrong side of that nasty one at Marlene's prison. Maybe it would be wise to at least try to raise that money, even though it seemed like such an enormous amount. She looked around to see if there was anything she could pawn. There wasn't much. She dug her little gold purse out of her big green one. That was something, she decided. There were also those cute moon earrings she had gotten to wear with her purple dress. They weren't expensive but they were quite attractive and she hated to let them go. Maybe if she did get a job and they were still at the pawnshop she would be able to buy them back. Other than those two things there was nothing else, the fire had taken everything. At least by pawning the earrings and the bag she'd be doing her part.

Through the front window in Dawn's apartment she sadly watched Matthew drive the Bounder away toward Bucky's. She sighed and grabbed the Yellow Pages from a shelf in the kitchen. It showed a pawn shop only five blocks away. Isn't that convenient, she thought drily, as she set out on foot.

Peaches didn't like to walk long distances. It made her feet hurt. So it took her a while to get to Ridge Avenue. Luckily there were a couple of benches along the route and she was able to sit and rest.

Hymie's Pawn Shop was grim. The windows needed washing, and as Peaches walked in, she noticed that everything was coated with dust. Behind the counter, Hymie looked like he needed a good cleaning too, with his sad grey sweater slung over his ample arms. Unkept grey hair framed his ashen face. His voice, however, was pleasant. "How can I help you?"

Reluctantly, Peaches pulled the little gold purse from her bag. She thought she'd save the earrings, revealing them only if she needed to.

"Nice little purse," Hymie said amiably.

Peaches nodded her head in agreement.

"Maybe I could do fifteen. Maybe sixteen."

"That's all? But you said it was a nice purse. I need $1,000." Hymie looked at Peaches for a moment.

"$1,000 you need? Well you ain't getting it from this purse. You got anything else?" He leaned over the counter and raised curly grey eyebrows in anticipation.

Peaches hesitated a moment before pulling out the earrings. He looked at them closely. "Nice earrings, I can give you maybe ten."

"Ten dollars?" Peaches questioned. "Oh that's great, now I need only," she calculated in her head, "$975." She tried to collect her thoughts and wondered how hard it would be to keep her mouth shut in jail.

"Let me look at that ring you're wearing." Hymie took out a magnifying glass from under the counter and examined it closely. "Hum," he said several times. "Hum." Before speaking, he looked at Peaches for a long time. He nodded his head. "I could give you a grand for this thing. You probably already know the ruby's real and those little diamonds are real too. It must be something special or you wouldn't have bothered with that other stuff."

"Really? I mean, of course it's special and I knew all that." Peaches thought quickly before she spoke again. "Is that all you'll give me for it? I mean, it does have real diamonds there, and the ruby. It is a family heirloom and probably at least 100 years old. My mother, Phyllis, wore it over from the old country." She tried to think what old country her mother could have come from.

"The old country, hey?" Hymie looked through his magnifier at the ring again and then peered over his glasses at Peaches before saying, "Two but not a penny more."

For once in her life Peaches knew what it meant to be walking on air. In her green bag was a check for $2000. Now she could pay that stupid loan off and if Matthew didn't need his half of the money back, she would have some left over. Oh no, she suddenly thought, Matthew went to sell the Bounder. She'd have no place to live.

She hurried along although she knew there was nothing she could do to stop him. He had left before she did. She rushed past one of the benches. There was no time to sit down. She had to get to Matthew. She pushed on and was winded when she finally caught sight of the apartment complex. Her heart sank when there was no RV in the street.

This was terrible. Why had she let Matthew talk her into selling it? The second bench was close by so she sat heavily on its wooden slats. It took awhile until her normal breathing returned and she slowly started for home. People were always messing her up. First Clute, then Dominick, now her brother, and always Dawn.

As she walked the last block and a half she thought about Dawn. Why did they irritate each other?

Peaches trudged into the apartment and was surprised to find that Dawn had already come home from work. Peaches' euphoria over her check deflated, then disappeared.

"What are you doing here?" Dawn greeted her.

Peaches drew herself up, "You expecting the queen of England?"

Dawn poured herself coffee. "No, but that would be a nice change, don't you think?"

"That's rude." Peaches turned to leave.

Dawn was quick to respond and said, "You'd know all about rude wouldn't you? At least I've got a concrete reason to be mad at you, you thief. But let's face it you've been holding a grudge one way or another ever since high school. High school, Peaches. That was over twenty years ago. Twenty years Peaches, do you hear me? I'll bet you don't even remember what made you so mad at me in the first place. I certainly don't." There was a long pause. "Well do you?"

"Why of course I remember and remember it very well. I don't like bringing up old business," Peaches said indignantly. Tears welled up in her eyes. How could Dawn possibly forget why Peaches was angry?

"It was so hurtful and demeaning," Peaches reminded her. "No friend would ever have put another friend through that. We had been best friends until you turned on me." Or, thought Peaches, was it that the other kids in her class turned and Dawn didn't stand up for her? Or maybe it was when Richie Barrett started liking Dawn better than her and Dawn didn't immediately break up with him. Peaches pondered that for a moment. Yup that's what happened.

"Peaches? I'm sorry, let's just drop it." Dawn's tone was

conciliatory.

"I'll tell you the problem," Peaches started with new energy. "It was Richie. You stole my boyfriend right out from under me. How could you forget?"

"Richie?"

"You know Richie. The one with the big hair. He lived over by the river. He was pals with Sherman, you know."

"Oh yeah, I know who you mean. But what does he have to do with--"

"You don't even remember. You stole Richie from under my nose. He loved me, he told me so and then he wasn't there because he was with you, my best friend." Tears ran down her face.

"Peaches, I started going out with Richie only after you dumped him. You said he had BO. I felt sorry for him. It's not my fault that you dumped him just before the prom. What was I supposed to do? Dump him too so that no one would go to the prom? I think I had a terrible time."

"You didn't even appreciate him."

"Peaches, I went out with him twice. You were right. He did have BO. Is this why you're angry with me? Richie, who I barely remember? Richie who had bad hygiene? That Richie?"

"It's the principle of the thing."

"What principle? All I know is that you've chosen to hold on to the memory of some stinky high school kid over me. You blew the whole thing completely out of the water and tainted our friendship for years. Maybe you should go find Richie. Don't worry I won't be anywhere around to come between you two. And if you don't get back for my party, we'll carry on without you."

Peaches had forgotten about Dawn's birthday party. Everyone was coming. That is to say Matthew, Mimi, and Dawn. Aunt Blossom was expected too.

. . .

Matthew felt proud of himself. He had finally gotten Peaches to address the whole theft issue. After all, having a sister convicted of taking money from a business owned by the father of the woman you're about to marry would not be a terrific way to start a new life.

He hadn't been able to find Bucky. In fact, he hadn't been able to find the used car dealership either. They were gone. So the Bounder was still theirs and as far as Matthew knew, they still needed money. He wasn't sure how he would tell Peaches.

As the apartment complex came into view he considered parking around the corner to keep the Bounder out of sight, but he was tired of playing games, and his sister had to grow up eventually. Inside the apartment he found only Dawn. "Peaches," she informed him, "was gone."

. . .

All that talk about the ideas she used to have, had churned up longings Peaches didn't even know were still in her head. She left Dawn's apartment and chose the sidewalk going downhill because it was easier. She walked to help clear her head, just in case any important thoughts might pop in. Walking was not easy, especially after that hike to the pawnshop and back. But she needed some sort of life changing correction and she wasn't going to find it sitting around Dawn's. Peaches knew she needed a good kick in the pants that would send her out into the world she knew she was meant to inhabit. In truth, she had no idea where this inspiration would come from or if she would even recognize it when it arrived.

She muddled through the notion that there must be another way to do her life. Peaches realized that if she didn't change something, the same things would happen. She cringed at the thought of settling for some dead-end, boring job because she didn't believe she could get anything better. She shivered at finding a do nothing guy that, after she was hooked, would be content to sit in his undershirt and burp at the TV.

If there wasn't that gun problem, she thought, prison would still be a viable option. But Matthew was right, she realized. Eventually, after many misunderstandings, she would literally end up a casualty of an experiment gone awry. Ideas and fragments of ideas splashed around her head with every step. Life was like this sidewalk, she thought, long, grey and hard with nothing much to speak of at the end. Then

Peaches made the bold decision to find Richie.

She was aware that a grown up Richie couldn't begin to hold up to the shining image she had of Dominick, even if he was unavailable. And Peaches knew that this former high school lover boy was just a curiosity and a destination for a bewildered woman with aching feet, in search of a life, nothing else. As she headed toward the river, she had a pretty good idea where his house had been, and with conviction, she knew he would still be living there. He had been somewhat weirdly attached to his house and his mother when he was in high school. Peaches was sure that not much had changed.

Luckily it wasn't too far away, because it was getting on toward four in the afternoon. And even though the street names weren't familiar, Wheeler, Chase, Barberry, she remembered the area.

That park, right across the street, with its big square jungle gym looked familiar. And eventually, she realized with cautious relief that she was almost there. She had absolutely no idea what she would do when she got there and she wasn't really sure why she was going in the first place, but she'd think of something.

Richie, she expected, would be sitting on his front porch in a tee shirt, even though it was a little chilly, with a beer in his hand, maybe even his fifth beer because he had failed to go to work that day. He would be waiting for his mother to call him in for dinner. Peaches expected to find the same unwashed, unkempt person that she'd gone to high school with, only a little older. Sadly, even though she wasn't interested romantically, except for Dominick, this was the type of guy she seemed to attract.

The neighborhood was nice enough. The development houses had matured since the late '60's when at 17, with her new driver's license, Peaches had driven by Richie's house a few times. And, even though the houses she passed now were still all the same shape, some had a little more color to them. Bushes helped, but honestly, Peaches thought, they were still small dull houses representing a vague stagnation of the human spirit.

Peaches sat on a bus bench to rest. Kids on bikes zoomed in and out of driveways. Some even rode in her direction curious to see who the new lady was. Legions of cars slowly brought husbands or wives home and neatly disappeared into garages. Peaches mused, all these people will sit in their identical kitchens for an early dinner of roasted chicken because it was on sale at Giant Eagle this week. But in spite of her criticism, Peaches' mouth watered at the thought. Would Dominick live on a street like this? Peaches thought for a moment, never. And neither would I. It's all so predictable.

There's no sense of adventure oozing from the windows. No, they would live in a motor home ready to see something new every day.

Wearily, Peaches decided that the Barrettes must live just around this next corner. She was sure of it. When it clearly was not, she chose the next corner and was rewarded with another bench.

As Peaches sat, she noticed a little girl who peddled her bike hard and came in her direction. The little girl wanted to get a closer look at the big woman sitting down rubbing her feet. As she coasted, the combination of loose gravel and broken curbing made her bike skid and fall. Peaches jumped up to help the crying child and together they discovered that the bike tire had deflated. Digging deep into her green bag, Peaches pulled out her bicycle pump.

"Let me fix that." And with great care, and a multitude of comforting words Peaches pumped up the tire. The bike chain was a little loose so Peaches dug a wrench from out of her bag as she explained that if the chain is on correctly, the axle nuts can be tightened. After that, the right axle nut should be loosened and the wheel pulled to give the chain tension. "Then," she explained, "that nut can be tightened too. With just these little adjustments, the chain will work better." Finishing by adjusting the bicycle horn, Peaches announced, "You're ready to go." As the little girl got back on her bike Peaches thought to ask about the Barretts.

"Dr. Barrett? He's my dentist. He lives over there." The little girl pointed to a gray house half way down the street. Peaches recognized it as the same house that Richie Barrett had grown up in. Only now, there was a large sign that announced his dental practice in the front yard.

Peaches felt weak and defeated as she tried to make sense of the Richie transformation. Once again, the unlikely of the unlikeliest had taken the lead. The realization that Richie Barrett could legitimately put a Dr. in front of his name and go through life like that was almost incomprehensible to Peaches. She was at least as smart as he was.

As this reality set in, her feeling of helplessness was replaced by anger. As it grew, it tightened her back and arms. The anger tensed the muscles in her neck and gave her a headache. Here she was again, just her plain ol' unaccomplished, directionless self and he was soaring.

Peaches jammed her feet back into her shoes. She grabbed the bicycle pump and the wrench. She threw them into her bag and started for Dawn's apartment. She was in no mood for a birthday party. As she walked back up the hill, Peaches tried to figure out how that dimwitted high school boy could get his stinky self to dental school, graduate and actually open a practice caring for people like that nice little girl?

"Dr. Barrett?" Peaches said out loud.

How was it possible? And where had she gone wrong? Maybe she was the drifter, the do nothing, the reject. If she hadn't been so angry, she would have cried.

She sat down on a bench, still deep in thought, and decided that the decision was the problem. Peaches was confident that once the choice was actually made as to what to do with her life, she would be able to go at it with full force. That's the way she did things. The worry was that she would get locked into something she'd hate, or not be very good at, or wouldn't be proud of.

She lumbered back toward the apartment and thought hard about a career and came to the conclusion that Richie's success could only have happened because his mother had pushed him into becoming a dentist. Peaches, on the other hand, had had influences like Clute, Matthew, Dawn and Marlene, none of them showing or knowing the way to success. No. She hadn't gone wrong. She hadn't even started. Unfortunately she'd gotten herself mixed up with the wrong people. Breathing heavily, Peaches was starting to understand why her life was so unfair with such regularity.

While her brain was energized by her anger, her feet and actually her legs felt like they belonged to someone else. Now the sun was going down.

She traipsed past a strip mall and noticed that Rite Aid and Lisa's Nail Shop flanked Martin's Mattress Store. I could be a mattress salesman, she thought. Those stores are never very busy and I'd be able to rest. Then she changed her mind. It would be so dull.

Even though she was tired, she made herself focus, everybody likes makeup, I could be a makeup artist. I know quite a lot about makeup from that little brochure I used to have, she reasoned. And it's really not that hard. I'd have a little uniform, like a candy striper. I wonder if they come in my size? She knew she would look silly in it but being a professional had its price.

Smoke from a barbecue wafted through the air and made her mouth water. It smelled like chicken. The scent reminded her of the house fire. She loved the motor home, but they wouldn't have had to buy it if the house hadn't burned down, but it did. Was it her fault? Was it Dawn's cigarette thrown in the trash? Or was it Blossom being sloppy with the Cognac? Exhausted, Peaches was confused. She tried to remember the events of that day more than a month and a half ago. Had Peaches left the burner on when she thought she had turned it off? One of these scenarios had to be true, but which one? Peaches didn't know the answer to that question either.

Desperate to make some personal headway, Peaches realized that Matthew and Dawn would never take her seriously if she came back without a direction. She could wile away the hours in Mimi's room, but eventually the whole living situation in that apartment would explode. She reasoned that it didn't really matter what her decision was, as long as she sounded like she meant it. And of course, she could always change her mind later.

. . .

Something magical happened when the exhausted woman came around the last corner, just before the apartment complex. She saw the Bounder. That big beautiful motor home she'd made her brother buy. Home sweet home sitting by the side of the road just waiting for her to move back in.

She suddenly felt better and had the warm feeling that things were finally going her way. No matter the real reason the RV was parked in front of the apartment building, the motor home was here. She had a $2,000 check in her pocketbook and now she had a place to live. She wouldn't have to stay with her brother and an unpleasant old friend from high school any longer.

She bustled up to the door and gave the knob a turn. It was locked. This meant that she'd have to walk into the apartment and ask her brother for the key. He might say that it had been sold and he had brought it back so they could remove all of their belongings. No matter the reason, Peaches wouldn't let it go away again.

Things were looking up, but she'd promised herself she'd have some kind of a job ready to announce to her brother and Dawn this evening, but she wasn't ready at all. And for god's sake, it was dusk and she didn't want to be out here on the curb without dinner. As she put her mind to it, she easily rejected most of the ideas her family expected her to do, like being a hairdresser or driving a bus, again. She realized with great clarity that she really liked fixing bikes, all kinds of bikes. She might be a little rusty at first, but she reminded herself, that for a brief period she'd been the best in her class. Kids could bring their bikes in to her for a checkup. Then eventually, she would have a section of the shop where she could fix motorcycles. There would be a little lift that would raise them to eye level because if she had to roll around on the floor trying to see what was underneath the carburetor she would probably get stuck. She would wear a cute jumpsuit instead of a candy striper's uniform and get her hands really dirty instead of marked up with blush and eyelash stuff that would be hard to get off. She would be a professional that she could be proud of. But frankly, she suspected nobody else would be proud of her. As she trudged down the hallway toward Dawn's apartment, Peaches made a decision.

CHAPTER THIRTEEN

Peaches surprised Dawn when she let herself in to the apartment. Dawn was working on her nails. Peaches' abrupt departure a few hours before wasn't mentioned. Matthew and Mimi were out with the dog, and Blossom had come over a little while before with food for Dawn's birthday party. She was in the kitchen and bustled into the living room to greet her niece.

"Florida was wonderful," Blossom assured her after giving Peaches a big hug. "You really missed a good time. What an upstanding devout group of people. In addition to the quick tour of Florida's east side we made a number of stops to spread the word and eat chicken barbecue." She indicated a pile of books in the corner of the living room. "I have Bibles for us all."

As she stood in front of these two women, Peaches awkwardly composed herself. She wanted to explain her new direction. After all a promise was a promise, especially to herself. She started enthusiastically, "I've decided. I know what I want to do."

Dawn broke in, "Peaches you'll find a job you like. A good job." She was reassuring but not really listening. "I have a job. And I'm not waiting around for Matthew to save me and you shouldn't be waiting around for Dominick or Richie or anyone else to save you either."

"But I'm not, really."

"You've always been like that," Dawn reminded her. "People don't change." Peaches regarded Dawn patiently as the woman continued, "When Matthew comes home, we'll all put our heads together and figure something out. Blossom's here to help."

"No Dawn, we don't have to put our heads together. I know what I want to do. I'm opening a bicycle shop."

"A what?" Blossom was confused. "Are you going to ride bicycles in a shop? I wouldn't do that if I were you, not with your size."

"No, Aunt Blossom, I'm going to fix them so other people can ride them. Motorcycles too."

Blossom acted as if she were going to faint. "Oh my dear, when? When are you going to do this bicycle thing? Maybe you'll need help. I could help in some way and Marlene could help too, although I don't think she knows anything about bikes. Do you? Do you know how to do that?" Then Blossom brightened. "Oh my god. Peaches, you're brilliant. Just think of all those biker men you'll meet. If you could lose a little weight, I give you six months before you're engaged. By then, Marlene will be out of jail and she'll take over the shop and meet someone too." Blossom held her hands to her bosom. "We could have a double wedding. I'll do everyone's hair." Peaches and Dawn both rolled their eyes.

Nodding in bewilderment, Peaches quietly left Dawn and Blossom and walked down the hall to Mimi's room. It didn't matter what they thought. She knew what she needed to do.

Through the closed bedroom door Peaches could hear the dog walkers return. She could also hear Dawn announce that his sister was back in the bedroom and could use a little help. Frantic to keep her strong frame of mind, she briefly wondered if Richie's mother was available. If that woman could transform her Richie, imagine, thought Peaches, how she could help her.

"Peaches, you in there?" Matthew knocked on her door. As he walked in, he gave her the news about the Bounder. "I couldn't find Bucky anywhere. Everything was gone. I guess it's ours for at least a little while."

Peaches was relieved to hear this and realized that Matthew knew nothing about the $2000 check in her pocketbook. She hesitated a moment before telling him. It was her money because the ring was hers from the drawer and he had gotten the socks. But she remembered her brother had offered her his half of the insurance money. Peaches had to admit that that was a really nice thing to do. She decided to tell him about the money, but not give him any of it unless he really needed it. And he wouldn't need it because he was looking for a job every day. Besides, Dawn had a job so they had money coming in and a roof over their heads. Peaches, on the other hand, would need whatever was left over from paying back that loan to set up her business.

The bed groaned as Matthew sat down beside his sister.

"Dawn said you're going to open up a bike shop."

Peaches trusted Matthew. He had a good heart and she knew he loved her. So, after inhaling deeply to focus, she told him everything.

She started out with Richie. Matthew didn't remember Richie from high school, but his transformation from cruddy school kid to a real dentist impressed him.

"How did he do that?" Matthew exclaimed. Peaches wasn't going to tell him the differences between the success driven people in Richie's life and the non-successful people in her life, so she told him about the bike shop and the motorcycles on the little lift and brightly reminded him how she had been the best in her class.

Matthew knew he would have to find just the right words although he had no idea what they might be. All he could say was, "Geez you went to school a long time ago." What he really thought was, why can't she do something normal? And then he realized that his sister had her own normal and what was normal anyway? So what he did say next was, "I think that's a great idea."

. . .

Aunt Blossom sprinkled copious amounts of coconut on Dawn's big round birthday cake as she gave her niece advice.

"It's all well and good to have made this decision about your career, now you have to make it happen. If you'll remember, I started a business too. It wasn't easy, but my hair salon thrived," she said proudly. "It was a lot of work. I'm sure you're prepared for that." Blossom reached for the candles and stuck half a dozen pink ones around the top. Peaches was reminded of the dessert that she had made for her brother's birthday two months ago. The fatal flambé that changed their lives.

"Carry this to the table, Peaches." Blossom licked her fingers and added. "As a precaution, we will not light those candles until it's in place. Let's not take any chances. You know what happened before." She gave Peaches a meaningful look.

That's silly, thought Peaches indignantly. Blossom is forgetting her part in the fire. She's blaming me and she's also forgetting that Dawn probably played a part too. But she carefully followed her Aunt's orders. As she balanced the large confection she made her way to the dining room where the birthday girl, Mimi and Matthew waited at the table.

There was excitement and surprise as she came through the door. Blossom was known for her good desserts and the cake was enormous. Suddenly, Peaches tripped on the carpeting and the cake sailed toward Dawn who had the seat of honor at the head of the table. In a split second, it lobbed into Dawn's head, slithered down through her dark brown hair and down the right side of her face. After sliding down her shoulder, it rolled across the front of her shirt, finally coming to rest in a messy heap in her lap.

Dawn's arms flailed as she cried, "You did that on purpose." She didn't dare stand up. Matthew and Mimi rushed to help, shocked that something like this could really happen. Blossom appeared from the kitchen, the box of matches in her hand and took control immediately.

"Thank goodness it wasn't lit. Dawn don't move. It can be salvaged."

When the commotion died down, five pieces of cake were carved from Dawn's lap and the remainder scrapped into a bowl. Dawn went to change.

"Now, don't stick up your nose, it's perfectly fine," Blossom reassured Mimi. "This is how it would look in your tummy. See, Butkus likes it." The dog had trotted in and licked fragments of cake from the carpeting. "It's too good to waste." After apologizing to anyone who would listen, Peaches sat down.

"You have so much trouble with birthday cakes." Blossom pointed out as she sat down and spread her napkin in her lap. "I've been reading about disorders. I want to be ready to help Marlene when she gets out. And from what I've read, you're both clumsy and distracted or the problem is psychosomatic, and that means this has nothing to do with your feet and everything to do with your head. Maybe this career thing you're gonna do is just too much of a burden. If that cake had been lit, we'd all be moving into the motor home or my house." Blossom shook her head and took a bite of cake. "I do like the idea of that bicycle shop because I don't see how you'd ever attract men without some help. Is that trucker guy still around?"

"I just tripped, Aunt Blossom. Everybody trips. And no, Dominick isn't around." Peaches realized she had defended herself a little too strongly and pulled the conversation back to the cause of the fire. "You were at Matthew's birthday party. I wasn't the only one in the kitchen when the fire started. It could have been Dawn. It could even have been you." Blossom regarded her niece over her glasses. "It wasn't me, I can tell you that," she said gravely.

Dawn returned with a wet head and fresh clothes. She added a new perspective when she said, "Why would you take responsibility for the fire or anything else, Peaches, when you can point your finger at someone else?"

"That's not fair." Peaches felt she was being attacked. "You were both there. Dawn are you sure you put your cigarette completely out, and Aunt Blossom we don't even know what you were doing over at the stove."

"It's always someone else," Dawn interjected. "Owning up doesn't make you bad, it makes you honest."

Matthew suggested they talk about something else but nobody heard him over the squabbling. Peaches felt her newfound direction, along with her serenity, melt away. She wished that Dawn's cake had been lit and caused just a little ruckus so they'd have something else to talk about.

Mimi quietly got up and walked over to Peaches' chair. She took her Aunt's hand and said, "Aunt Peaches if you made that fire, I still love you."

Peaches looked down at her niece with a little smile. The child obviously didn't understand, so Peaches was going to emphasize again that it was not her fault when she stopped. She paused a moment and realized that admitting the mistake would not be condemning herself as a person, people made mistakes all the time. She was tired of defending herself.

She lifted the small child to her lap and gave her an affectionate squeeze, she looked around at her family and managed to say, "Maybe it's possible. Maybe I did cause that fire."

CHAPTER FOURTEEN

At first Matthew felt a little lost with Peaches out of the apartment. She lived in the Bounder now. He had been use to her advising him at every turn but now it seemed that he was on his own. It was nice. While Mimi had always looked up to her Dad, Dawn now looked up to him for guidance and suggestions too.

"I'd like to get a car. Matthew, what do you think?" Dawn asked him one evening. He was a little surprised that he did have thoughts and that those around him took him and his thoughts seriously. Of course Peaches was right outside in the Bounder and always available with her advice, but now she was preoccupied planning her new business. They didn't see much of her.

"I'm right out here if you need me," Peaches pointed out. "We're neighbors now."

Like Peaches, Matthew felt that this was the time to get a real job, especially because he and Dawn were getting married soon. Being the caregiver for his father certainly had been work, but not a serious career choice.

Matthew liked driving, but memories of his bus driving days were scarred by that horrific experience of driving that great big bus down that dead end street, and having all of those commuters shrieking at him. Even now it made him shudder.

Matthew was making an honest effort by pouring over the classified pages of the *Post-Gazette* every evening. He knew he would hate wearing a suit and tie. He didn't want a desk job and he didn't want to be a bank teller. It made him shudder to think of himself as a traveling salesman or even a trucker. He was worried he wouldn't find anything.

"How about a school bus driver?" Dawn suggested. "You'd have the same schedule as Mimi and we wouldn't have to get extra daycare for her."

"I could do that." Matthew was elated with the idea. "I'd have summers free to help Peaches when the shop got busy."

With a doable direction, Matthew was relieved and planned to head down to the bus garage in the morning, to file an application.

• • •

The loan/theft problem was paid off using the rest of the life insurance money and some of the pawned ring money so that problem was out of the way. Best Deals Used Cars did not, however, want Peaches back as an employee any time soon.

All Peaches' textbooks and manuals about motorcycle and bike repair and maintenance had been lost in the house fire, but after hunting through books and catalogues at the local library, Peaches found some information that would get her started. Moving back into the motor home gave her the quiet study situation she needed. The superintendent of Dawn's building allowed her to park the motor home in the back parking lot for a month or so until she figured out what she was going to do. Mimi would regularly find Peaches at the dinette, surrounded by a hero sandwich, a bowl of potato chips, a diet soda and her books. Peaches had taken Mimi's small pink two-wheeler apart and put it back together several times.

There was still the problem of where to open her bike shop. Everyone in the family was on the lookout. Aunt Blossom called Dawn's apartment at least once a day with a message to be delivered to Peaches about vacant stores near her house. Blossom thought it might be easier for her to help out at the shop if it was located close to where she lived. She even offered her garage. She reasoned that having a bike business right on a service road, next to a highway would be the ideal location. She was a little disappointed when Peaches rejected her offer.

Matthew took a job driving a school bus and almost instantly became a hero with the kids on his bus when he was able to avoid a collision with McGregor, an unusually large grey Great Dane that leapt from his owner's side into the road, directly into the path of the bus. Matthew didn't think it was such a big deal. After all, he just put on his brakes, but the kids on the bus and especially Ed, the owner of McGregor could not praise Matthew's quick-witted action enough. It turned out that Ed was a realtor and after finding out that Matthew and his family needed help finding a commercial property, he was happy to help and knew just the place.

Ed gave him the address of a vacant store that was small and a little run down, but in a good location, not too far off a fairly busy street. The rent seemed reasonable.

The next morning all the Packers drove across town in the Bounder to see the shop. The small clapboard building had started out as a residence, turned into a bakery, and then a cheese shop. Now it was vacant. Peaches was thrilled with it and thought it was a good omen that so much food had passed through its doors. She also noted that there was an attached garage where motorcycles could be driven right in for repair. That afternoon, with great excitement, she signed the lease as Matthew, Dawn and Mimi looked on and Aunt Blossom called out an encouraging, "We won't burn this one down."

Ignoring the landlord's look of concern, Blossom reached for the cooler she had brought and pulled out an ice cream cake to christen the deal. It was a nice cake that had an odd looking bicycle on top that she had fashioned herself out of blue icing.

"Morton would be so proud. He biked once in a while, you know. And here's a Bible for good luck." Blossom pulled the familiar black book from her large purse and placed it on Peaches' new workbench. Peaches thought that that was a pretty good gift for the shop, especially if it came with a little luck. By now, each member of the family had one or two.

After cake, Matthew suggested they all go out to dinner to celebrate. "How about Luigi's? Isn't that your favorite place Peach?"

"It was my favorite place." Peaches sobered.

But they couldn't agree on another favorite restaurant so they settled on Luigi's.

Excited about the occasion, they all piled back into the Bounder as Peaches drove them across town and parked in the rear of the one story restaurant. Inside, they found a nice table in a quiet corner.

This may have been a bad idea, thought Peaches as she glanced toward the table where Dominick and his date had sat. But she soon forgot that awful night as Matthew made an attempt at a school bus joke and the appetizers came. For her main course, Peaches had her favorite, eggplant Parmesan with extra spaghetti on the side. For dessert, everyone had Luigi's Good Luck Cheese Cake.

They all had a nice evening and Peaches was grateful for the celebration.

She drove everyone home to the apartment complex and then parked the RV in the back lot. It had been an exciting day. Her new career was getting launched in record time. They would start fixing up the shop when Matthew got home from work the very next day. She was to meet him there at five to go over improvements he had agreed to help with.

Motorcycle driving lessons would start for Peaches the following week. She was nervous about them. She had planned to reduce a little before starting those classes, but this license was necessary soon because things were falling into place faster than she could ever have imagined. Who else would test those bikes out?

As she pulled Matthew's chicken quilt up around her chin, she felt excited and content. She was working hard at her studies and that felt good. She was working hard to get everything in place, confident that this was the right direction for her. But deep in her heart, she had the gnawing feeling that something was missing.

. . .

Exactly one month and a day after the lease was signed Packer's Bike World opened for business. Blossom organized an open house with fancy cookies. Matthew and Dawn helped behind the counter and Mimi handed out cups of lemonade. They had a good turnout. Peaches was a little surprised at this and suspected that in addition to their curiosity, the sugar cookies in the shape of two wheelers brought in enthusiastic kids from the neighborhood.

It had been a rush getting the place painted inside, and a challenge figuring out tools and manuals Peaches would need. The outside paint color caused great consternation, but they finally agreed on a soft shade of orange with green trim. Peaches had put her heart and soul into organizing the shop.

Matthew, grateful that Peaches had a real direction, offered his help eagerly. In the middle of the open house they had to coax the heater to work to keep the place warm. It was the end of October and getting chillier each day.

Peaches knew it might have been smarter to have the opening in the spring when people were getting their bikes out for the season. In April, she hoped the store would be flooded with tune-ups and repairs. Business would be slow through the winter months but Peaches wasn't worried. She would take the winter to get used to her new life. She had a new slogan: *Turn right in to roll right out.*

Because the motorcycle lift was back ordered until February, Peaches rigged up a ramp so she wouldn't be crawling around on the floor. The winter delay would give Peaches a little more time to practice on that old bike she had had Matthew pick up for her.

Blossom was in and out of the shop several times a week just to check on things. She made it her business to bring cookies, brownies, or some other finger food adding to the ambiance and the smell of the place.

"I love having people to cook for," she would frequently repeat.

Peaches had invested in a good supply of parts, which she figured would also add to traffic. Already she had had a middle-aged man stop in for a motorcycle headlight. He intended to install it himself and had been pleased that Packer's Bike World was there because the other motorcycle repair shops were across town. Blossom kept watch from the back and gleefully pointed out to Peaches how, "Men are just flocking in."

Peaches wasn't much interested in the flocking or in Blossom's predictions. For the first time in her life she was content on a daily basis.

. . .

The hours of operation were nine a.m. to six p.m. and open every day but Monday. Bike World had already been in business for a few weeks, and the weekends were important for business. It was Sunday and Peaches was working late. She had received a delivery of bicycles to sell for Christmas and was busy putting one together. This one was purple and Peaches thought Mimi might like it. Her niece was growing fast and her pink one was too small.

From the back workroom, she heard the front door bell ding-a-ling. Peaches pulled herself to her feet, wiping her hands on her jumpsuit. Glancing at the wall clock she noted that it was almost six thirty. She probably should have locked that door, especially since she needed to finish the bike. She walked from the back room to behind the counter and hesitated. Motionless, her heart began to pound. She wanted to hide.

"Dominick?"

When he turned around, he smiled, "It's a nice store, Peach."

She smiled back and steadied herself at the counter. "I did it myself. Well Matthew and the others helped."

"You didn't really need anyone, Peach." He moved closer.

"No Dominick, I still need you."

Purchase other Black Rose Writing titles at www.blackrosewriting.com/books
and use promo code PRINT to receive a 20% discount.

CPSIA information can be obtained
at www.ICGtesting.com
Printed in the USA
FFOW05n0445300316